TALKING OF THE DEAD

MICHAEL DYLAN

Tuesday 22nd November

1

Wise had nearly cancelled his visit to Belmarsh Prison a dozen times that morning alone. With all the arrests his team had made the day before, there was plenty to be getting on with back at Kennington, without wasting time with his own private investigation. Especially since he didn't have any doubts about his twin brother's guilt anymore. Not after Tom's threats against Wise's family.

Despite all that, Wise still found himself making the hour-long drive from Kennington over to Thamesmead, where the category A prison was located. Built in the early nineties, Belmarsh was now home to only the most violent and dangerous prisoners.

The worst of the worst resided inside a prison within the prison. The High Security Unit, known as The Box, was hidden behind twenty-foot concrete walls. Access was only granted by the prison's central command.

It was where Elrit Selmani had his cell.

Wise had put the man behind bars for the murder of a prostitute. However, someone had coerced his partner, Detective Sergeant Andy Davidson, into attempting to kill the only witness in the case, in the hope that Selmani would go free. Armed Response Officers had shot

Andy before he could do it, though. Now, Wise believed the man behind that plot was his twin brother. Hopefully, Selmani would confirm that suspicion.

Walking through The Box, Wise could feel his claustrophobia ratchet up another notch every time another door slammed shut and a lock engaged. Everywhere he looked were white walls, concrete floors, and metal doors. Daylight was something to be glimpsed through thick glass windows. He knew the prisoners spent at least fourteen hours a day locked up in cells twelve feet by eight feet, sharing that space with one or two other prisoners. For Wise, it was the very definition of hell.

Eventually, the prison guard stopped in front of a steel door, painted white. 'Here you go.' He used his lanyard to disengage the locks and opened the door, then stepped back to let Wise enter.

Wise walked into the visiting room, then stopped dead when he saw who was waiting for him.

It wasn't Elrit Selmani.

Instead, DCI Rena Heer from Specialist Crime and Operations 10, and her colleague, DS Brendan Murray, were sitting on one side of the small table.

'Hello Inspector,' said Heer. 'It's nice to see you.'

The door slammed shut behind Wise. The lock engaged.

Detective Inspector Simon Wise stared at the two people sitting at the table, shocked that they were there waiting for him, yet unsurprised at the same time. It'd been over a month since he'd last seen Heer and Murray. They'd turned up at Kennington Police Station, just after Wise and his team had arrested David Smythe, the Motorbike Killer. They'd brought along a picture, taken by a covert operative, of a man they claimed was waging a war to seize control of the London underworld.

The detectives had wanted to know if the man in the picture was Wise.

After all, Wise did look identical to the subject of the photograph. Except it wasn't Wise. He'd been in Birmingham at the time the picture was taken, interviewing someone with DS Hannah Markham.

However, that didn't mean Wise didn't know who the man was. He knew only too well, in fact.

It was his brother, Tom. His twin.

Of course, Wise hadn't told Heer or Murray that at the time. Instead, he'd lied and denied any knowledge.

Now, that picture now lay on the table in front of Heer and Murray.

'We'd like to talk to you about your brother, Tom.' Heer pointed at the chair on the other side of the table. 'Take a seat.'

With a shake of his head, Wise did as he was told. It wasn't as if he had any choice in the matter. He was in an interview room in Belmarsh Prison with the door locked behind him. There was no way Wise could just turn around and walk away. In fact, there was more than a good chance Heer and Murray might want him to stay there no matter what he did.

'You both look good,' Wise said with a smile. 'Life treating you well?'

'I see you've still a mouth on you,' Murray said. 'You should be careful though. No one likes a smartarse.'

'That so?' Wise said, spreading his hands out on the tabletop. 'You talking from personal experience?'

Heer tapped the picture. 'Why didn't you tell us this was your brother?'

Wise shrugged. 'I didn't know it was him.'

'Oh, come on,' Murray said. 'He looks identical to you.'

Wise glanced over at the detective. 'It's just a picture. I wanted proof before saying one way or another.'

'Is that why you're here to see Selmani?' Heer asked. 'To get some sort of proof?'

'That was the plan originally,' Wise said. 'But two days ago, Tom made threats against my family because he'd found out I'd been making enquiries into his life. I figured that was proof enough that you were right.'

'So why come here if you knew already that he was bent?' Heer asked.

'Because I'm an idiot?' Wise said with a smile.

'You should've told us the truth weeks ago.'

Wise nodded. 'I know. And I'm sorry — if that's any consolation.'

'Not much,' Murray growled.

'Well, now we're all here,' Wise said, 'what do you want to know? Because I don't know much. Tom and I haven't really spoken for twenty years.'

'You have a falling out?' Murray asked.

'You could say that.'

'What happened?' Heer asked.

'He killed someone and went to prison,' Wise replied. 'And he was a bit upset that I wasn't serving time with him. He stopped speaking to me after that.'

'Should you have been?' There was a coldness to Heer that Wise appreciated. She wasn't a hothead like Murray.

'At the time I thought I should've been,' Wise said. 'Looking back now though? No.'

'What happened?'

Wise looked around the bare meeting room. 'I take it there's no chance of a coffee?'

'No,' Murray said. His Richard Gere eyes were nothing but narrow slits, probably in some attempt to intimidate Wise, no doubt. Not that it worked.

'Tom wasn't always a bad man,' Wise said. 'Sure, back when we were kids, he and I caused a bit of trouble every now and again at school. Maybe we kept our parents up worrying a bit later than we should've done sometimes, but it was all innocent stuff. The sort of nonsense two hyperactive kids get up to all over the world.

'Then our mother died when we were thirteen. Cancer. It was awful. It took nearly a year for her to go from diagnosis to coffin. A year when all we could do was watch her suffer and wither away. It was hell.' Even talking about it right then brought back the pain as if it was yesterday. Then again, grief never really disappeared. It just lurked away inside, waiting for its moment to reappear as bad as ever before.

'Once she was gone, me and Tom... well, we went off the rails. We were hurt. Angry. Scared. Lost. And we covered all that up by getting into trouble. By fighting, mainly. We liked a good ruck, Tom and I. Causing pain to hide our pain.'

'A therapist tell you that?' Murray said.

'She did, actually. Her name's Doctor Shaw. I see her once a week,' Wise said. 'I can give you her number, if you want. You could talk to her about your anger issues.'

Heer put a hand on Murray's arm, stopping him from replying. 'You were telling us about your falling out with Tom.'

Wise nodded. 'As we got older, we liked fighting more and more. We also liked going to the football. Luckily, back then, both our interests went hand in hand. Most Saturdays, we'd go see the Chelsea play, then have a punch up with the other team's fans. By the time we were sixteen, we'd got really good at it. So good, in fact, that we got noticed by some older heads and they invited us to run with them.

'Me and Tom were thrilled. We'd felt we'd made it. We'd found a new family to be a part of.'

'I take it that it didn't work out,' Heer said.

'It did for a while. We had a lot of fun,' Wise said.

Murray scoffed. 'Beating up people was fun?'

'Have you ever been really good at something?' Wise asked. 'I mean really, really good? So good that it's obvious you're leagues above anyone else you know at doing it? So good that you can do things that others would find impossible to do? That they wouldn't even dare to do?'

Murray just stared back.

'Well, that's what Tom and I were like at fighting. We were big, but it was more than that. We'd get into a fight and we'd not be scared or worried. Because we knew we could beat anyone who was standing in front of us. And that power was exciting. Thrilling. And the more we did it, the more we wanted to do it.'

Wise leaned back in the chair, the plastic complaining about his weight. 'Anyway, on the third of April, 2004, Chelsea played Spurs at White Hart Lane. They won one nil. Jimmy Floyd Hasselbaink scored. A tap in from a few yards out. The win allowed the Blues to move within a few points of Arsenal at the top of the table and we were starting to believe that maybe — just maybe — Chelsea might be able to win the Premiership at long last.' He didn't know why he told Heer and Murray the details of the match. Maybe it was because he wanted them to think it was important, but the truth was, he could barely remember the game itself. It was everything else he could still recall in vivid detail. Even after twenty years.

'We went to the match with our usual crew, after meeting in a pub near the Bridge to have a few pints first.'

'You were sixteen at the time?' Heer asked.

Wise nodded. 'No one cared that we were underage. We were with some of the older lads anyway, seasoned fans. More than a few of them claimed they'd been members of the notorious Headhunters back in the day and, having been in a few punch ups with them, I could believe it. They were never shy about getting stuck in and they could definitely handle themselves. For wannabe thugs like Tom and I, they were people to look up to. People to admire.

'By the time we all left the pub and headed north, there was nearly fifty of us. Quite the force to be reckoned with. It felt good marching along together, singing, shouting and scaring anyone out doing their Saturday shopping.

'We took the Victoria Line to Tottenham Vale Station. It wasn't the closest to the stadium, but that was a deliberate choice. It meant there were less police about and the thirty-minute walk gave us lots of opportunities to have a little fun.'

'And by fun, you mean fight,' Murray clarified.

'We started singing the moment we were off the train. Singing *Carefree* so loud, it rattled around the houses. Tom and I were at the front. There was this bloke, Mad Errol, on one side, a right hard nut who'd had his face spliced open with a Stanley knife once upon a time. If anyone asked him about the scar, he'd just smile and say, 'You should see the other guy.' There were others too; Disco Biscuit, Two-Pint, Chinese Dave and Little Mark. All of us clapping our hands and singing away, proudly wearing our colours.' The memories came back to Wise like it was yesterday. It took balls to walk through enemy territory like that, but Wise had felt invincible at the time. He couldn't wait for someone to try and have a go. That was what they all wanted.

'Some Tottenham fans were waiting for us in the park. They had about the same numbers as us. We fought.'

That was true, but didn't really convey what happened. In fact, there was something medieval about what happened next as the two opposing groups of fans ran full-tilt into each other, beating each other with their fists, boots and whatever else they had to hand. There were knuckle dusters, truncheons and saps in the melee. Maybe a few knives too. Wise didn't care though. The fight was why he'd gotten out of bed that morning. It was what he'd been looking forward to all week.

He was super-charged with adrenaline, flattening anyone dumb enough to come near him.

He had smacked someone right in the face, pulping his nose, before kicking another lad in the balls so hard that he was probably still singing soprano twenty years later. Wise ducked under a club, then stamped on the club-owner's knee. The man went down quick and got rewarded with a boot to the head for good measure.

Someone tackled Wise to the ground, and he had struck back with a flurry of rabbit punches to the bloke's kidneys. It was like hitting a punch bag for all the good it did. The ugly bastard weighed a tonne too and Wise could feel the air being squeezed out of his lungs as he was being squashed into the mud. That was when Wise bit the man's nose as hard as he could. Blood filled his mouth as he heard the man scream.

Then he was gone. Tom had kicked the bastard off Wise and the Spurs fan had run, clutching his bloody nose, howling like a girl.

'You alright?' Tom had asked, sticking out a hand to help his brother to his feet.

Wise spat something out and grinned. 'I'm good.'

'Is that the geezer's nose?' Tom asked, staring at the lump of flesh on the ground.

'Yeah,' Wise said. Looking back now, Wise wondered if that was what sent Tom over the edge later, because Mad Errol and Two-Pint came over and they were patting Wise on the back like he'd done something special. When they went to the match, the nose-biting incident was all anyone wanted to talk about.

'What happened next?' Heer asked.

'When the game finished, Errol pulled Tom and I aside and asked if we were interested in joining his crew,' Wise said. 'His work crew. He said he needed lads like us who could handle themselves and wouldn't mind if the odd law got bent in the process. When we said yes, Errol told us we'd have to pass an initiation test first.'

'A test?' Heer clarified.

'More of an initiation, really. He told us we had to walk into this Tottenham pub, wearing our Chelsea shirts, and have a pint,' Wise said. 'If we could do that, we were in.'

Murray looked up. 'What pub?'

'You Spurs?' Wise asked.

'I am.'

'You know the Bishop's Crown on Whitehall Street?'

Murray winced. 'You had to go in there wearing blue?'

Wise nodded.

'I'm amazed you made it out of there alive.'

'Well, we weren't entirely stupid. We waited maybe three or four hours after the match before we did it. When most of the Tottenham fans had gone home or gone elsewhere. Even so, I was crapping myself when we walked in. Everyone, even the old grandads and grannies gave us evil looks as we sauntered up to the bar. The barman refused to serve us at first and told us to jog on but, when he realised we weren't going anywhere, he gave us a pint each and told us to drink it quickly.'

'How much of the pint did you get to drink?' Murray asked.

'We had about two sips before these four lads came over and it kicked off. We all knew that was what we were there for, after all.

'It was pretty much a straightforward scrap at that point. Four of them against the two of us but Tom and I were winning — if there was such a thing. Anyway, someone must've called the police because

I heard sirens and I saw the flashing blue lights wash over the pub. I turned to grab Tom so we could leg it, but he was kicking this lad, who's on the ground. Kicking him bad.' Wise could see Tom's face so clearly in his mind, despite the long years between then and now; all twisted and contorted, full of fury, full of hate. 'I tried pulling him away. I told him the police were there. I did everything I could to get him to leave, but he just kept on kicking the lad. In the end, I legged it out the back as the police came through the front. Tom got arrested and I ran home.'

'I'm surprised you didn't get a knock on the door,' Murray said.

'Tom said he didn't know the bloke with him,' Wise said. 'He never grassed me up either. Not even when he was sent down. But that didn't mean he was alright with it. He said I should've dragged him out of there, that I just ran to save myself and left him to get nicked. He refused to speak to me after that. I tried seeing him once, when he was in Feltham. I went along with my dad but Tom... Tom attacked me. The guards had to drag him off me and he got banned from having any visitors for four months.'

'Any reconciliation since then?' Heer asked.

'The first time I saw him after he got out was back in September. I went over to see my dad and Tom was just leaving when I got there. We exchanged words but Tom made it clear that things were still bad between us,' Wise said.

'Was that when he threatened your family?'

'No. That was this past Saturday. I knew he seeing my dad again, so I went over to get his car reg so I could run a PNC check on it. His driver spotted me, though, and told Tom. Tom then rang me and made some not very subtle threats against my family if we should ever accidentally run into each other again.'

Heer glanced over at Murray, then turned her attention back to Wise.

'If your brother's threatened you,' Heer said, 'you need to take it seriously.'

DS Brendan Murray leaned forward. 'Most people he threatens end up dead.'

'We've got twenty-eight bodies against his name at the moment,' Heer added, the pair of them a little tag-team of information. 'But the real count's much higher.'

'And, if we count the people who've died because of him — people like your old partner, then we're talking hundreds.' Murray grinned. He was enjoying this. He could see how much his words hurt Wise and he wasn't holding anything back.

'Have you told your wife?' Heer asked.

Wise shook his head, stunned by what he'd just heard. 'No, I've not told her about any of it.'

'You should. Your brother's about as dangerous as they come.'

Wise didn't reply. That was another conversation he didn't want to have. God only knew how Jean would react.

'Did you get his car details?' Murray asked.

'Yeah, he drives a BMW Five series, but it's registered to a Melanie Hayes. She's a solicitor at Trelford, Mayers and Jenkins,' Wise said.

Murray whistled. 'They're big money.'

'Where do I know the name Melanie Hayes from?' Heer said.

'She was the one who got Harold Sumner off a twenty million quid heroin bust and forced the Met to issue an apology,' Wise said.

'Of course,' Heer said. 'She's not very popular up at the Embankment.' The Embankment was New Scotland Yard.

'What is she to your brother?' Murray asked. 'Brief? Girlfriend? Partner?'

'Your guess is as good as mine,' Wise said. 'But you don't hang out with London's top criminal solicitors unless you're up to no good.'

'Quite,' Heer said.

Wise rolled his neck. 'And that's all I've got. I don't know where he lives, what he's doing day to day or anything like that. I don't even know if the car details are useful anymore because he knows I was checking his motor out. There's a good chance he'll have swapped it for something else now.'

'I wish you'd told us all this back in September,' Heer said.

'I know and I'm sorry about that. It's just taken me a while to get my head around it.'

'And how do you feel about it now?'

'If Tom's doing what you say he's doing,' Wise said, 'then I want him arrested. It doesn't matter if it's my brother, father or friend. If they break the law, they go to prison.'

'Or end up dead on a rooftop in Peckham,' Murray said.

A red dot appears as it always does and dances across Andy's shoulders, seeking his head, finding its spot, stopping on his temple, dead still.

Wise blinked. 'Yeah. That too.'

'Well, that's quite the story, Inspector,' Heer said. 'But you've put us in quite the predicament. On one hand, you're the brother of quite possibly the most dangerous man in London and you've already lied to us in order to protect him and yourself.'

Wise went to interrupt her, but she held up a finger.

'Let me finish,' Heer said. 'Because my gaffer thinks we should bang you up. He reckons you're a bad one — like your brother.'

'What do you think?' Wise replied, very aware of the walls around him and the locked door behind his back.

Wednesday 7th December

2

It was 4 a.m. and Karen Metcalfe was fit to drop. Unfortunately, she wasn't even halfway through her shift at the Emergency Operations Centre in Newham. She didn't think there was enough coffee in the world to get her through the next three hours, answering all the 999 calls coming in.

The centre in Newham was only eighteen months old and had the best tech money could buy to help process London's six and a half thousand 999 calls a day. But, when you broke it down, that meant the team of one hundred and fifty responders had to deal with four or five calls a minute between them. It was a mental pace at the best of times but, with Christmas around the corner, the volume of calls had gone crazy.

To make things worse, the bloody World Cup was on, so that meant on top of all the normal festive bollocks, domestics were up, bar fights were up and other drunken incidents and accidents were off the charts.

Karen hadn't had two minutes to herself since her shift had started, but, then again, no one else on her team had taken a break all night long. And it didn't look like that was going to change anytime soon.

Her call light flashed.

'Emergency services, how may I help you?' she said, feeling that familiar surge of adrenaline she got with every call.

'Yeah, I need someone to come around my house,' a man said, his words slurred. 'It's an emergency.'

'Okay,' Karen said. 'What type of emergency is it? Do you need the police, ambulance, or fire brigade?'

'Whoever can get my door open,' the man said.

'Your door?'

'Yeah, my front door. I've lost my keys, and the missus won't let me in. The bitch said I'm ... I'm drunk.'

Karen closed her eyes and took a deep breath. Another dickhead. 'I'm sorry, sir, but we deal only with life and death emergencies. Perhaps you should call a locksmith.'

'This a bloody life or death emergen... emer... emergency I'm freezing my nuts off out here.'

'I'm sorry, sir, but I can't help you,' Karen said. 'I'm sure if you apologise to your wife, she'll let you in.'

'Apologise?' the man roared. 'To that c—'

Karen ended the call. How many cranks was that tonight? Too many. The saddest fact of all was, out of those six and a half thousand calls a day, over half were for non-emergencies. Everything from people complaining about a restaurant being overbooked to demanding help to change a flat tire. Christ, someone even called 999 the other day because their local KFC was shut. Their stupidity made Karen's job near impossible.

And, no doubt, if England lost to France at the weekend, people would inundate the centre with calls demanding the arrest of Gareth Southgate.

Her call light flashed again. Jesus. It had better be a genuine emergency, or she'd scream.

She answered the call, putting on her business voice. Fake posh, her mum had called it. 'Emergency services, how may I help you?'

'Oh, hi,' a man said. He sounded young, scared. Karen straightened. She knew straight away this wasn't a nonsense call. 'I need an ambulance urgently. There's this man. He's not moving, and he's covered … covered in blood.'

'Okay,' Karen replied, keeping calm, her tone friendly, as if a body covered in blood was just one of those things everyone had to deal with. The man wouldn't panic if she could make him feel like everything was under control. 'Let's start with your address, just in case we get disconnected. Where are you?'

'Yeah. It's … er … it's Friary Road. Wilmsden Terrace Flats.'

'Okay. I've got that,' Karen said. 'And what number are you?'

'I'm in flat eight, but the guy's in the flat below me. The ground-floor flat.'

'Okay. You're doing really well. I've got help on its way to you already.'

The man let out a sob. 'Thank God. Thank you.'

'Can you tell me your name?'

'My name?'

'Just so I know who I'm talking to. That's all.'

'Leon. Leon Tomoral.'

'Okay, Leon. You're doing really well. Now, you said the man is bleeding. Is he conscious?'

'I don't think so, but I only went down for a quick look. I saw him through the window — but there's so much blood. He's covered in it.' Leon paused. It sounded like he was sniffing back tears. 'He wasn't moving. I think he's dead.'

'What made you go down to have a look in the first place?' Karen asked as she typed the information into the system, triggering calls to the nearest police station and ambulance service.

'There was shouting. Lots of shouting. I couldn't really hear most of what they were saying, but it sounded bad, you know. Nasty. Lots of threats and stuff. I nearly called you lot then, but it went quiet. So, I went down. Had a look.'

'And what did you find, Leon?'

'The door to the flat was open, man, but I didn't go in, 'cause I could see through the window. And the bruv, he's lying there and the light's on, and I can see the blood.'

'Did you go inside to check if he's alive?'

'I didn't want to go in. I didn't want to. I couldn't.' Leon sobbed again. 'He looks dead.'

'That's fine,' Karen said. 'I'm sure it must be very frightening.'

'I'm petrified,' Leon replied. 'What if whoever did this comes back?'

'I have people on their way to you now,' Karen said. 'But you can stay on the phone and talk to me until they get there.'

'Thank you.'

'Is there anyone else in the flat with you?'

'No. I'm on my own.'

'Okay. Well, you've got me now,' Karen replied. 'Do you know the man that lives in the flat downstairs?'

'No. He's new. I think he moved in about a month or so ago.'

'Does he live on his own like you or does anyone else live there with him? Anyone we should be concerned about?'

'I don't know,' Leon said. 'I think he lives there on his own but there's always lots of people coming and going, you know. All day, all night.'

'Is there anything else you can think of that can help us?' Karen asked.

'After the shouting stopped, I heard a car drive off. Real fast, man. Wheels spinning and screeching, you know?'

'Did you see the car?'

'Nah. I kept my head down, then went to check on the bruv downstairs.'

Karen checked her monitor. 'All right. Thank you, Leon. I'll ask you to stay in your own flat for the moment, please. The police are four minutes away.'

'Thank you,' Leon said.

'You're welcome,' Karen said as she listened to him cry.

3

Wise woke with a start, his heart racing, his body soaked in sweat. He might have even been screaming. He had been having The Dream again. The Dream, in which Armed Response Officers shot and killed his old partner, Andy Davidson, on the rooftop of the Maywood estate in Peckham.

He picked up the glass of water from the nightstand next to his bed and took thirsty gulps as he tried to force his heart rate back to normal. It would be nice if he could just make it through one night without reliving that terrible moment. His psychiatrist told him it would take time to get over everything that had happened that night, but it had been six months. Surely that was long enough? He'd give anything for eight hours of uninterrupted, guilt-free sleep.

Wise looked over his shoulder, to check if he'd woken his wife, Jean, only to find her side of the bed was empty. He reached over and touched cold sheets. Jean hadn't been in bed for a long time. A touch of guilt ran through him. Jean was normally a good sleeper — unlike him — but the last week hadn't been easy on her.

Not since he'd told her about Tom and his run-in with SCO10 at Belmarsh Prison.

Putting the empty water glass down, Wise glanced at his watch. It was just gone 5. He got out of bed, shivering as he did so. The central heating hadn't come on yet and there was a chill to the air that didn't sit well against his sweat-soaked skin. Wise pulled off the damp t-shirt that he'd slept in and swapped it for a hoodie that he'd left lying on the chair in the corner of the room.

Wise picked up his phone next. No one had messaged him during the night. That was something, at least. He could do with no work dramas for a while.

Slipping the phone into the pocket of his pyjama bottoms, he slipped out of the bedroom and went looking for Jean. He passed his children's bedroom doors. Ed had his door slightly ajar, just wide enough to let some of the light that always had to be left on in the bathroom opposite into his room. Claire, though, had her door firmly shut. Even though she was six years old, the dark never bothered her. Of course, that might have something to do with the army of stuffed toys that guarded her bed from any monsters foolish enough to try entering her room.

Jean wasn't in the bathroom, so Wise headed downstairs. He wished he'd put socks on as the wooden floorboards were just as cold as the rest of the house. Probably more so. His father had laughed when he'd seen the house after they'd had the floors done. 'Still saving up for the carpets?' he'd said and then his mouth had dropped open when they told him how much it had cost to have the wooden floorboards done up.

In the end, Jean was easy enough to find. The light was on in the kitchen at the back of the house. They'd talked about knocking down the various walls that separated the kitchen from the dining room and living room, so it was all open plan but, for now, the downstairs still had the original Fifties cramped layout from when the house was built.

Jean sat at the small, round kitchen table where the family ate all their meals, wrapped up in a white dressing gown and clutching a cup of tea. She looked up as Wise entered, and he didn't need to be much of a detective to see that she'd been crying.

'Hey,' he said, keeping his voice low. 'You okay?' It was a stupid question because it was obvious she wasn't.

'I'm fine,' Jean lied, her voice thick with emotion.

Wise slid into the seat next to her and squeezed her shoulder. 'What's wrong?'

'Nothing.'

A smarter man might've taken the hint and left things there, but Wise could be pretty dumb sometimes. 'Something's upset you.'

'Something?' Jean spat the word out as if its very utterance by her husband was an insult. 'Something?' It didn't sound any better the second time she said it. Worse, in fact.

'Is this about Tom?' Wise said, even though he knew it had to be. Tom, his twin brother, had been the only topic of conversation recently. Well, when the kids were asleep or out of earshot, at least.

'Don't you mean Tom the gangster? Tom the killer? Tom who bloody threatened our family?' Tears sprung up in the corners of Jean's eyes.

'I don't really think he'll hurt any of you,' Wise said, not for the first time. 'He just said it to get me to stop looking into his affairs.' It sounded just as unconvincing as it had on all those other occasions he'd said it.

Jean smiled but there was no humour there. No laughter. Her lips clenched tight. Pained. 'That's right. He only wanted you to stop your unauthorised investigation into his criminal empire. An investigation that's put all of us at risk. Put your job at risk.'

'I just wanted to make sure Tom was guilty of what they suspected him of doing. That's all.'

'But it's not your place to do that. You told me they've got a whole special task force set up to investigate him. A task force you've been interfering with.'

'Have you told your wife?' Heer asks.

When he returned home from Belmarsh, Wise had told Jean everything. It hadn't been a pleasant conversation. No mother wants to hear a criminal has made threats against her children. No mother wants to be told to be careful and to keep an eye out for anyone who might be watching her or the kids. Someone who might do them harm.

'I'm sorry,' he said, as he had done so many times since he'd first told her. And, like all those times, it did nothing to make the situation any better. And two weeks of thinking about it, of worrying about it, hadn't made Jean any less forgiving for being thrown into something that she and the kids didn't deserve to be in.

Wise didn't blame her for being angry about it all. He just wished he could fix it somehow.

He glanced over at her cup. 'Can I make you another cup of tea?' An Englishman's answer to everything.

Jean pushed her near empty cup towards him.

Picking it up, Wise got up from his chair, walked over to the kettle, and turned it on. Then he opened up the coffee machine next to it and popped a capsule in. He put a cup of his own in front of it before pressing the power button. It gurgled into life and Wise winced at the noise it made, unwelcome in the early morning quiet, and hoped it wouldn't wake the kids up. That would be all he needed. It was bad enough that Jean was upset about Tom without provoking her fury further by disturbing the children.

By the time his cup was full, the kettle had boiled. He threw a tea bag into Jean's cup, filled it with hot water, and then dug a teaspoon out of the cutlery drawer. All the while, he could feel Jean's eyes on him, full of accusation and resentment. He squeezed the tea bag with the back of the spoon, then fished it out of the cup and dropped it in the bin, thinking how annoyed his father would be at the waste. That man got at least two, if not three, cups out of every bag. Finally, Wise added a splash of milk to Jean's tea before placing it in front of her. 'There you go.'

In the past, she would've said thank you but now there was only silence and, somehow, that hurt more than angry words. As he sat down with his coffee, the small table felt more like a wall between them that was only growing bigger by the day.

'Have you heard what that DCI's going to do about you?' Jean said, eventually.

'No,' Wise said.

'*My gaffer thinks we should bang you up,*' Heer says. '*He reckons you're a bad one — like your brother.*'

'*What do you think?*' Wise replies, very aware of the walls around him and the locked door behind his back.

Wise wasn't in trouble just for hindering their investigation. There was the fact that he'd lied when he'd applied to join the Met all those years ago. Wise hadn't mentioned that his brother was in prison for manslaughter, and he'd kept that fact hidden from every background check since then. The Met didn't like people doing things like that. He'd be lucky if he kept his job, let alone his rank, by the time the higher ups decided what to do. And that was something else Jean wasn't happy about. He was the main wage earner. His salary paid the mortgage.

There was never a good time to lose your job, but now? In the middle of a cost-of-living crisis, when a pack of butter cost an arm and a leg? And it wasn't as if there'd be lots of people lining up to hire an ex-police detective who'd been forced out because of his dishonesty.

Wise took a sip of coffee as he wondered what to say — what he could do — to make things better. As usual, he didn't have a clue.

More tears appeared in the corners of Jean's eyes.

'I'm so ...' Wise's phone rang, cutting off another useless apology. He pulled it out of his pocket, saw DC Sarah Choi's name on the screen. 'Sarah,' he said on answering.

'Hi, Guv. Sorry to call you so early,' Sarah said. 'But we've got a body.'

4

Wise had to admit he was glad he'd been called out and had an excuse to leave the house. He hated seeing Jean upset like that, but he didn't know how to fix things. He didn't believe Tom had been serious with his threats against his family, but it was also obvious Wise didn't have a clue what his brother was capable of.

The sky was still as black as it got. Dawn wasn't even a promise in the sky as he set off towards Peckham in his battered Mondeo. Rain slashed down, forcing the windscreen wipers to work overtime, and they squeaked and groaned with the effort. Wise had his car's heater on full blast as well to fight the December cold, but it was as knackered as everything else in the Mondeo, and was losing the battle.

He'd put in a request for a new service vehicle, but as with everything else in the Met, he'd been told in no uncertain terms that he was going to be waiting a long time. In the meantime, he just hoped his car could soldier on a little longer.

At least, it was only a fifteen minute drive from Wise's home in Clapham to Friary Road in Peckham, especially as London was only just waking up. Lights were coming on in houses as people made their morning cups of tea and coffee and tried to pluck up the courage to face another miserable day. Christmas was only a few weeks away and yet there seemed to be very little festive cheer going on. Most people were just struggling to make it to the end of the year in the vain hope that 2023 would be miraculously better.

Wise, on the other hand, had a horrible feeling things were only going to get worse in every way. He turned the radio on as he drove, needing its noise to distract him from his thoughts. The news from the World Cup in Qatar was on and Wise half-listened to the commentators pumping out the usual hysteria about the England team's prospects of finally winning a trophy after coming so close at the last World Cup and at the Euros. England were playing France in the quarterfinals in a few days' time, though, and Wise wasn't so sure that the team had it in them to win against such good opposition. England had enjoyed quite an easy qualifying group, scoring plenty of goals against Iran and Wales, but they'd struggled against the US, the only half-decent team in their group. Playing France was going to be an even tougher ask. Still, he'd watch if he could and pray the lads got a result.

He drove up through Brixton and along Coldharbour Lane, to Denmark Hill, then turned right by the Camberwell Bus Garage. The red single and double deckers were already heading off to pick up the first commuters of the day. He passed them, grateful that he didn't have to rely on busses to get around, as he turned into Peckham Road.

Wise was halfway along it before he realised where he was.

The Maywood estate.

The giant monstrosity stood out amongst all the neighbouring buildings, full of all its ghosts from that fateful night in June. He slowed down without thinking, remembering the army of emergency vehicles parked around the base of the building, washing the neighbourhood in strobing blue lights as they brought him down off the roof, carrying Andy's body on a stretcher behind him. All those police officers watching him as he came out wrapped up in a silver-foil blanket, talking about him, judging him.

Nausea rose in Wise as he stared at the Maywood. He gripped his steering wheel tighter and tighter, feeling his throat constrict, and sweat popped out across his brow. He turned the heater off and opened the window, letting the freezing air in, carrying the stink of the streets with it. Even with the rain pelting down, he could smell the skunk and the shit, he could hear the gunshot ...

Andy tumbles forward, red mist leading the way, his brains and blood already splattered across the rooftop.

Wise blinked the memories away, focusing his mind on the road, back on the present, not on the past. It wasn't the time to get caught up with thinking about Andy again.

And it wasn't as if he didn't have enough on his plate. Leading a Murder Investigation Team in London kept him more than busy enough, with an average of one hundred and thirty murders a year in the capital. Things wouldn't slow down anytime soon, either, especially with all the budget cuts and personnel shortages. His own team was running at half-strength and yet they had a workload for double their number.

And he now had a fresh case to work on. He only hoped this one was a lot more straightforward than the last couple of big cases his team had handled. He'd had enough of serial killers to last a lifetime.

Wise put his foot down, eager to get to the murder scene and leave his bad memories behind.

Rain pelted his face through the open window, so he quickly buzzed it back up and turned the heater back on.

He turned left into Southampton Way then right onto Commercial Way, passing more and more council housing, blocks of flats and apartment buildings, ranging from the run-down to the brand-new. Past Victorian terrace houses and multi-million-pound developments. When he reached the Duke of Sussex pub, he turned left into Friary Road and immediately spotted the police vehicles clogging up the narrow road.

Wise found a spot to park the Mondeo, grabbed his phone and coat from the passenger seat, and got out into the wind and rain. He didn't waste a moment getting his overcoat on and buttoned up, but it wasn't fast enough to stop any lingering warmth from his car blowing away in the wind.

Wilmsden Terrace ran along the left-hand side of Friary Road. Built back in the sixties, the decades since had seen the block of flats endure more than their fair share of wear and tear. The concrete building now stood stubbornly unloved by all its residents. There were boarded up windows here and there, graffiti covered walls and all the paintwork looked in desperate need of a few hundred coats of fresh paint. The ground floor flats had garden areas, but it appeared most residents used the space for dumping anything from prams to bed frames. The front doors of the flats had once been painted a myriad of colours, perhaps in some vain attempt to inject some individuality to the terrace, but now each shared the same unloved, weather-beaten tones. The only nod to modernity were the satellite dishes that sprouted along the length of the terrace, all aimed west, to pick up the latest in mass entertainment from around the world, no doubt linked up to the biggest TVs the small flats would allow.

The victim's flat was at the far end of the terrace, opposite the old Friary that gave the street its name. It jutted up into the dark sky in all its gothic splendour, looking out of place amongst the low-cost housing that now made up the neighbourhood. No doubt in the future, some developer would take over the Friary and turn it into luxury apartments in the next step in the area's gentrification.

When Wise reached the blue and white police tape that cordoned off the road, he showed his warrant card to the scene guard, who noted down his name, rank, and time of arrival. Once he was logged in, Wise ducked under the tape and headed towards the inner cordon, marked by red and white tape. Scene Of Crime Officers — SOCOs — were already on site. They'd covered the front of the victim's flat with white tenting to protect it from the elements as well as prevent any passersby from having a morbid look at what was going on.

Amongst all the white suited forensics officers, Wise spotted Detective Sergeant Hannah Markham waiting just outside the tents.

Her all-weather, waxed motorbike jacket was done up tight to the top of her neck but she looked as cold as Wise.

'Hannah!' he called out.

She looked over on hearing her name and smiled. 'Guv. It's a lovely morning for a murder.'

'It is a murder, then? Sarah was lacking details on the phone,' he replied.

'Oh yeah. There's a IC3 male inside with his throat cut,' Hannah said. 'I don't think it was a shaving accident either.'

'Who's in charge of the SOCOs?' Wise asked.

'Do you know Helen Kelly?'

'Name's familiar,' Wise said. He couldn't remember where from, though.

'She seems good. Switched on.' Hannah glanced back at the tents. 'She's certainly not wasted any time getting things organised here.'

'What about the Home Office pathologist?'

'Your good friend, Doctor Singh, is on her way.'

Wise was glad. Singh was smart and damn good at her job. 'What about the rest of our team?'

'Hicksy's here. He's chatting to the bloke who called 999 in a flat upstairs. Apparently, he heard an argument, then saw a car speed away, so he came down to investigate and clocked the body,' Hannah said. 'Callum and Donut are here as well, doing some initial house-to-house enquiries.'

Wise nodded. As things stood, that was most of his active team. Sarah was back at Kennington, getting the incident room ready, and Brains would be with her doing what he did best — crunching data.

On a perfect day, he'd have ten officers on his team, but it'd been a long time since they'd had a perfect day. DC Louise 'Madge' Thomas had transferred out of the team after Andy's death, Jono was off on sick leave while he dealt with his cancer and Dan 'The Man' Turner had quit after a bout of long Covid ages ago. His team was now running with the bare minimum they needed to do their jobs.

A SOCO came out of the white tent and pulled their hood off, revealing a woman in her forties with curly brown hair tied back from her face. Wise recognised her, even though he still wasn't sure from where. When she spotted Wise and Hannah, she waved and headed over.

'Simon, isn't it? Simon Wise?' she said. The SOCO looked tired, with dark shadows under her eyes.

'That's right,' Wise replied.

'We worked together on that murder over in Tooting earlier in the year,' Helen said.

'Ah, yes,' Wise said as memories slipped into place. 'The bus driver.' It had been a particularly brutal and senseless killing. The bus had arrived late because of traffic congestion, and a passenger had got more than a little irate about it. So much so, he'd stabbed the driver a dozen times with a kitchen knife he just happened to be carrying. 'It's good to be working with you again.'

'Likewise.' Helen grimaced suddenly. 'I was sorry to hear about DS Davidson. He seemed an excellent officer when we worked together.'

The bullet takes the top of Andy's skull off a heartbeat before Wise hears the crack of the gun.

Wise looked away for a moment as he gathered himself, angry that any mention of Andy still triggered him. 'This is DS Markham,' he managed to say in the end, introducing Hannah.

'We've already met,' Hannah said.

'I take it you'd like to have a look around?' Helen said.

'If that's okay,' Wise replied.

'There's not a lot of room in there but get suited and booted and I'll give you the ten pence tour.' Helen pointed to a forensics van parked in the middle of the street. 'Changing room's over there.'

'Okay. Give us a minute.' Wise and Hannah headed over to the van, providing their details to another SOCO who gave them a set of the one-size-fits-all suits to put on. Wise had his customary battle to fit his bulk into the thing without ripping it, much to Hannah's amusement.

He gave her a glare as he zipped the suit up to his neck. 'It's not funny.'

'It is a bit,' Hannah replied before making a show of forcing the smile from her face.

Helen waited for them outside. 'You know the rules. No touching anything when we go in and keep to the metal treads.'

'I promise to be good,' Wise replied.

The two detectives followed Helen into the tent. It covered the whole of the front garden, protecting all its weed-riddled glory from the pelting rain. Metal treads led into the flat to ensure the comings and goings of the SOCOs didn't trample any evidence the killer might have left behind.

'The front door was already open, apparently, when the 999 caller came down to check on the flat's resident,' Helen said. 'There are signs someone tried to force it open at some point, but we don't know whether that was last night or last year.'

'In this neighbourhood,' Wise said, 'both are possible.' He spotted numbered yellow plastic cards on the ground just inside the door. As Wise got closer, he could see twenty-pound notes lying next to them. 'Interesting.'

'There's about two hundred or so quid scattered around inside,' Helen said. 'Maybe this is a robbery gone wrong.'

'The 999 caller said he heard sounds of an argument,' Hannah replied.

'He also said he didn't enter the flat and that he saw the dead body through the window.' Helen pointed to the windows by the front door. They were small, about forty centimetres high and twenty across, covered by net curtains on the inside. 'But, unless he's got x-ray vision like Superman, I'm not sure we can trust his account.'

Wise went over to the windows and peered through. The glass was so dirty, though, he could just about make out a shape on the floor, but he couldn't see clearly who or what it was, let alone any blood. 'I always wanted to meet Superman.'

'Maybe he killed the victim,' Helen said.

'It wouldn't be the first time a killer has rung 999 hoping to give themselves some sort of alibi,' Wise said.

They all pulled their suits' hoods up over their heads and then

Wise and Hannah followed Helen into the flat. The front door opened straight into the living room. A sofa was against the far wall, its cushions overturned, creating an immediate impression that someone had been searching for something, especially as there was a sideboard next to it, with its drawers open and half their contents dangling out or scattered on the floor.

A glass coffee table stood in front of the sofa, with four bottles of beer on it: two Stellas and two Luz Solars, one of which had been knocked over. Wise also noted two small plastic bags with some kind of powder in them. 'Drugs?'

Helen nodded. 'Looks like it.'

The dead man lying to the right of the door, face down in a pool of blood, by a drinks cabinet in the corner, a bloody gash under his chin. Wise walked over and bent down to have a better look.

The man wore black Nike trainers, black tracksuit bottoms and a grey Stone Island jumper. There were three gold rings on his left hand and one on his right. He looked young but Wise couldn't tell if he was eighteen or twenty-eight. Life had a way of aging people around that part of London. 'He's still got his jewellery. So, if it was a robbery, the gold wasn't what they were here for.'

'Maybe Top Boy here was selling,' Hannah said. 'That would explain the gear on the table.'

'Or buying,' Wise said. 'That would explain the cash.'

'Either one's a dumb reason to get killed for.'

Wise looked up at Hannah. 'There's never a good reason to kill someone.'

5

By the way the body was positioned, it looked like the man had been facing the drinks cabinet set up by the far wall when he'd gone down. A kitchen knife was next to his right hand, marked by another yellow plastic card. 'That the murder weapon?' Wise asked.

'We don't know but we'll send it along with the body to the morgue. The pathologist will be able to tell us if it matches the cut,' Helen replied.

There was an overturned waste paper bin by the victim's head. Its lid lay tucked up against the wall but there was nothing inside. Wise looked closer. 'Is that powder on the sides?'

'We think so,' Kelly replied. 'We'll know for certain after we've sent it for testing.'

Wise stood up. 'No one did a taste test then?'

Helen laughed. 'This isn't the nineties. By the way, there are two mobile phones on the floor by the sofa. One's an iPhone and the other's an ancient Ericsson.'

Wise glanced over. More yellow cards marked the phones' locations. 'I haven't seen an Ericsson in years.'

'Those old phones are still a lot of dealers' first choice,' Hannah said. 'You can call or text, but people think we can't track them as well as a smartphone.'

'They're wrong about that,' Helen said. 'We'll get these off to Digital Forensics and see what they can get from them.'

'Do we have an ID for the victim?' Wise asked.

'The flat's rented to a Cameron Nketiam. Twenty-four. A recent resident of Wormwood Scrubs.' Hannah pulled out her phone, brought up a mug shot and showed it to Wise. 'That's him.'

'May I?' Wise asked, holding out his hand. Hannah passed him her phone, and he bent down again to compare the picture with the man's face. 'Looks like him. Did Sarah say what he was inside for?'

'Take a guess.'

'Possession with intent to supply?'

'Bingo.'

'Don't quote me on it but I think the assailant hit the victim over the head, then cut his throat once he was down on the ground,' Helen said. She pointed to the spot at the back of the man's head. 'There's a massive dent here and, if his throat had been cut while he was standing up, the far wall would've been decorated with arterial spray from top to bottom. As you can see the wall's clean.'

Wise glanced up at the wall above the drinks cabinet. 'I'm not sure clean is the word I'd use to describe it but you're right. There's no blood.'

Wise stood up. 'I've seen enough here for now. We'll get out of the way of your team, Helen.'

'Thanks, Simon. I'll be in touch if and when we find anything of interest,' Helen said.

'Appreciate it,' Wise said. He headed back outside, with Hannah following. 'How long has Cameron been out?'

'Three months,' Hannah replied. 'Long enough to get back into his old life.'

'So, he either got whacked for his stash or for his cash.' Wise stepped out of the tent and pulled his hood down. It was still pouring, but not as hard as before. Wise raised his face to the sky, enjoying the rain's icy sting. It was nearly as good as coffee in washing the cobwebs away.

Despite the early hour, a sizeable crowd had gathered around the blue and white tape of the outer cordon. Most had phones out, filming the police at work, looking for gossip or something to post on social media. There were some mothers with prams, a few kids on bikes, their heads covered with hoods, plus a smattering of others with umbrellas up who looked like they were on their way to work, and plenty of others who appeared to be on their way home from wherever they'd spent the night.

'Get someone to have a word with our audience,' Wise said to Hannah, 'and see if we can get their names and addresses. Who knows? Maybe someone saw something.'

'In this neighbourhood?' Hannah said. 'They're more likely to have collective amnesia if they have to talk to the Feds.'

'We have to try, anyway.'

The two detectives returned to the forensics van and removed their suits, giving them to a SOCO to bag up and dispose of later. With a crime scene, no one took any chances of corrupting the evidence by transferring something from one place to another. Someone reusing a forensics suit from another crime scene by mistake would do that only too well.

Back outside, Wise looked across the street. In marked contrast with everything else in Friary Road, the Georgian terraced houses opposite Wilmsden Terrace were in perfect condition despite being three hundred years older than the surrounding buildings. The white paint on the various doors, columns, and window frames looked like it was freshly painted a few days before. In a street where everything else could do with demolishing, the properties looked like they had multi-million-pound price tags.

'Let's check out those houses as well,' Wise said. 'I'd imagine they'll have cameras for security. Maybe they caught our killer running away.'

'I'll do that now,' Hannah said.

'Thank you.' Wise watched her duck under the tape and head

over to the Georgian houses, feeling grateful that Hannah was on his team. Her presence had made the world of difference to everyone after what happened with Andy.

'You weren't thinking of leaving without saying hello?' A voice said from behind him. Wise turned around to see Doctor Harmet Singh. The diminutive pathologist smiled at Wise.

'Doctor,' Wise said, with a nod of greeting. 'How are you this fine morning?'

'All good,' Singh replied. 'Still waiting for that drink you owe me, though.'

Wise winced. He'd promised to buy the pathologist a thank you drink after her discoveries had helped catch David Smythe, the Motorbike Killer, back in September. 'Sorry. I've been a bit busy. Soon?'

'Sure. I've only been waiting three months. Perhaps we can sneak a drink in by the year's end?'

'I'll do my best to make that happen,' Wise said.

Singh nodded towards the forensic tent. 'Have you been in to have a look?'

'I have.'

'And?'

'I think you'll find he's dead, but I'll let you confirm that.'

'I heard the victim had his throat cut,' Singh said.

'You heard right.'

'Should be an easy one then.'

'Don't say that. They always turn out to be the worst,' Wise said with a smile.

Singh raised an eyebrow. 'I never took you for the superstitious type.'

Wise held up both hands. 'I'm not. I just don't believe in tempting fate.'

'Okay. I won't argue the logic of that,' Singh said. 'I better get inside and see the body.'

'We'll speak soon,' Wise said.

'Oh, we will,' Singh replied. She sauntered off to the forensics van to get her own suit, leaving Wise alone for a moment in the rain. The sky was brightening at least, the day finally feeling brave enough to show its face.

Wise yawned. He needed coffee as a matter of urgency. He'd not had one since the argument with Jean.

Wise pulled out his phone, opened WhatsApp, flicked through to the conversation with his wife, and typed *I am sorry. Everything will be okay. I love you. XX.* He hit send and heard the whoosh as it disappeared into the ether.

Jean would be getting the kids ready for school, chasing them to get dressed no doubt, and making sure they ate their breakfast. He knew she'd not have time to reply, even if she was in a mood to, but he still stared at his phone screen, hoping she would, desperate for any sign that things would be okay.

But no message came back.

The screen remained blank.

'Guv!'

Wise looked up. Hicksy was walking towards him, his chin tight against his chest, his eyes in shadow under his furrowed brow.

'Everything okay?' Wise asked.

'I think you need to come and have a word with the geezer who called 999, Guv,' Hicksy said.

'Why's that?'

'I've been in this game long enough to know a lying little toe rag when I see one — and Leon Tomoral is definitely telling porkies,' Hicksy growled before wiping some snot from that jagged mess of his nose. 'About what though, I don't know.'

'Come on then,' Wise said. 'Let's have a word.'

6

The upper-level flats were accessed via a central staircase that was open to the elements. Despite the wind and rain howling through, the smell of skunk and urine still lingered, as if great quantities had been absorbed into the brickwork over the years, so that nothing could ever wash it away.

Wise followed Hicksy up the stairs, stepping over discarded fag butts and scrunched up shopping bags, past graffiti-scrawled insults and puddles of who knew what, until they reached the third floor and they stepped out onto a landing with more badly painted front doors.

Hicksy headed straight to Leon's flat, directly above the victim's. A uniform stood guard outside, but she stepped aside to let the two detectives in.

The interior wasn't much different from Cameron's downstairs. The living room was smaller, but it was even more sparsely decorated than the one below it and what little he did have looked like Leon had rescued it from skips. Wise noted that the only new items were a Sony sixty-six-inch flatscreen TV and the PS4 connected to it.

Leon Tomoral himself was perched on the sofa, looking very unhappy with life. His right leg bounced up and down like a jackhammer while he chewed away at the fingernails on his left hand. He'd already bitten all the ones on his right hand to the quick. He wore blue Adidas tracksuit bottoms with a black Nike hoodie. A toe poked out of one of his not quite white socks.

'Alright, Leon,' Hicksy said, looming over the lad. 'This is my governor, Detective Inspector Wise.'

'Hello, Leon,' Wise said.

Leon looked up, his eyes wide and fearful. 'Hello.'

'I imagine you've had quite the morning so far,' Wise said.

'It's been horrible,' Leon replied.

Wise smiled. 'How old are you, Leon?'

'I'm ... I'm nineteen,' the lad replied.

'And do you live here alone?'

'No. I've got two flatmates. We're students at St. Martins.'

'That's the art school, isn't it?'

'Yeah. That's right. I'm studying fine art.'

'Very impressive,' Wise said. 'I can barely paint a fence, let alone a picture.'

'Why don't you tell my boss what you told me?' Hicksy said.

'Sure.' Leon took another bite of a fingernail. 'I was asleep when I heard shouting. It sounded real bad, so I went outside to have a look.'

Wise pointed to the walkway. 'Out there?'

'Yeah. That's right,' Leon said. 'That's when I heard them. The blokes in the flat downstairs.'

'How many blokes?'

'Two — I think.'

'And was it one person shouting, or were they both shouting at each other?' Wise asked.

'I don't know. It was hard to make out. I think both. One shouted, "You got this coming!" and the other told him to put the knife down. Then one of them was calling the other one a ... a ...'

'It's okay. You can say whatever it is,' Wise said. 'I doubt it's nothing I haven't heard before.'

'He called him a cheating cunt.'

'Charming,' Hicksy said, as if butter wouldn't melt in his own mouth.

'What happened then?' Wise asked.

'There was this scream. Blood-curdling, it was,' Leon said. He looked down, examining his fingernails for a moment. 'I ducked down out of sight, then I heard this car screech off, wheels spinning and stuff like that. So, I thought something bad must've happened, so I went down to have a look.'

'That was brave of you,' Wise said.

'No lie, I was shitting myself, man.'

'What did you find?'

'The door was open, but I didn't go in,' Leon said. 'It didn't feel right, so I peered through the window and that's when I saw him. The man. On the floor. And I knew he was dead. So, I ran back up here and called you lot.'

'You didn't go inside? Check to see if he was still breathing?'

'No one with that much blood around them was going to be alive, man. No way.'

'And you saw all this through the window?'

'That's right.'

Well, Wise knew that was impossible for a start. 'Okay. That's all good to know. We'll need you to come down to the station and make a formal statement.'

'I will?' Leon said.

Wise smiled. 'One of my officers will be in touch. Until then, try to relax. This sort of thing doesn't happen too often.'

'What if whoever did this comes after me?' Leon said. 'Because I'm a witness?'

'They won't,' Wise said. 'You didn't see whoever it was running to their car, did you?'

Leon kept his eyes on the floor. 'No.'

'Did you see the make of car or a numberplate?'

'No.'

'So, you're not actually a witness to anything,' Wise said, 'and, therefore, you have nothing to worry about. However, if there's something you're not telling us...'

'There isn't,' Leon said far too quickly. 'I saw nothing else.'

'You'll be fine then,' Wise said, glancing over at Hicksy. 'If you are concerned at any point, just call and we'll be straight here.'

'Thank you.' Leon went back to chewing his fingernail.

'We'll show ourselves out,' Wise said.

'Well?' Hicksy asked once they were back on the street.

Wise looked up at Leon's flat. 'He's definitely lying about something. Let's see what the door-to-door enquiries come up with and maybe they'll tell us what about. We can then bring in him to the station for a proper chat.'

Hicksy gave him a nod. 'I'll go check with Donut and School Boy. See how they're getting on.'

'Cheers. I'll see you back at the nick.'

As Hicksy walked off, Wise checked his phone but there were no messages from Jean. Shit.

He dialled Hannah instead, to let her know he was heading back to Kennington.

'Any luck with any CCTV footage?' Wise asked when Hannah picked up.

'Not yet, Guv, but a few of the houses don't seem to have anyone home. One place has a camera above their door that might cover the victim's flat. I've left a note asking them to call me.'

'That's good.'

'I did speak to one person who saw a Honda Civic driving away at speed at just gone 4 this morning. She didn't get the number plate though.'

'What was she doing up at that time of the night?'

'Apparently her dog needed to go for a wee.'

'Of course. And she's sure it was a Civic?'

'Yeah,' Hannah replied. 'She'd walked past it a few minutes before. She said it was orange, maybe red.'

'Great. Let Sarah know. Hopefully she can track the car to

wherever it was going.' Wise smiled. 'You never know, maybe the killer used his own vehicle to commit the crime.'

'That would be nice.'

'It certainly would be. I'm going to head over to Kennington,' Wise said. 'I'll see you there.'

'Okay, Guv.'

Wise ended the call and slipped his phone back into his pocket as he watched the crime scene over the heads of the gawping crowd. Maybe Singh was right. Maybe this was going to be a simple case for his team. God only knew they were due something straightforward after the last couple of big cases they'd investigated.

Then he shook the thought from his head. This was London. It didn't do easy.

7

As Wise drove to Kennington police station, he had to admit that he was glad that he had another case to focus on. Something else to think about other than himself and his own problems. A chance to forget about the mess his own life was in.

Unfortunately, his mind didn't want to focus on the body in the Peckham flat.

Instead, his thoughts drifted back to the Maywood estate, to that awful summer day in June when everything unraveled: the family barbecue ruined by a phone call, the rush to find Derrick Morris before he got killed, Wise unaware that the greatest danger to the witness was his partner, who it turned out was a drug addict and who might've murdered the prostitute blackmailing him.

Even now, it was hard to believe.

Wise had always said that it wasn't just the murder victims he needed to find justice for. It was for all the family members, loved ones and friends who got caught up in the horrific aftermath caused by a sudden death. Their lives got ripped apart and sometimes — a lot of times — they could never put them back together again. He'd personally discovered the truth of that after Tom killed Brian Sellers in that pub in Tottenham. And it was proving to be even more true after Andy's death. Whatever life Wise had built over the twenty years since he'd become a police officer — his career, his happy family — had been damaged by what had happened that night.

His confidence in himself was hit worst of all. Wise had always prided himself on his copper's instinct, that gut reaction he had when he came across things that weren't what they should be. And yet he'd not noticed anything wrong with his partner at all. He didn't have a single suspicion that Andy was up to no good.

But how could that be — especially once the magnitude of Andy's corruption was exposed?

He knew others in the Met felt the same. There'd been too much talk that Wise must've been on the take as well. After all, how could his partner — his best friend — be so bent without Wise noticing? The sad thing was Wise didn't even blame anyone for thinking that. He'd think the same if it was another officer in his situation.

All in all, the scandal had nearly broken Wise. So much so that he'd even thought about driving into the Thames and ending it all at one point, but he was glad he hadn't. Especially now he knew he was slowly getting better.

Recent successes at work had helped, but it was his weekly session with Doctor Shaw, his police appointed psychiatrist, that had really done wonders for him. Still, it was slow progress. He wanted to be better now. Not in a year or two years' time. He wanted his nightmares to stop. He wanted his life back the way it was — Jean feeling safe and happy, his job secure, his mind focused.

To do that, he needed the man responsible for Andy's downfall behind bars.

He wanted his brother, Tom, nicked.

So why hadn't anyone from SCO10 been in touch? He'd not heard anything from them since the meeting in Belmarsh.

'My gaffer thinks we should bang you up,' Heer says. 'He reckons you're a bad one — like your brother.'

Wise drove past Burgess Park, turned into Denton Road, and then headed up the Old Kent Road. Like everywhere in London, the area was going through the gentrification process at a rapid rate. Modern buildings mingled with Georgian terraces, an old fire station converted into apartment blocks, with a cafe taking up the ground floor, and the old building next door was now a posh school for rich kids.

The morning commuter traffic was at its peak and his progress was painfully slow as everyone battled to get to wherever they were spending the day. Boris Bikes lined the side of the road, left unwanted as the rain pelted down.

He took St. George's Street up to the cathedral, then turned left into Lambeth Road. It was a straight run from there to Kennington Police Station and, thankfully, the wider road allowed the morning traffic to move faster.

The entrance to the station car park itself was off Mead Road. The blue steel gates buzzed open as Wise approached, allowing him to slip through and into an empty parking slot. He didn't head into the station after he got out of his knackered Mondeo, though. Instead, he headed back out into the street, crossed Kennington Road and walked quickly over to Luigi's coffee shop.

As much as he relied on caffeine to keep him on his feet and functioning, Wise was still fussy about how it tasted and, as far as he was concerned, Luigi's made some of the best he'd ever tasted.

The cafe was quiet inside for a change, having finished its morning rush and with hours to go before the lunchtime madness. Customers sat around a couple of tables, but Wise was glad to see there was no queue at the counter.

'Hello, my friend,' Luigi said as Wise walked over. 'A late start today.'

'Unfortunately, it was an early start elsewhere,' Wise said.

'Ah,' Luigi replied, filling the word with all the wisdom gained from serving food and drinks to police officers for too many years. 'Not so good.'

'How's things with you?' Wise asked instead, happy to change the subject.

'We're okay,' Luigi said, looking round at his wife, Maria, behind the till, and his daughters, Sofia and Elena, who were busy prepping food for the lunch service. 'Big game for England soon, eh?'

Wise nodded. 'Big game. Have you watched many of the matches?'

Luigi waved the question away. 'A World Cup without Italy is like a meal without pasta. It's okay but never as good.'

'So why have you been watching every game then?' Maria called out, without looking in her husband's direction. 'Every night, it's football, football, football.'

Luigi shrugged. 'A man still needs to eat, eh?'

'Indeed,' Wise replied. 'Can I have a double espresso and a large Americano to go?'

'Of course, coming straight up.'

'Thank you, my friend.' Wise shuffled along the counter to the till and smiled at Maria, although she always seemed angry with the world.

'Six pounds ninety-nine,' Maria grunted.

'And worth every penny,' Wise said, holding up his debit card.

Maria's eyes took in the piece of plastic in his hand, then slowly moved up to fix on Wise's face. To say she didn't look happy was an understatement. 'You want to pay by card?' She managed to ask the question with so much disdain that it was easy to imagine that he'd asked to pay with coat buttons.

All Wise could do was smile more. 'Please.'

Maria tutted as she entered the cost into the card machine, then pushed it towards him. Before Wise could tap the payment through, he noticed the screen now asked him to add a tip to the cost with a starting option of fifteen percent. As his finger went to select it, Maria made a noise that could've been a growl. It was enough to make Wise select the twenty percent option instead. Going after some of the toughest criminals in London didn't bother him, but Wise was just a little bit scared of upsetting Maria. God only knew what it was like being married to her.

As the payment went through, Luigi handed Wise his drinks. 'Have a lovely day, Detective Inspector.'

'You too, my friend,' Wise said and hurried out of the cafe before Maria could add on another charge.

As he walked back to the nick, he looked at the nineteen fifties concrete block of a police station and wondered if it, too, would end up as an apartment building in its future, like everything else in London seemed to these days. Wise hoped not. As run down as the station was, it was his home, and he had a lot of affection for the old building.

When Wise walked into Major Incident Room One, or MIR-One as it was known, DC Sarah Choi and DC Alan 'Brains' Park were the only ones there. The bespectacled officer hadn't just got his nickname because of his uncanny likeness to the *Thunderbirds* puppet. The man was also a genius when it came to working the Met's ancient computer systems. Even now, he was tapping away at his keyboard, oblivious to Wise's arrival, illuminated by the glow from his monitor.

Sarah stood by the three whiteboards that covered the far wall, marker pen in hand. One of the boards said, *What do we know?* The second said, *What do we think?* and the third, *What can we prove?* Those boards and the questions posed on them were the heart of every investigation as far as Wise was concerned. Every detail that his team uncovered went up on them, alongside any theories that came up. Wise would often spend hours just staring at their information, looking for patterns and connections. They also helped him feel connected to the victims of the crimes his team investigated as they told a tale of their lives before they came to abrupt ends.

Sarah was his right hand in managing this aspect of the investigation. In the same way Brains was a genius with computers, Sarah would coordinate Wise's team of detectives like an orchestral conductor. The diminutive officer also had an amazing eye for going over CCTV footage. It wasn't a popular job with most officers but, with London one of the world's most heavily monitored cities, it was an essential element of the modern detective's job and not much missed Sarah's attention.

She'd been busy, filling details of that morning's incident on the board marked *What do we know?* There was a mug shot of Cameron

Nketiam stuck up in the centre with his date of birth and his Friary Road address. She'd also added his previous criminal record. Wise walked over and had a closer look. 'Possession with intent to supply, GBH, possession of a firearm, resisting arrest, possession of a class A drug, possession of a knife ...'

'For a twenty-four-year-old, he's covered most of the greatest hits,' Sarah said. 'Stints in youth detention centres and the Scrubs didn't deter him, either.'

'When you're in the life, you're in the life,' Wise said. He stared at the picture of Cameron, still so young, and yet his eyes were those of an old man who'd seen too much of life and none of it good. Wise wondered what chance he'd ever had to be anything other than what he was. Not many people were waiting to hand out opportunities to ex-drug dealers straight out of prison. It was all too understandable when people like Cameron just went back to what they knew best. Getting nicked and banged up for a stretch were just part of the gig.

Maybe that was what it was like for Tom too, after he got out of prison. He'd been locked up since the age of sixteen, with only hardened criminals for role models. Was it any wonder he was now a professional gangster?

'Cameron's got an ex-wife, Nadine, and a two-year-old daughter, Maxine,' Sarah said. 'They live down the street from him on Peckham Park Road. They've got a restraining order against him though, so it wasn't an amicable break up.'

'Has anyone gone around to break the news to them yet?' Wise asked.

'Not yet. Everyone's tied up at the scene.'

'Can you do that? Take Donut with you.' He took the lid off his double espresso and blew on the coffee to cool it down. It probably didn't make a difference, but it at least made him feel better about downing the scalding hot drink. Despite burning his mouth and throat, the caffeine immediately made Wise feel better.

Sarah arched an eyebrow at the suggestion of going with Donut. 'I'd rather go on my own. It's only a death notice. I don't need backup.'

'Donut's okay.'

'Yeah? Try sitting in a car with him. That man stinks. You should have a word with him.' Sarah shook her head. 'It's not right.'

'I think I'll leave that job to HR,' Wise said. Sarah did have a point, though. The body odour of DC Ian 'Donut' Vollers made everyone's eyes water. However, the man was blissfully unaware of the harm he was doing to the team's nasal passages. Someone had even given him aftershave and deodorant as secret Santa gifts, but the hints hadn't sunk in.

'By the way, Doctor Singh has already called,' Sarah said. 'She's doing the PM this afternoon and asked if you could come down around 2 p.m. to go over whatever she's found.'

'She's not wasting any time. That's good.' Wise looked back at the board. 'Try to find out who Cameron worked for. Maybe he set up shop on someone else's turf and that's what got his throat cut? Or maybe he was cheating on his boss?'

'I will — as long as Donut doesn't poison me on the way over to the ex-wife's,' Sarah said. 'Then you'll need to find some other fool to do that for you.'

'You know I can't afford to lose you,' Wise said. 'Maybe drive with the window open?'

8

The morgue was bitterly cold as usual when Wise and Markham entered through the main doors at the back of King's College Hospital in Camberwell. The temperature hovered just above freezing all year round. It was the optimal setting for the work that went on inside, essential so bodies wouldn't deteriorate after being removed from the storage freezers, but it made it uncomfortable for the people who worked there.

Wise wished he could've kept his overcoat on, but there was no way it would fit under the blue forensic suit he had to wear if he was to go into the examination suite. It was hard enough getting himself into the damn thing without the extra bulk.

Hannah tried not to laugh as she watched him struggle. 'Have you ever thought about getting some extra-large suits made just for you?'

'Apparently, these are as big as they get,' Wise replied, wiggling an arm in. 'And last time I asked, I got told it'd be easier if I lost twenty-five kilos instead.'

'Didn't you tell them it was all muscle?'

'Yeah. They told me to lay off the steroids.' Wise managed to get his other arm in and then began the perilous task of zipping up the suit. This was the point they normally split on him as the material stretched tight across his chest. He hoped it wouldn't happen this time as he couldn't face going through the ordeal again.

Hannah paused getting into her own suit and gave him a quizzical look. 'You're not on the juice, are you?'

Wise laughed. 'No. I can be pretty dumb on occasion, but not that dumb. I've always been big, and I just make sure I eat properly on top of exercising. Plenty of good protein, limited carbs and too much coffee.'

'Ah. You do admit you drink too much, then?'

'Oh yeah,' Wise said. 'Unfortunately, it's about the only thing that keeps me going most days. If I gave up the coffee, I'd have to give up The Job.'

'I don't want you to do that,' Hannah said and seemed to mean it. That thought perked Wise up. He had a very different working relationship with Hannah compared to the one he'd had with Andy but, after everything that had happened, that only had to be a good thing. He certainly liked her the way she thought, and he really liked the way she made him think. Considering how challenging their first cases together had been, the pair of them had still managed to results and put some very bad men behind bars.

They left the changing room and walked towards the examination suites. 'I don't know how you find time to work out,' Hannah said. 'I used to enjoy running, but now I just look at my trainers sitting in the bottom of my closet and feel guilty.'

'I've got a small gym set up in the back of my garage,' Wise said. 'It's nothing fancy, but it does the job, and I can use it whenever I have some spare time.'

'Lucky you.'

Wise didn't add that he was in there most mornings now, trying to exorcise his demons as well as exercise his body. It might not be curing him of his ills, but it was, at least, keeping him sane — aided, of course, by his sessions with Doctor Shaw.

It hadn't been easy trusting his shrink at first. Wise came from a long generation of South London men who didn't talk much, if at all, about their feelings. Emotions were things to be bottled up inside, to be dealt with on very rare occasions by excessive use of alcohol or violence. All things considered, Wise had been lucky that his father hadn't resorted to either after his mother had died but, looking back now, it would've been healthier for all of them if they'd actually talked about their feelings and the grief they were going through. Instead, his father had just retreated into his shell, barely noticing that Wise and Tom were going off the rails. It was only after Tom was arrested that his father returned to the world. Just when it was all too little, too late.

'You think you're hard, do you?' Tom screams as he kicks the lad in the head. 'Well, you're not so fucking tough now, eh?' His boot flies in again and again and Wise can hear bone breaking, the rattled gasps of a man dying. Strobing blue lights wash through the windows of the pub, making everything out of synch with reality. Tom doesn't even notice. His face is contorted, full of hate and anger — no, not anger. Tom's happy. He's enjoying himself. He lifts his foot up, so his knee is level with his waist, and then he stomps down. Like he's squashing an...

'Guv?'

Wise blinked and saw Hannah was looking at him with her head cocked to one side. He tried a smile. 'Sorry. Miles away.'

Hannah nodded. She was probably used to him drifting off into the past like that. Hopefully one day she'd get to work with him without ghosts haunting his thoughts.

They found Singh and her team hard at work in Examination Room Two. They all wore green smocks, hats, masks and gloves. One assistant helped Singh while another videoed the procedure.

Cameron Nketiam lay naked on the metal table in the centre of the room, his organs already removed and weighed. Stripped of everything — especially his life — it was hard to imagine Cameron as the career criminal he was. Now, he was just another person who'd lost their life far too soon.

'Inspector,' Singh said without looking up. 'You're on time for once.' She was checking the fingernails of the victim's left hand. 'That makes a pleasant change.'

Wise winced. He hated being late for anything, but London's

traffic made that an inevitability more often than not. 'Good to see you too, Doctor.'

'Not much to report with this one,' Singh said. 'He sustained a fracture to his occipital bone prior to death and then had his throat cut.' Singh pointed to the jagged wound across his neck. 'No surprises there.'

'When you say "fracture to his occipital bone",' Wise said, 'what do you mean by that?'

Singh reached up and touched the back of her head. 'This is the occipital bone. Someone whacked our friend here in the back of the head with something small but heavy. A cosh, perhaps, or a small club or truncheon.'

'The head SOCO thought he might have been hit there. So, he was definitely unconscious when he died?'

'Absolutely. In fact, there was probably no need to cut his throat,' Singh said. 'Death would've taken longer, but the victim wasn't getting up again after the damage done to his head.'

Wise turned to Hannah. 'Can you check with the SOCOs and see if they found anything that could've been used to deliver the blow to the head?'

Hannah nodded. 'Of course.'

'What about the knife, doctor?' Wise asked. 'Is that the one used to cut Cameron's throat?'

'It is,' Singh replied. 'Judging by the angle and depth of the cut, the killer was standing over the victim and cut into the throat in much the way we'd carve a joint of meat. There are signs that the knife moved backwards and forwards as they cut deeper into the neck.'

Hannah shivered. 'Jesus.'

'Whoever did this wanted to do the job properly,' Singh said.

'Any other injuries?' Wise asked. 'Any defensive wounds that might suggest a fight or anything like that?'

'Nothing,' Singh said. 'Just the bump to the head and the cut throat. We've sent his fingerprints and DNA off to be checked but, when we ran his prints through IDENT1, we got a match for a Cameron Nketiam.'

IDENT1 was the new Home Office major national database of fingerprints. It contained all fingerprints gathered by the police when they took someone into custody. Anyone convicted of a serious crime may have their fingerprints stored on the database indefinitely. People arrested or charged in connection with a serious crime may also have their fingerprints stored on the database for up to five years, or indefinitely if they were convicted of another crime.

Wise nodded. 'We thought it was Cameron.'

'I'll be in touch if we come across anything else that might help you,' the pathologist said. 'But that's all we've got for now.'

'Thanks ever so much,' Wise said.

'And don't forget you still owe me that drink, Inspector.'

Wise and Markham left the examination suite and headed back to the changing room to dispose of their forensic suits and retrieve their coats.

'What do you think, Guv?' Hannah asked as they got changed.

Wise screwed up the blue suit and shoved it into the waste bin. 'This feels like a robbery to me. Cameron knew whoever killed him. The killer's gone around to his place, had a drink and a chat. Then, when Cameron got up to get something, maybe to make another drink, our killer smacked him over the head, knocking him down, then cut his throat to make sure he wouldn't get up again and come after him for stealing whatever it was.'

'Whatever they nicked was valuable enough to kill for, then.'

'Yeah. Drugs or money. Maybe both,' Wise replied, putting on his overcoat. 'And the killer was sneaky about it all, so that makes me think whoever did this knew they couldn't win in a straight fight.'

'Cameron didn't look all that tough in there,' Hannah said.

'You don't have to be a giant to be dangerous. Cameron's rap sheet was testament enough to how violent he was.'

'Okay. So, we're looking at friends, acquaintances and customers then?'

'Looks like it to me.' Wise's phone rang. He pulled it out of his pocket. It was Sarah. 'Yeah?'

'Traffic's just been on the phone. They've got your getaway car,' Sarah said. 'Orange Honda Civic, stolen sometime this morning from Carline Mews.'

'That's quick work,' Wise said. 'Well done.'

'I can't take any credit,' Sarah replied. 'Whoever nicked it dumped it shortly after the murder and set fire to it.'

'Where did they torch the car?' Wise asked.

'The Maywood estate.'

Wise closed his eyes. Of all the places in London, it had to be there.

Shit. 'Alright. We'll head over and have a look.'

9

Sarah was in hell.

There was no other way to describe it. She was on her way to see Cameron Nketiam's ex-wife, Nadine, with Donut, and it was a wonder she hadn't thrown up because the man stunk worse than ever. She'd tried opening a window, but it was still pissing down and, no matter how slight she kept the gap, the rain found a way in to soak her. It was freezing cold too, so Donut had the heaters on to stop the windscreen fogging up. That only made her suffering worse, though, as the warm air was swirling his body odour around even more.

Sarah had tried holding her nose, but it hadn't made any difference.

And now, because God clearly hated her, they were crawling along Peckham Park Road at a snail's pace, making their fifteen minute journey take three times that so far.

Donut, of course, was oblivious to her suffering and was blabbering on about the World Cup. For some reason, he seemed to think she gave a shit about football.

All in all, she wanted to scream.

She knew she couldn't do that, of course. So, Sarah got out her pack of cigarettes, grabbed one, stuck it in her mouth and lit it.

'Hey!' Donut said, instantly outraged. 'You can't do that in here.'

Sarah ignored him, inhaling deeply and holding the glorious smoke in her lungs for as long as possible before blowing it out.

'Fucking hell, Sarah,' Donut said. 'You can't smoke in here.'

Sarah looked at him out of the corner of her eye. She didn't think she'd ever despised someone as much as she despised Donut. 'Why the hell not?'

'It's against regulations, that's why! It's a healthy and safety risk. I could get second-hand cancer.'

Sarah took another long drag of her cigarette and then blew the smoke straight at Donut. 'Good.'

'What the—' Donut started coughing and waving at the smoke. 'You can't do that!'

'Oh, I can.' Sarah set her eyes on the slow-moving traffic and inhaled another lungful of beautiful smoke. Then her window buzzed down and rain quickly rushed through the gap, soaking her. 'What the fuck?'

It was Donut using the controls on the driver's door.

Sarah immediately pressed the button to wind the window back up but, as soon as it went up, Donut pressed his button for the window to go down again.

'What are you doing, you idiot?' Sarah snapped, winding the window back up.

'If you're going to smoke, then you have to have the window down,' Donut said. 'I'm not dying because of your filthy habit.'

'My filthy habit?' Sarah couldn't believe her ears. 'Why, you —'

'Don't you go calling me names. You're the one smoking in here.'

'And do you know why I'm smoking in here?'

'Because you're an addict.'

'No. I'm smoking because you stink, Donut, you dumb-arse. You stink so much I want to vomit. At least, this way, I don't have to smell you.'

'Oi, there's no need to get personal,' Donut said. 'I'm not being unreasonable because I don't want to breathe in your smoke.'

Sarah buzzed the window down, threw her cigarette out and buzzed it back up. 'Happy?'

Donut just glared at her.

Well, sod him. Sarah was in no mood to piss about. 'Donut, do you actually realise how bad you smell?'

'I don't smell.'

'You fucking do. Why do you think no one sits near you in the office?'

'That's just the way they set the office up,' Donut replied. 'It's got nothing to do with—'

'It has everything to do with the way you smell,' Sarah said. 'Everything. Christ, have a shower in the morning. Use soap and some deodorant and do us all a favour.'

Donut stuck his nose in his armpit and gave it a sniff. 'I don't smell. That's just normal.'

'Are you having a laugh right now, Donut? Because if you're not, then you need some serious mental help.'

'Christ, just because I don't like your smoking, you don't have to attack me.' Donut turned off Peckham Park Road into a side street and pulled into a parking spot near Nadine's block of flats. Freshly painted bright blue fencing on every floor gave the building an air of decency. 'We're here.'

He got out the car, leaving Sarah inside, feeling like shit for having a pop at him. The idiot really didn't know. With a sigh, she climbed out of the car as well. Donut had his back to her as he stared up at the flats. 'Donut, look. I'm sorry. I shouldn't have said what I said the way I did, alright?'

He gave her a sideways look, like some sulky five-year-old. 'She's on the second floor.'

Sarah tutted. Oh well, she'd tried to apologise. At least now, they were outside for a few minutes, even if it was freezing cold and raining, and his smell wasn't a problem. 'Come on, then.'

She stomped off towards the building entrance, a set of double doors painted as bright blue as the rest of the place. There was no intercom system. No security. No locks. Sarah just dragged the door open and marched inside. The door shut before Donut could follow her and Sarah allowed herself a little smile as she set off up the stairs.

Nadine's flat was easy enough to find and Sarah knocked on the door. No one came to answer but she could hear the TV on and a baby crying, so she knocked again, louder this time.

The door swung open, revealing a short, well-built woman with her hair in a net. 'Yeah?'

'Nadine Nketiam?' Sarah held up her warrant card. 'I'm Detective Constable Choi.'

The woman didn't move. 'I'm not Nadine Nketiam anymore. The surname's Ake. My maiden name. I'm not married to that waste of space, thank God.'

'Well, I need to have a chat with you about your ex-husband, Ms Ake,' Sarah said.

Donut appeared on the landing and half-jogged towards them, all red-faced and panting.

'Who's that?' Nadine asked, not looking impressed.

'He's a colleague.' Sarah glanced at Donut. 'He's staying outside.'

'Come on in, then.' Nadine stepped aside and Sarah entered the flat, smiling as Nadine shut the door in Donut's face. The flat was small but clean and well looked after. The living room was full of toys and children's books, all stacked neatly around its edges. A young girl glanced over as Sarah walked in, then went back to watching *Peppa Pig* on a big TV. A baby crawled on the floor in front of the girl, crying its eyes out.

Nadine went over and picked the baby up. 'I've got to feed her. Can we do this in the kitchen?'

Sarah smiled. 'No problem.'

The kitchen window overlooked the walkway and the car park below. Sarah couldn't see Donut and wondered if he'd had to take shelter from the rain somewhere else. Not that she cared. She was just glad he was outside and she was inside.

Nadine put the baby into a highchair next to a small table. 'Have a seat.'

Sarah did so as Nadine opened up a cupboard, took out a yellow plastic-looking pouch of something, unscrewed the top and gave it to the baby. The baby immediately began sucking on it, eager for its contents.

'Do you want tea or anything?' Nadine asked.

Sarah smiled. 'I'm fine.'

Nadine sat down next to the baby, putting a hand on the child's leg. 'So, what's that twat done now?'

'I'm afraid he'd dead, Ms Ake.'

Nadine's mouth dropped. 'Dead? How?'

'Someone killed him this morning. Unfortunately, I can't tell you any more than that.'

'Fuck.' Nadine sat back in her chair and shook her head. 'Bloody hell.'

'When was the last time you saw your husband?'

'I told you, he's my ex-husband. And I ain't seen him for months. He turned up here just after he got out, all big smiles and wanting to play happy families again. Then he clocked Esme here, and it all kicked off. I had to call the police to get rid of him before he smashed the place up.'

'I take it Esme isn't his?'

Nadine laughed. 'Put it this way. Cam was away for two years and Esme here is ten months old.'

'Ah.'

'Yeah? So what? He was dumb enough to go to prison, and we were getting divorced anyway. He had no say in who was in my bed. His only obligation was to pay me money for the one that was his and he couldn't even do that.' The baby threw the pouch onto the floor. Nadine picked it up and gave it back to Esme. 'Whoever killed him really dropped me in it. We were due in court next week because he ain't paying me what I'm owed. Now I'm never going to see any child support.'

'I'm sorry,' Sarah said.

'Why? It's got nothing to do with you.'

'Do you know what Cameron was doing for money now he was out of prison?'

Nadine looked at Sarah like she was an idiot. 'He's a drug dealer. Always was. Always will be — well, if he wasn't dead.' She reached over and tickled her baby's cheek. 'It was fun when we were kids, going out with a gangster and all, but drugs and babies don't go well together. When we had Maxine, I told him he had to sort himself out, but the boy only knew the life, you know? In the end, I had to get out of there.'

'That's understandable.'

'Do you know he sold our dog because he needed some ready cash once? He took her down to the pub and flogged her for fifty quid. I had to tell Maxine she'd run away. She was heartbroken.'

'How much about his business do you know?'

'Like what?' Nadine straightened in her seat, and Sarah could see her defences come up.

'I'm not trying to get you into trouble. We just need to build a picture of who he worked for, stuff like that.'

'You might not want to get me into trouble, but you could get me killed if I go telling you shit and it gets out.'

'I know,' Sarah said. 'But I promise you, whatever you tell me will stay confidential.'

'If anyone hears I told you ...'

'They won't.'

Nadine leaned over and fed the last of the food pouch to her baby. She took her time, wiping Esme's mouth once she was done.

Sarah was happy to sit and wait. Every minute away from Donut was a minute to savour.

'Ollie Konza.' Nadine's voice was so quiet that Sarah almost didn't hear her. Almost. But Sarah heard her well enough and wished she hadn't. To make matters worse, Nadine said it again. Louder this time. 'He worked for Ollie Konza.'

Shit. 'He did?'

'Yeah. They grew up together.'

Ollie Konza was one of the biggest drug dealers south of the river. He was a right dangerous bastard. 'Okay. That was really useful,' Sarah said, standing up, eager to go. She got out a card and passed it to Nadine. 'If you think of anything useful, call me. It doesn't matter what time of day it is, what day it is. Call me. That's my direct number. Don't bother speaking to anyone else. Okay?'

Nadine took the card. 'I will. Cheers.'

'Thanks for your time. I'll see myself out.'

When she left the flat, she saw Donut huddled against the side of the door, his hands stuck deep into his pockets, face bright red from the cold. 'Thanks for leaving me out here.'

Sarah walked straight past him and headed for the stairs. She needed some air. Needed to think. Ollie Konza was right at the top of her list of people not to fuck with.

Donut ran after her. 'Did you learn anything useful?'

'Yeah, Cameron Nketiam was a shit who sold his kid's dog to buy drugs. And he was due in court because he hadn't been paying his wife child support.'

'What a wanker.'

'Whatever.' She took the stairs down as quickly as she could, her mind racing. Sarah knew what she had to do, even though she didn't want to do it. She didn't feel any better when she got outside, with the rain pelting her face, the wind pinching her skin.

Sarah turned around when she heard Donut come out through the doors. 'Go wait in the car. I have to make a call.'

'Who to?' Donut asked.

'None of your fucking business,' Sarah snapped back. 'That's who.'

'Is it your period or something?' Donut said. 'You're even more miserable than you normally are.'

'I'm going to ignore you said that.' Sarah turned her back on the git and got her phone out. She did nothing else, though, until she heard Donut get in the car and shut the door.

Only then, confident she couldn't be overheard, she opened her phone, scrolled though her contacts, and stopped on one named

NAILS. She hit the call button and took a deep breath before putting the phone against her ear. With any luck he wouldn't answer, and Sarah could say she'd at least tried to contact him.

Of course, the phone didn't even ring twice before he picked up.

'Long time no hear,' the man said. 'I was beginning to think you didn't like me anymore.'

Sarah closed her eyes. Just hearing his voice made her want to throw up. 'You've got a problem.'

10

Wise stood in the car park of the Maywood estate, staring at the burnt-out remains of the Honda Civic. The killer had done a good job on it, too. By the time the fire service had reached it, the car was a ball of flame. Once they'd put the fire out, anything that might've had some DNA on it was long gone.

'This is a waste of time,' he muttered, rain splattering across his face. The fire crew had left now the fire was out. Three uniformed officers stood watch nearby, waiting for the tow truck to arrive and remove the wreck.

Hannah looked around. 'Is there any CCTV covering this area?'

Wise pointed to a camera on a nearby lamppost. It dangled from its mounting, the front end clearly broken. 'It's one of the most replaced cameras in London. The locals smash it so no one can see what they're up to, we replace it, and they smash it again, sometimes within minutes of the new one being installed and so on it goes.'

'Great,' Hannah said. 'I don't suppose there's any point in getting some uniforms down here to knock on doors? In case anyone saw anything?'

'Nah. We'd have to send them in mob-handed to ensure our

people were safe and that could start a riot in itself. Besides, no one here will talk to the police.'

'Do you think our killer's in there?'

'If he is, he's chosen a good place to hide. There's something like eighty or ninety flats in that building. Unless someone talks, we haven't got a hope of finding him.'

'Shit.'

'Yeah, that just about sums it up.' Wise's eyes drifted unbidden to the rooftop, the grey concrete almost camouflaged against the winter skies. It had been six months since that night and yet it felt like yesterday.

He remembered only too well blue-lighting it over from Kennington with Madge, both of them in shock at the thought of Andy betraying them. They'd rushed into the building, full of fear, and found Tasha Simcock's flat with the door kicked in. Wise had then gone up to the roof by himself.

Dear God. Wise closed his eyes, feeling his heart speed up, feeling his anxiety climb.

It's June. Hot and sweltering. And everything feels so desperate. Wise steps through the doorway and onto the roof, dreading what he'll find there, praying he's not too late.

Then, he sees them and it takes a moment to accept what's happening before his very eyes. Derrick Morris, the missing witness, wearing only a pair of trousers, is holding onto his girlfriend, Tasha Simcocks. Both of them are on their knees and crying. Andy's behind them, pointing a revolver at their heads.

'Andy!' Wise calls out.

Andy flinches at hearing his name, then turns to face Wise.

'What the fuck are you doing here, Si?' Andy says, his eyes bulging, tears running down his face, flecks of powder on his nose and chin. The gun shakes in his hand. 'You shouldn't be here.'

'You alright, Guv?'

Wise jerked back to the present. 'Sorry, I got distracted for a second there.'

'You were shaking.'

'Was I? Sorry, it's just the cold and the rain.'

'You sure?'

'Yeah,' Wise said, trying to compose himself. It'd been a mistake to go to the Maywood. What had he been expecting to find out from a wreck anyway? 'We should go.'

'Okay.' Hannah didn't say anymore but Wise could see she wanted to.

They walked back to the Mondeo and climbed in. Wise turned the engine on and whacked the heater up, even though he doubted it'd do much to dry his clothes out.

The moment Hannah had her seat belt on, Wise put his foot down and wheel-spun the Mondeo out of the car park. He could see Hannah looking at him out of the corner of his eye, but he kept focused on the road ahead, not wanting to invite a conversation.

Wise needed to get away from the Maywood estate and sort himself out. What he didn't need was to talk about the past. Not with Hannah, anyway.

As they trundled through the traffic back to Kennington, though, the silence grew uncomfortable, and Wise felt guilty about the way he was behaving. Hannah had been a great asset since she'd joined the team, and a lot of their recent successes were down to her. And she wasn't an idiot. She knew something was up.

'Hannah,' he said as they turned onto the A2. 'I'm sorry about earlier. It's just ... being at the Maywood brought back a few unpleasant memories.'

'It's okay,' Hannah replied. 'I know what happened there.'

She knew. Of course she did. Everyone in the Met knew what happened there.

Andy's head jerks as the bullet hits him. Red mist erupts from the other side of his head. His brains hit the concrete roof a heartbeat before Andy's body.

Wise took a deep breath. 'I know I shouldn't let it bother me anymore, but it does. A lot.'

'Were you and DS Davidson close?'

'Yeah, I thought we were. We worked together since day one in the Met. He was best man at my wedding, godfather to my kids. I was the godfather to his kids.' Wise shook his head. 'I thought I knew him, but I didn't. No one did.'

'Did he do all those things they say he did?'

'Yeah — and probably a lot more besides. Professional Standards are looking into every case Andy was involved in to see if he perverted the course of justice in any of them. They've not found anything yet, but who knows? I pray nothing's going to turn up. We put away a lot of bad people over the years.'

'That must play on your mind a lot,' Hannah said.

'Just a bit,' Wise said in the understatement of the year.

'I'm sorry.'

'Yeah. Aren't we all?'

They drove on again in silence, but it wasn't as awkward as before, and Wise felt better for saying something. Maybe it was like the TV ad said: it was good to talk.

If only he could get that advice to work at home.

By the time they reached Kennington, it was pitch black, and the rain hadn't shown the slightest intention of stopping. Wise parked the Mondeo near the main entrance, and the two officers dashed from the car into the building.

It was close to 5 o'clock, and Wise and Hannah's footsteps on the concrete stairs echoed through the now near-empty station. Most of the admin personnel, who seemed to make up the majority of the people who worked in Kennington, had gone home. Even MIR-One was quiet when they walked through its doors.

Sarah and Donut were back, and Brains was at his computer, but that was it.

'Thanks for your help today,' Wise said to Hannah. 'Why don't you call it a day and head home?'

'You sure?' Hannah said. 'I don't mind staying if you need me.'

'It's okay. I'm going to go soon, anyway. I need to get out of these wet clothes before I catch the death of me.'

'I will then. Cheers.' Hannah grabbed her bike helmet and headed back out of MIR-One.

'That goes for the rest of you,' Wise said, turning to face the others. 'Go home if you've not got anything urgent to do.'

'Cheers, Guv,' Donut said, not needing to be asked twice. He practically jumped out of his seat in his hurry to get away.

'I've got a bit more to do,' Sarah replied, not looking happy.

Brains poked his head up. 'Me too.'

'Alright, but don't be here all night,' Wise said. Leaving them, he entered his small office and took his wet coat off, hanging it up on the back of the door.

Wise walked over to the window and gazed out over Kennington Road. He hated that fact that it got so dark this early. It made everything feel utterly miserable. That was winter, though. Travelling to work in darkness, going home in darkness with just a patch of grey in between, grateful if it wasn't raining on top of everything else, which it always was.

The Christmas lights did their best to add some cheer to the gloom, blazing away in all their gaudy colours, dangling as they did from shop windows or stretched out across streets, but there was only so much magic they could work.

The pub opposite seemed to have doubled, if not tripled, the lights it normally had around their exterior and they flashed on and off in a desperate attempt to encourage passersby inside. A chalkboard by the front door proclaimed: 'Have your Xmas party here!'

Looking at it now, it was hard to believe it was nearly the end of the year. Wise hadn't even spoken to Jean about their plans for Christmas or what to get the kids for presents. They normally had his dad over and sometimes her parents too but, right then, he didn't fancy the idea of having a noisy get-together in a packed house, full of stress, hard work and endless small talk. Maybe it'd be better if it was just the four of them; him, Jean, Ed and Claire. Keep it quiet. Keep it simple. Get through it somehow with no dramas.

Then he remembered the conversation that morning, the coldness in the kitchen that had little to do with the December weather. Things between Wise and Jean were hardly conducive to chatting about tinsel and what size turkey to get.

Shit. Wise rubbed his face. He was tired. Maybe Dan The Man had the right idea about leaving The Job.

Then again, maybe Wise wouldn't have much of a choice about that. He still had no idea what DCI Rena Heer was going to do about him.

Someone knocked on Wise's door.

'Yes?' he said, putting his mask on, playing the perfect boss.

Sarah poked her head around the door. Wise could smell cigarette smoke overpowering the perfume she had on. She'd obviously just been out for a quick one before coming to see him. 'You got a minute?'

'Sure,' Wise replied. He indicated the chair in front of his desk. 'Have a seat.'

'I just wanted to let you know about our visit to see Nadine Ake, Cameron's ex, this afternoon,' Sarah said, sitting down.

'How did that go?'

'Let's just say the divorce wasn't amicable. She hated Cameron's guts. In fact, the only thing she was upset about was that she wouldn't get the child support he owed her.'

'Why did she have a restraining order against him?'

'Apparently he wasn't happy about the birth of her daughter as he'd been in prison for two years and therefore wasn't involved in her conception.'

'I can imagine that would piss a lot of people off.' Wise pursed his lips for a moment. 'Do you think she was involved in his death in any way?'

'No. She was genuinely shocked when I told her he was dead.'

'That's good to know at least,' Wise said. 'What about any other titbits about his business that could help us?'

Sarah shook her head. 'Not really. She said he was dealing drugs again, and that once he sold the family dog for some ready cash, but that was it.'

'Did she have any idea who he worked for?'

'No, I'm afraid not.'

'Do you believe her?'

'Yes. I do. She broke up with him because she didn't like what he did for a living once she had her first daughter. I think staying ignorant was her way of staying innocent.'

'But she was happy taking his money. That makes her guilty, no matter how she spins it.'

Sarah shrugged. 'That's not an option now.'

'Alright,' Wise said. 'Thanks for letting me know.'

Sarah stood up. 'Night, Guv.'

'See you in the morning.'

Sarah smiled but there was a sadness to it — to her — that Wise hadn't noticed before. 'Everything okay, by the way?'

Sarah flinched. 'What do you mean?'

'Nothing. Just asking.'

'I'm fine.'

Wise nodded, but after spending so long hiding his own feelings, he reckoned he was becoming an expert in spotting when others were doing the same. And he was pretty damned sure Sarah wasn't being honest about hers. But he'd asked. It was up to her if she wanted to talk about whatever it was. 'Good night.'

Sarah left his office and Wise rose from his seat, wincing at the feel of his wet suit trousers. It was time to follow his own advice and go home.

He only hoped tomorrow would be a better day.

11

Hannah parked her Ducati in her building's car park and chained it up. The underground space was one of the main selling points when she and Emma had first come to look at the flat they now called home. Her bike was her pride and joy, and the last thing she wanted to do was leave it outside somewhere all night. Chained up or not, some scrote-bag would nick it within a week if she had to do that. In fact, when they were looking for somewhere to live, Hannah had decided she'd happily trade living space if it meant she had a safe spot to park her bike. Not that she'd told Emma that. She wouldn't have understood.

Like everything else Emma didn't understand.

Hannah walked over to the door leading to the lift and stopped before she went in. As tired as she was, going upstairs was suddenly the last thing she wanted to do. She didn't want to hear about Emma's day at school and how little Tommy wasn't learning his times tables as quickly as he should. She didn't want to sit in front of the TV and pretend she was interested in whatever crap Emma was binge watching on Netflix either. And Hannah didn't want to make out that she'd had a good day either, doing 'this and that.'

So, after chaining her helmet to her bike, Hannah turned on her heels and took the exit out into the street. Two minutes later, she was on Mitcham Road and walking away from her flat. The high street was busy, despite the freezing wind that rattled the cheesy decorations that stretched from one side of the road to the other. A week earlier, the council had hired some actor who'd once been on *Eastenders* and had done a stint in the jungle to come down and turn the lights on. Emma had gone to watch — of course she had — but Hannah hadn't bothered going with her. In her mind, it summed up everything wrong in their relationship.

Hannah walked past the fake KFC, the fake McDonalds, and the cheap Indian. Past the chippy and the curry house. Past the second-hand mobile shop and the knock-off luggage shop. She crossed the road, striding between the slow-moving traffic, and headed straight into the pub on the corner of Bickley Street. The Gazelle was a bit on an anomaly in Tooting, a gastropub with aspirations to serve quality meals in the middle of a deep-fried, fast-food hell.

Warmth and noise hit Hannah in equal measure as she stepped through its doors. Despite it being a Wednesday night, it was packed to its artfully decorated rafters with people determined to have a good time. *Hide and Seek* by Stormzy soundtracked the laughter and the chatter, its bass throbbing in Hannah's bones as she squeezed her way to the bar. Finding a spot near the corner, she unzipped her jacket, immediately feeling like she could breathe again.

The Gazelle always had a good crowd, full of young up-and-comers that were attracted to Tooting by the still reasonable rents. Artists mixed with yoga instructors, DJs mingled with fashion designers, and TV producers got drunk with content creators. Emma hated the place, finding it too noisy and full of people she claimed were pretentious, but that made Hannah like it even more. It was her refuge from the world, a haven where no one knew she was a copper, where she could be left alone to drink at the bar if she wanted and the music was just loud enough to make it almost impossible to have a serious conversation.

After spending the day with the dead, it was wonderful to be amongst people so desperately alive.

Hannah was happy to see Nikki was working behind the bar, her tank top proudly displaying her well-toned arms with full sleeves of tattoos. Her dreadlocked hair was tied back for once, revealing the curve of her cheeks. She handled the waiting punters with ease, dancing along the line as she served those who'd been waiting longest and ignoring anyone flapping money or cards at her, expecting her to do their bidding as a result. She dished out smiles with pints and somehow always heard the shouted orders over the hullabaloo. Better than that, the moment she spotted Hannah waiting, she mouthed 'the usual?' at her.

Hannah nodded and, thirty seconds later, there was a large Tanqueray and tonic with a slice of lime and a short straw in front of her. Hannah held out her credit card, but Nikki waved it away. 'First one's on me. You look like you need it,' she said.

'Cheers,' Hannah replied but Nikki was already pouring a Guinness for someone else.

Hannah stirred her drink with the straw, enjoying the rattle of the ice cubes as *Unholy* by Sam Smith and Kim Petras pounded out of the speakers.

The first sip tasted glorious. The second was even better, and Hannah could almost convince herself that she wasn't still thinking about a young man with his throat sliced open.

Nikki was back before she'd had the last mouthful. 'Ready for another?'

Hannah looked from her drink to the beautiful bartender, then risked a guilty glance at the clock above the bar. 8:30. An image flashed through her mind of Emma sitting in their flat with a meal of some sort waiting on the table. It was easily blinked away. 'Yeah. A double this time, please.'

Nikki beamed her a thousand-watt smile. 'You got it.'

The second drink was better than the first, so much so that Hannah thought Nikki might've put more than a double in it, but she wasn't complaining. It went down easily enough, washing away any guilt she might've felt about not going home. Not that there was much guilt to begin with.

Her phone beeped. It was a message from Emma. Of course it was. *Everything ok?* Hannah didn't answer. Better to ignore it than lie. Better to ignore it than tell the truth. She just slipped the phone back in her jacket pocket. Easier to forget now it was out of sight. She'd go home soon enough. After the next one. The day she'd had, she deserved that much time to herself.

What was wrong with having a quiet drink, anyway?

She caught Nikki's eye and held up her near empty glass, signalling for another with a smile and was happy to see she got a smile back.

'You're a life saver,' Hannah said when the drink arrived. She held up her card to pay.

'You going to be here awhile?' Nikki asked instead. 'You can run a tab if you are.'

All thoughts of leaving after the third drink vanished as Hannah looked into the eyes of the bartender just a little bit too long. 'A tab sounds good.'

'Excellent.'

Hannah watched Nikki walk away, enjoying the tang of the ice cool gin on her tongue. Felt the tang of Tanqueray solving all her problems. For now, at least. Maybe it'd be creating a few more later. She hoped so at least.

Maybe the right thing to do was the wrong thing. Maybe the way to feel good was to do something bad.

She could blame it on the alcohol. She could blame it on The Job. Hell, she could blame it on Emma being so goddamned boring. Her safe little wife, sitting at home with the dinner ready.

Hannah drained her drink, watching Nikki, thinking about the dead, wanting to feel alive.

She held up her empty glass, signalling she wanted another with a smile. She wanted that and so much more.

Thursday 8th December

12

Wise was feeling good by the time he got back to his house, his run done. He'd left early, fleeing from his dreams, and had welcomed the stinging rain and the night chill as he made his way down to Clapham Common. The run hurt in a good way, washing away the cobwebs, waking him up, making him feel in control.

Even so, the weather had made a mockery of his all-weather running gear. It seemed even the best water-resistant material had a point where it gave up and just let the rain and the cold in. Still, it didn't matter. It was nothing that a hot shower couldn't sort out, helped along by a coffee or two.

Of course, Wise wasn't expecting to see Jean in the kitchen when he came in through the back door. After all, it wasn't even 6 a.m. Normally, she'd get up just before the kids, around 7:45.

'Couldn't sleep?' Wise said, doing his best to sound happy and breezy despite the rain running off his face and the dread in his gut. He grabbed a tea towel to mop up the worst of it, but he'd need a hundred of the things to make a real difference.

'Yeah, well. You're not the only one who can't sleep these days,'

Jean said, her eyes red for the second day running. Or maybe the third.

'I'm sorry,' Wise said, feeling guilty. He'd done this to the woman he loved, who'd held him together when he was falling apart, who'd done nothing but give him unconditional love right until now.

It was no surprise she answered his apology with a shake of her head and a glare that would scare the dead. How could saying sorry repair all the damage done?

The trouble was, Wise didn't know what else to say or what to do. He just stood there, feeling lost in his small kitchen, the drip of rain from his jacket onto the tiled floor the only sound in the room. He couldn't even leave to dry off, either. It would look like he was walking out on her when she needed him the most, abandoning her to deal with all her fears alone.

Christ, he'd rather be facing a man with a gun than his wife in her dressing gown in that kitchen.

Then again, the last time he'd done that, things hadn't gone well. Not well at all.

'I spoke to my mother last night,' Jean said, not looking up, not meeting his eyes. 'Mum's invited me and the kids over to stay once they break up for Christmas. I said we'd go.'

'You and the kids?' Wise repeated as if he didn't know what she meant when he knew only too well.

'Yeah. Me and the kids.' She looked up then. Met his eyes. Showed him her pain. Her anger. 'It'll be safe for us there.'

'It's safe here,' Wise said, the words sounding almost as worthless as his apology.

'It doesn't feel like it.'

'I can keep you safe.'

'Like you did Andy?' Jean spat the words out, filling them with venom, wanting them to hurt, knowing they would.

It took everything Wise had to stay on his feet, to stay breathing.

Time slows as Andy tumbles forward, red mist leading the way, his brains and blood already splattered across the rooftop.

Jean stood up, the damage done. 'We leave next Thursday. Try not to put us in any more danger until then.' She left the kitchen and headed back up the stairs without so much as a backward glance, leaving Wise alone in the kitchen, a puddle forming around his feet.

Feeling helpless.

He didn't know how long it was before he braved the stairs himself. He was vaguely aware of having a shower as his mind replayed the conversation from the kitchen over and over again, until his imagination took him forward in time to next Thursday, watching his family leave him.

When he came out of the bathroom, he could hear Jean crying on the other side of their bedroom door. He knew he should go to her, but he also knew that to do so could provoke another fight. That would only make things worse, never better. So, he headed to the spare room where he still had clothes hanging in the wardrobe and dressed there. On went a starched light blue shirt, followed by a dark blue suit, the creases in the trouser legs razor sharp. Wise stared at himself as he did up the tie, his hands moving automatically as he tightened the knot, aware of how fragile the life he'd built actually was.

After Tom had killed Brian Sellers and gone to prison, he'd done everything he could to be a better man and make up for his part in that tragedy. He'd become a police officer so he could help other victims of violent crime find some sort of peace and resolution. No longer a hooligan, he'd become a family man, a pillar of the community.

But all it had taken was Tom to reappear to make all of it crumble. The consequences of that night rippling through the years to wash away his life.

He left the spare room, grateful that his kids were still asleep and Jean hadn't come out to throw more harsh words at him.

We leave next Thursday.

Grabbing his coat, he headed out into the dark. Running away like he always did. Looking after the dead, the perfect excuse to go.

It was cold and damp inside the Mondeo. His windscreen misted up the moment he climbed inside, making it impossible to make a quick getaway. Just his luck.

Wise turned on the engine and turned the vents on full blast. A sliver of clear glass appeared at the bottom of the windscreen, growing bigger by the second, but not fast enough for Wise. He watched its painful progress as he fought the urge to scream. This was Tom's fault. Andy's too. He'd had his life under control before they'd ruined everything for him.

Now though?

He had one week to sort things out. To save his marriage. Save his family.

Christ.

It felt impossible.

13

The drive into Kennington gave Wise a chance to calm down and think. By the time he walked into MIR-One, clutching a coffee from Luigi's, he felt like he had a plan. He nodded to Brains and Sarah, who were already at their desks, before heading into the sanctuary of his office.

After hanging up his coat, Wise stood by his window, watching people brave the elements as they went about their business, the slanting rain fighting with the bitter cold to make it as unpleasant as possible for everyone.

The Christmas decorations, robbed of their neon cheerfulness, just rocked back and forth in the wind, looking sad and out of place in the morning gloom. Buses, cars and trucks inched their way up and down Kennington Road, driving past ads promising better clothes, better holidays and better lives.

Wise drank his coffee, savouring its flavour, needing its caffeine. Buying himself time. Putting off what he had decided to do. It was stupid really. Even if it was his plan.

Turning away from the window, he put down his coffee and pulled out his phone. Scrolling through the contacts, he found the number he wanted. Hit dial.

She answered on the second ring. 'DCI Heer.'

'It's Simon Wise,' he said.

'Ah.'

'It's been a couple of weeks since we had our chat.'

'Has it?' Heer replied. 'I'd not noticed. I've been busy.'

'I'm sure you have. Has Tom been behaving himself?'

Heer laughed. 'I can't tell you that.'

'Have you spoken to your boss about me?'

'Of course, We've spoken several times about you, in fact.'

'And?' Wise asked, getting annoyed at the back and forth.

'And what?' Heer said, sounding equally pissed off.

'Last time we spoke, you said he wanted me banged up,' Wise reminded her. 'He said I was a bad one.'

'Can you blame him?'

'He's wrong about me — but, if he's going to put in a complaint about me, if he wants me kicked off the force or arrested, I have a right to know. I have a job, a family. I can't have his whims hanging over me.'

'You should've thought about that before you lied to everyone,' Heer said, as cold as ever.

'I apologised for that.'

'And you think that makes everything okay?'

Christ, it was like talking to his wife again. 'Look, whether I had a brother or not didn't matter for twenty years, and I would've preferred for it to stay that way. But Tom had other ideas. Now we all have to deal with it.'

'Not "we," Simon. This isn't your problem. It's mine and my team's,' Heer said. 'We've made that clear. Even your brother has told you to keep out of it.'

'Yeah, I remember that,' Wise said through gritted teeth. 'He threatened my family. Now my wife's petrified and wants to go hide somewhere.'

'I don't think that's a bad idea.'

'Well, I do. I'd rather it was Tom that had to go away. Somewhere nice like Belmarsh.'

Heer sighed. 'Look, Simon. We all want that. But we need to do things properly.'

'Then let me help you,' Wise said, seizing the opportunity. 'I want in.'

'You've got to be joking. I can think of a hundred reasons why that's not going to happen.'

'I want to go undercover into his operation.'

'You've gone mad.'

'Think about it. Imagine the places I could go, the people I could talk to because people would think I was Tom. Think about what information I could get. You could wire me for sound and vision, and it wouldn't even cross anyone's mind to check me because they'd think I was their boss.'

'You'd get killed within a day if we tried that,' Heer said.

'Or I could save you years of hard slog,' Wise replied. 'You had an undercover officer in Tom's gang for six months before they could even find out who was in charge.'

Heer went silent.

Wise let her think without interruption. He knew it was a mad plan, but he knew it could work.

'Look. I can't talk about this now,' Heer said eventually. 'Let me discuss it with my boss.'

Wise smiled. That was as much as he could've hoped for. 'Alright. I'll leave you to it. Have a good one.'

'Simon, I will get back to you but, in the meantime, don't — and I mean don't — get in our way,' Heer said. 'Don't go off being a cowboy again. You hear me?'

'Loud and clear.'

The line went dead.

Wise looked at his phone and opened WhatsApp. He clicked on the chat with Jean and started typing. *I'm sorry about this morning. I'm sorry about everything. It'll all be ok. I love you.*

He hesitated for a moment with his thumb hovering above the send button, rereading his message, knowing it was just more apologies. But he could see a way out now, a way to fix his life, save his marriage. All Heer had to do was bring him on board her investigation.

And break every rule in the book.

Wise hit send. There was a whoosh as the message pinged off to find Jean's phone. He imagined her reading it and writing a reply. Imagined her hitting send back.

He waited for the ping that said her reply had arrived, staring at his phone screen so he could instantly read what she'd said.

But there was no ping. No message back.

He could hear MIR-One getting busier on the other side of his office door. Phones ringing. People talking. Day two of their investigation was underway.

Wise sighed and put his phone away. It was time he got to work too.

14

It wasn't even 8:30 a.m. and Hicksy was already in a foul mood. Granted, it took little these days to get him going, but he was starting to think this was something of a record, even for him.

But who could blame him for being a right grumpy bastard? He'd spent yesterday knocking on doors, getting soaking wet, trying to be all smiles as he asked around for the slightest bit of information that could help the investigation, getting more than his fair share of doors slammed in his face. It wouldn't have happened in the old days, of course. Back then, no one would've dared to treat him like that. But now? They just saw a tired old man who couldn't do jack shit without it becoming some sort of PR nightmare.

He still wasn't sure why the governor had him looking after the house-to-house enquiries. He was hardly Mr. Charm School. As he glanced around MIR-One, he couldn't help but think that any of the others there would be better at it than him. Even fucking Donut.

Of course, that realisation didn't help his mood. Far from it. It just made him feel even more unnecessary.

Even more redundant.

It wouldn't have been so bad if Jono was with him. They had their old dinosaurs act down pat, watching each other's backs as they fought against the bloody Wokerati taking over the Met. At least, he could roll his eyes at his mate when someone brought up their pronouns or wanted to talk about their feelings.

Back in his day, if you felt stressed, you went and got leathered down the boozer with the lads. If you were being too sensitive, you had the piss ripped out of you until you twigged that you needed to toughen up.

And if some Herbert didn't treat you with respect on the street — well, they got a good slapping until they saw the error of their ways. But now, it was all about de-escalation and being polite even if someone was spitting in your face.

Christ, he should've known the writing was on the wall when they banned smoking at your desks. He'd still been a young man, twenty-something years ago. If he'd got out then, he could've done something else with his life, but he was stuck now, working with colleagues he couldn't relate to, doing a job that didn't want him around anymore, and dealing with people he downright despised.

Every morning and every night he wondered why he didn't just quit. He'd done his years. He had his pension, and he could easily pick up some security work or a private detective gig to help on top of that.

Then his eyes drifted over to the whiteboards, taking in the pictures of Cameron Nketiam. Some were from when he was alive, and others were from yesterday when he was very much dead. Even if he was a scumbag, that man's killer needed catching.

Then he thought about that toe rag, Leon Tomoral, who had the sheer audacity to lie to Hicksy's face. If ever there was someone who was guilty of something, it was him. Hicksy was going to enjoy nicking him for whatever he'd done — and that was a pleasure he'd not get walking around some warehouse in a blue uniform and a peak cap, pretending to have some authority when he really had none.

Hicksy watched Hannah walk into MIR-One. That was unusual because she was normally in the incident room well before he rolled in. She didn't have her motorbike helmet with her either and that had to be a first as well, considering she drove that Italian pimp machine of hers no matter what the weather.

Hannah looked over and caught his eye for a moment, then looked away even quicker. That made Hicksy perk up. He was a master at spotting someone trying to hide a hangover, and Hicksy would happily put down a tenner that dear old Diversity was suffering something rotten. He turned around to say something to Jono but there was only his empty chair.

'Bloody cancer,' he muttered. He stood up, stretching back, in need of an industrial strength cup of tea and a fag. 'What time's the DMM starting?' he asked Brains.

The boffin stuck his head up. 'Nine.'

'I'm going to grab a quick brew,' Hicksy said, but Brains was already lost in his computer again. The thought of having some banter probably hadn't even crossed his mind. No doubt too busy hash-tagging and whatnot with his online pals.

Whatever. The man was a loser anyway.

Still, Hicksy knew what would cheer him up more than a cup of tea. He wandered over to Hannah's desk as casually as he could. She was struggling to log into her computer. 'Morning.'

She looked up and saw his grin, and her own face got grimmer still. 'Whatever it is, I'm not in the mood.'

'I was just going to ask you if you wanted a cup of tea or something,' Hicksy said, cheering up by the second.

'I'm fine,' Hannah said through gritted teeth.

'Big night last night, was it?'

'Fuck off, Hicksy.'

Hicksy wagged a finger at her. 'Ooh, I might have to report you for using inappropriate language in the workplace.'

Hannah glared daggers at him. 'Says the walking violation.'

'Fair enough. It's just nice to see you're human after all. Try not to puke over your desk.' Hicksy gave her a wink and sauntered off, whistling as he went. Seeing Hannah in pain had really perked him up. Maybe there was a bit of an old school copper in her after all.

Deciding he needed tea more than a smoke, Hicksy headed to

the canteen on the first floor. It had a bad rep in the station because it didn't serve fancy hazelnut decaf soy lattes, but Hicksy liked the tea well enough. It was good old-fashioned bricklayers, after all. Strong enough to stand up a spoon. Proper tea, as his old mum would say.

'Alright, Roy?' Doris, the old girl behind the counter, asked. She'd been working in the canteen long before Hicksy had started at Kennington.

'How you doing, Doris? All good?'

'I've not won the lottery yet, love, but otherwise I've got nothing to complain about,' Doris replied as she passed him his mug.

Hicksy took it and raised the cup in salute. 'Cheers, darling.'

With his brew in hand, Hicksy headed over to an empty table in the corner, next to a window that overlooked the carpark. He'd have a sit down for ten minutes before the DMM started.

'Can you help me?' a voice said from behind him. A voice Hicksy knew oh so well. 'I'm looking for a right grumpy bastard.'

He turned around, grinning like a kid at Christmas. 'Jono! You wanker. What are you doing here?'

His mate grinned. 'My missus has had enough of me making her miserable at home, so she sent me here to make your life miserable instead.'

'As if my life wasn't bad enough as it is.' Hicksy put down his tea and gave Jono a hug. 'God, I've missed you.'

'Alright, you big nonce,' Jono said, breaking the embrace. 'I wasn't gone that long.' That might well be, but Hicksy could see his friend had lost weight over the last few weeks and his face had more of a grey hue to it instead of the drinker's ruddiness that it used to have. His hair was longer, too, hanging down the sides of his face from a centre parting that was getting wider by the day.

'You could've got a haircut while you were away,' Hicksy said. 'You look daft.'

Jono laughed. 'The missus said it makes me look like Paul Weller.'

'How much had she had to drink at the time?'

'Not enough for me to get lucky.'

'Outrageous,' Hicksy said. 'Surely you've had a few sympathy shags out of the whole cancer thing?'

Jono shook his head. 'You'd think so but no. She's tough, my old girl. No mercy in her.'

'Do you want a cup of tea? I just got one.'

'Nah. I'm okay for now. I've got to go see the governor. Tell him I'm back,' Jono said. 'You got much on?'

'Yeah. It's never quiet. We're looking into a drug dealer who got his throat cut yesterday.'

'Well, drink your tea and I'll see you in MIR-One in a bit.' Jono gave him a wink. 'It's good to see you, mate.'

'You, too. More than you'll ever know.'

'Aw, you soft git.' Jono slapped him on the shoulder. 'You'll be making me cry next. Now, drink your tea. I'm off to see the boss.'

Hicksy took his seat and watched Jono walk out of the canteen, feeling happier than he had in a long time. Then he realised he hadn't asked Jono how he was and a quick rush of guilt and just a touch of fear took away some of his good mood. He was being stupid though. Jono wouldn't have come back if he wasn't up to it. He hoped not, anyway.

15

There was a knock on Wise's door.

'Come in,' he called out and, a beat later, Jono poked his head around the door.

'Hello, Guv,' Jono said. 'Got a minute?'

Wise shot to his feet, a smile across his face. 'Of course, come in. Sit down. It's good to see you.'

The two men shook hands. 'And you, Guv.'

'Are you just popping in to say hi or are you back to do some work?' Wise asked as the two men sat down.

'I'm back to work, if you'll have me,' Jono said.

'Of course, I will — if you're up to it.'

Jono took a breath. 'As long as it's only desk work for now, I'll manage. It'll be a while before I'll be any good at chasing bad guys.'

Wise smiled. 'How's the treatment coming along?'

'I've had one session of immunotherapy so far and the doctors are happy,' Jono said. 'I felt like crap for two or three days afterwards but, otherwise, it's pretty easy.'

'How often are you having treatments?'

'Every six weeks. I'll let you know when the next one's coming up as I'll have to take a few days off.'

'Whatever you need.'

Jono nodded his head towards the incident room. 'It looks like you could do with the extra hands. It seemed pretty quiet in there.'

'We've been short-staffed for so long that I'm slowly coming to realise that we're never going to get any more help. The team is what it is. But having you back will make a big difference. You've been missed.'

Jono waved the comment off. 'I just had all that nonsense from Hicksy. Don't you start.'

'Alright. Point taken. I'll —'

Someone else knocked on Wise's door. It was Sarah. She did a double take when she saw Jono and a massive grin spread across her face. 'Hey! What are you doing here?'

Jono got up and hugged the petite detective. 'I couldn't have you doing all the work around here. It's bad enough you have to put up with that bunch of losers outside.'

'Oh my God. I've missed you,' Sarah said.

'And I've missed you, darling.'

Sarah stepped back and wiped the corner of her eye. 'Don't make me cry.'

Jono chuckled. 'You won't be the first woman I've had in tears.'

Sarah turned to Wise. 'I was going to tell you that everyone's here. And it turns out they are.' She whacked Jono playfully on the arm.

Wise stood up. 'Okay. Let's get everyone briefed and Jono up to speed.'

'Lovely,' Jono said, rubbing his hands. 'I can't wait.'

They walked out into MIR-One and anyone else who hadn't seen Jono return rushed over to say hello. All except Hannah, that is. She was at her desk with her head in her hands, looking like her world was about to end. She managed to look up and wave a greeting, but that was all.

Wise, surprised at the state of her, walked over. 'You okay?'

'Yeah. Just feel a bit rough,' Hannah replied.

That was quite the understatement. Even Jono looked better than Hannah did at that moment. 'Are you coming down with something?'

Hannah winced, her cheeks colouring. 'I'm sorry. I went out for a few drinks last night and got a bit carried away. I'll be alright in a bit.'

'Okay,' Wise said, doing his best not to feel frustrated. 'Go get yourself a coffee or something from the canteen. We're going to be busy, and I need you firing on all cylinders.'

Hannah nodded. 'I will. Sorry.' She got up sheepishly from her desk and headed out of the incident room. Wise watched her go, wondering why she'd gone out on a bender right at the start of an investigation. It wasn't like her at all. He hoped there wasn't anything behind it other than a poor decision on her part to let off some steam.

With a shake of his head, he headed over to the whiteboards, then turned to face his team. 'Good morning, everyone. This is day two of our investigation into the murder of Cameron Nketiam in his flat on Friary Road. But, before we get started, I'd just like to formally welcome Jono back. He's not a hundred percent fighting fit, so go easy on him.'

'He's never been a hundred percent, Guv,' Hicksy called out. 'To be honest, most days, he's not even at twenty percent.'

'Ah, but my twenty percent is like you at five hundred percent,' Jono said.

Hicksy grinned. 'Never said it wasn't.'

'Right,' Wise said. 'Yesterday morning, after being alerted via a 999 call made by a Leon Tomoral, uniformed officers found the body of an IC3 male lying on his living room floor with his throat cut. We now have it confirmed that the victim is Cameron Nketiam. Twenty-four years old. A recent resident of Wormwood Scrubs.' Wise pointed to the list of priors that Sarah had jotted down next to his mug shot. 'As you can see, Cameron has had plenty of run-ins with us in the past. Mainly for drugs and violence.'

The door to MIR-One opened and Hannah reappeared, clutching a paper cup in one hand. But she wasn't alone. Following on her heels was Helen Kelly, dressed in her blue SOCO jumpsuit and with her curly hair tied back. 'I hope I'm not interrupting anything,' she said when everyone's heads turned to face her.

'We're just going over the case at the moment,' Wise said.

'Ah, perfect timing then,' Helen said. 'I was nearby, so I thought I'd pop over and update you in person.'

'Excellent,' Wise said. He indicated the space next to him. 'The floor's all yours.'

Helen weaved her way through the desks and joined Wise. 'Cheers.'

'Everyone, this is Helen Kelly. She's leading the forensics on this job,' Wise said to the others.

'Hello,' Helen said. 'If I'd known I'd be making a group presentation, I would've done my hair and make-up.' She smiled. 'Not that it would've made much difference.'

'How are you getting on at Cameron's flat?' Wise asked.

'We had a long day there yesterday,' Helen said. 'And I imagine that we'll be there for a few more. The big problem is that there is almost too much evidence. We've found so many fingerprints, that it looks like all of Peckham have been in the flat at some point.'

'Understandable if he was dealing drugs.'

'Oh, I think it's safe to say that he was. Apart from the couple of bags left on the coffee table, we've found traces of heroin and cocaine in drawers, cupboards and especially in the metal bin that was in the living room.'

'But only traces? No actual drugs?' Hicksy asked.

'No,' Helen replied. 'Whatever was there, the victim had either sold or had stolen.'

'Depending on the quantity Cameron might have had in his flat, I'd say robbery was a good motive for murder,' Wise said.

'We do have something interesting though,' Helen said. 'There were some bottles of beer on the coffee table. Two Stellas and two Luz Solars.'

'I remember,' Wise said.

'The Stellas have Cameron Nketiam's fingerprints all over them. We also found some more bottles of Stella in the fridge, again with his fingerprints. So, no surprises there. But the Luz Solars had some interesting fingerprints too. Fingerprints that belong to Yusuf Ozdemir.'

'I know that name,' Wise said. He knew it well. 'The Turk.'

'That's the one,' Helen said.

'Who's the Turk?' Callum asked.

'Brains,' Wise said. 'Can you put Mr Ozdemir's details on the big screen for us?'

Brains tapped way at his keyboard for a couple of seconds and then a mugshot appeared on the monitor by the whiteboards. Caucasian and bald, the dark eyes of Yusuf Ozdemir stared out across MIR-One. 'Born in Istanbul in Nineteen Sixty-Six,' Brains said. 'Moved to the UK in Eighty-Nine. Sentenced to ten years for heroin smuggling in Nineteen Ninety-Three. Served seven. He's been arrested a few times since then but not charged with anything.'

'He's the biggest importer of class A substances in South London,' Wise said. 'Allegedly.'

'Fucking hell,' Hicksy said. 'So, he was having beers with Cameron before he died?'

'Looks like it,' Helen said.

'That doesn't make sense,' Wise said. 'Ozdemir is big time, at the top of the ladder. Cameron's maybe one or two rungs off from the floor. I'm amazed they even know each other, let alone talk.'

'Maybe Cameron was working for Ozdemir?' Sarah suggested. 'Maybe Cameron was stealing from him and that's why he got his throat cut?'

'Both possible — but I just don't see the Turk popping around to Wilmsden Terrace for a quick beer with Cameron before cutting his throat,' Wise said.

'Fingerprints don't lie,' Sarah replied.

'Okay. Well, let's find where Ozdemir is, so we can have a chat,' Wise said. 'Hicksy, did you get anywhere with the door-to-door enquiries yesterday?'

Hicksy rolled his neck. 'Not really. They don't like the police much down Friary Road. However, no one we spoke to said they'd heard a fight, though. Apart from our friend, Leon. It might be something or it could just be no one wants to get involved.'

'Well, we know he's lying to us about something. Maybe he made up the fight for some reason?' Wise replied. 'Have we got Leon's fingerprints and DNA?'

Hicksy nodded. 'Yeah, we told him that we needed to eliminate him from our enquiries.'

Wise glanced over at Helen. 'Can you prioritise processing Leon Tomoral?'

'Yeah,' the SOCO replied. 'No problem. I'll call the lab after I leave here.'

'Do you want me to bring him in for a formal interview?' Hicksy asked.

'No, not yet,' Wise said. 'Let's wait until we've got a bombshell to drop on him first. But we should keep our eyes on him for now. Make sure he doesn't do a runner.'

Hicksy scratched his armpit. 'I can ask the scene guards to keep a look out. They can call us if he goes anywhere.'

Wise nodded. 'It's not ideal but, considering how short staffed we are, it'll work for now.'

Helen looked at her watch. 'I better be off, but I'll shout as soon as we find anything else, and I'll tell the team to look out for any matches with Leon.'

'Thanks. I appreciate you coming down,' Wise said.

'No problem.' The SOCO weaved her way back through the desks and left the incident room.

'Anyone else found anything useful?' Wise asked.

'I have, actually,' Sarah said.

'Oh, yes?'

'I tracked the Honda Civic from Friary Road to the Maywood estate,' Sarah said. 'CCTV footage has nearly the whole journey covered.' A video replaced the mug shot of Ozdemir. 'It left Friary Road at 4:05, turned right onto Commercial Way, then right onto Sumner Road before parking up at the Maywood at 4:09.'

The team watched the car make the four-minute trip via different CCTV cameras.

'Now, we haven't got any footage of the car park at the Maywood, but I did catch the car burning from a camera on Sumner Road that covers the turning into the estate.' Sarah froze the video and pointed to a bright light in a sliver of space between two blocks of flats. 'Now, watch this.' She hit play again. The team watched the flames burn bright in the distance and then there was a flash of light as the petrol tank went up. As the flames reduced in size, Wise could see a figure running towards Sumner Road.

Wise stepped closer. 'Whoever that is, they're in a hurry.'

'He is,' Sarah said.

'He?' Wise repeated.

'He,' Sarah confirmed. They watched the figure run straight towards the camera. Whoever it was wore all black clothing with their hood up and had a sports bag in one hand. However, as they reached Sumner Road and passed under a streetlight, they looked up, showing their face. Sarah froze the film once more. 'That's our car thief.'

'One thing's for sure, that's not The Turk.' Wise looked at the picture of the man on the TV screen. The film was grainy. It was dark. But the streetlight had found the man's smiling face well enough, despite his hood. As pictures go, it was about as good as it got. 'IC3 male. Young. Late teens? Early twenties?'

'Yeah. I'd say younger than older,' Sarah replied.

'He certainly looks happy with himself.'

'Maybe it's got to do with what he has in the bag?' Hicksy said. 'Looks big enough for a load of stolen gear.'

'Brains, do you think you could get us an ID with this?' Wise asked.

'I'll give it a go,' the detective replied.

Wise looked over at Sarah again. 'Do you know where he goes?'

'To a point,' Sarah said. She hit play again and the video jumped from one camera viewpoint to another. 'He heads north up Sumner Road, all the way up to the park, then turns left onto St Georges Way. I think he goes into the flats in Bibury Close. Or at least that's where we lose him on the CCTV.'

'That place isn't much better than the Maywood,' Jono said.

'There was a domestic there in the summer that escalated into a mass brawl in the streets once the uniforms turned up.'

'Fucking hell,' Hicksy said. 'I remember that. Half the Met ended up down there in riot gear.'

'That's as may be. But it doesn't put the place off-limits to us. It just means we have to be careful,' Wise said. 'Anyway, we must find out who our car thief is first. Once we know his identity, hopefully that will help us track down where he's living. But just because he's the driver of the Civic, it doesn't mean he's our killer.'

'Yeah, but driving away from the scene at high speed and then torching the car aren't exactly the acts of an innocent man,' Hicksy said.

'We also need to look closer at Leon and find out what he's lying about and then we have the Turk to chat to. Why was he having beers with Cameron? What's their connection? Was Cameron one of the Turk's dealers? Or someone trying to make a move on Ozdemir's territory? We've got lots of questions to answer for now.'

Wise paused for a moment, as he looked around MIR-One at the faces of his team. 'Let's go at them hard but be careful. These are dangerous people in dangerous places. Stay in touch with each other, stay alert and, most importantly, stay alive.'

16

Sarah normally smoked in the station car park, right by the main doors. It was easier, more than anything. The amount Sarah smoked, after all, it made sense to just pop out, puff away, then head back in. She couldn't afford wasting time by going for a wander. In winter, who wanted to walk about anyway? It was always so bloody cold and miserable.

Now, though, Sarah left the station and turned onto Kennington Road, hugging herself to keep warm. She only had a jumper on because she'd not wanted to draw any attention to herself by picking up her coat.

She stuck her cigarette in her mouth and lit it with shaking hands. She sucked greedily on the smoke, half to keep warm and half to calm herself down. How the hell had she got herself into this mess?

With her cigarette clamped between her teeth, Sarah pulled her phone out, scrolled through her contacts and found NAILS. Just seeing that contact, that number, made her feel sick. Was this what it was like for Andy?

She took another drag of the cigarette, needing the hit before she hit dial, then blew the smoke out into the cold, grey day as she listened to the phone ring. Praying all the while for him not to answer.

For all the good it did her.

'Hello, darling.' The man's voice sent shivers down her spine.

'We've got three suspects,' she said, needing to tell him everything before she lost her nerve or maybe gained some courage. 'Leon Tomoral, who made the 999 call, an unidentified man who was seen driving away from the scene and Yusuf Ozdemir.'

The man laughed. 'Fuck off. The Turk? You're pulling my leg, you are. No way is the Turk involved in bumping off little Cam.'

'We found his fingerprints on beer bottles in Cameron's flat.'

'Then the bloody tooth fairy put them there because King Charles is more likely to pop around to have a drink with Cam than the Turk,' the man said. 'Still, your lot can go bother him as much as you like. After all, he's not part of my crew. Unlike dear Ollie.'

'I've made sure his name's not come up,' Sarah said, taking another drag, hating how much her hand shook.

'Good girl. I knew you wouldn't let me down,' the man replied. 'Just make sure you tell me who nicked Ollie's gear before you nick them, because I want my drugs back. I don't want them seized as evidence.'

'How much did they take?'

'Three keys.'

Shit. Sarah closed her eyes, imagining that volume of drugs. She'd need a bag if she was going to snatch them. If she could. 'Simon doesn't send me out of the office much. I don't know if I can—'

'Stop right there,' the man snarled. 'Andy gave me all the same bullshit excuses and you know what happened to him.'

Sarah said nothing. She knew only too well.

'All you need to do is give me a name and I'll sort the rest out. Don't you worry.'

'Okay. Okay. I can do that,' Sarah said, but the line had gone dead. The man didn't care what she could or couldn't do. Only that she did what he told her.

Putting her phone away, she hurried back to the nick, smoking what was left of her cigarette furiously, a hundred emotions going through her head.

One thing was for sure, it was a good thing Andy was dead. If he wasn't, she'd kill him herself for getting her in this mess. He'd introduced her to that bastard, telling her it was an easy way to make some quick money. Money that would take all her problems away. Money she deserved.

'No one will get hurt,' he'd crowed to her in that Geordie accent of his. 'No one innocent at least. And who cares about the scumbags, eh?'

Sarah should've told him to fuck off there and then. Maybe reported him too. But she'd done neither. Instead, she'd gone along and met the bastard.

That had frightened the life out of her, for starters. Sarah thought she'd been set up when she'd seen him in the pub. She thought that Andy had tricked her, because it looked like the governor was waiting for her. But when she got closer, she realised it wasn't Simon Wise sitting there, no matter how much alike they looked. It wasn't just the clothes — the lack of a suit for starters — but it was the cruelty in the man's eyes that made him stand apart from Wise. The darkness.

Again, she should've walked there and then but no, she'd sat down like an idiot and taken the man's goddamned money. And now she was trapped, just like Andy had been.

Sarah took one last drag of her cigarette and threw the butt onto the ground. Rain started to fall, pecking at her face, so she hurried back through the gates, jogged across the car park and up the steps in the building.

All the lights were still on, fighting to keep away the day's gloom, despite it being 10 a.m. The ancient heating was gurgling away in the background as well, but it did little to relieve the chill in her bones.

Sarah took the lift up to the third floor, needing a few more seconds by herself to shake away the guilt and the shame. She took deep breaths, feeling worse by the second. When the lift doors opened, she had to force herself to step out into the corridor. Walking to MIR-One, she wondered if she could pull a sickie and head back home, hide there, but if she did that... well, she wouldn't be able to get the information the bastard wanted. And if she didn't do that, she knew what would happen next.

She'd be dead like Andy. Or wish that she was.

Her hands were still shaking when she pushed the door to the incident room open. Most of the team were still there; Jono, Hicksy, Donut, Brains and Callum. No sign of Hannah or the governor though. That was a good thing, at least.

A few heads turned to see who it was as she walked in, but they all quickly returned their attention back to their work. No one asked why she looked so scared, so maybe she'd managed to hide it after all.

Sarah felt better when she was back behind her desk.

Then she caught Donut looking at her.

'What?' she snapped.

Donut shrugged. 'Nothing.'

Was it really though? Paranoia swept through her. Had he seen anything? Maybe he'd been looking out the window and seen her on her phone out in the street.

No. She was just being stupid. Feeling guilty. 'Do you know where the governor is?' she asked instead, trying to cover up how flustered she felt.

'Yeah,' Donut replied. 'He's gone with Hannah to see the Turk. Apparently, he works out of a strip club in Bermondsey. Why, do you need him for something?'

'I was just wondering, that's all. Forget I asked.' Sarah stuck her head back down so all she could see was her monitor and hit play on the next bit of CCTV footage. She wanted more footage of the car thief. Hopefully, a clip where she could clearly see his face.

She'd called in footage from around Carline Mews, covering the hour or so before he pinched the car. For some reason, crooks always worried about being spotted while they were committing a crime and afterwards. They didn't worry about the ten minutes or so beforehand.

If one was patient, and Sarah was, it was just a matter of sifting through all the possible approach routes to find what one needed. One time, she'd backtracked a masked and hooded man, who'd stabbed and killed someone. She'd found him at a KFC on Kentish Road, where he'd been happily captured on multiple cameras eating and chatting with his mates before going off to commit the murder. The jury had taken all of about ten seconds to find him guilty after they'd seen her movie of the crime all cut together.

Hopefully, it'd be the same here. Maybe she'd even be able to track the thief to his home.

Maybe.

Of course, if she found anything, she'd have to tell the bastard first before she told his brother. Then God only knew what would happen.

What a mess. What a bloody awful mess.

17

Jono had to admit he was damn glad to be back at work. Even if he didn't have that much to do right then. It was just good being back in MIR-One, listening to the banter, taking the piss out of Hicksy, feeling useful instead of feeling dead.

And, after the last few months, that was a feeling to be savoured. They'd been plenty of times when he'd thought he wasn't going to make it. Especially when he'd ended up in hospital with blood clots in his lungs. Even the doctors had thought it was all over for him then.

Of course, being grateful to be alive didn't stop him from going stir crazy at home. Even Pat, his wife, had had enough of his moaning and moping. She'd practically pushed him out the front door that morning to send him on his way. No doubt, she'd have her feet up, watching *Loose Women* or something, enjoying the peace and quiet. God only knew she deserved a bit of time to herself. She'd been a saint, looking after him like she had.

The phone on his desk rang. An outside call.

'Murder Team,' he said on answering.

'Oh, hi,' a woman said with a trace of an accent. 'I was trying to reach a Detective Sergeant Markham?'

Jono glanced over to Hannah's desk, even though he knew she'd gone out with the governor. 'I'm afraid DS Markham's not here at the moment. Can I leave her a message for you?'

'Well, I live on Friary Road opposite the flats where the man was murdered,' the woman said, 'and DS Markham left me a note asking if we had any video from our Ring camera that might be of use.'

Jono sat up, feeling a little burst of adrenaline. 'And do you?'

'We do but I don't know if it'll be useful or not,' the woman said.

'Give me your name and address and I'll pop over to have a look with a colleague of mine.'

'It's Christina Osakara,' the woman said and reeled off her address.

'Er... how do you spell that?'

'O-S-A-K-A-R-A.'

Jono scrawled it down, already dreading having to try to pronounce it himself. 'Lovely. My name's DS Jonathan Gray. I'll see you shortly.'

'I'll be waiting,' Christina said.

Jono ended the call.

'Who was that?' Hicksy asked.

'Some woman who might have some CCTV footage of the murder,' Jono said, grinning. 'I said we'd go have a look.'

'Why didn't you just ask her to email it over?' Hicksy said. 'You're not supposed to leave your desk.'

'Aw, come on. It's not like we're kicking down doors. I'm going to sit in your car while you drive me. We'll go see this Christina woman, maybe have a cup of tea, watch the video and then drive back. It's hardly going to be stressful.'

'Yeah but you're on desk duty. Pat will kill me if something happens to you just because you got bored of being in the office.'

'Mate, I'm not going to bloody die. Besides, it'll be good for me to see where this drug dealer got murdered. You know, get a feel for the place and all that.'

Hicksy shook his head. 'No way.'

Jono just laughed and stood up. 'Well, if you're not going with me, I'll go on my own.' He picked his coat up and headed for the door.

'Jono!' Hicksy called after him, but he was already in the corridor and heading for the lift. Sure enough, he heard Hicksy running behind him and had to hide a smile.

The two men stood next to each other without speaking while they waited for the lift to arrive. When the doors opened with a ping, both men climbed inside.

'I'm only going in case you keel over and need some CPR,' Hicksy said as the lift juddered its way back down to the ground floor.

'In your dreams. You just want to slip me some tongue while you give me mouth to mouth.'

'Aw, God. I'm going to be sick. You know I wouldn't do that. I'd let you die first,' Hicksy said. 'Anyway, your missus made me promise not to kiss anyone else while I'm shagging her.'

The two men were chuckling as they walked out of the station and headed over to Hicksy's car. God, it really did feel good to be back.

'I'll tell you one good thing about your near-death experience,' Hicksy said as they pulled out into Kennington Road. 'I don't have to put up with your fags stinking up the car anymore.'

'Which means I don't have to put up with all your moaning about it, either,' Jono replied. 'Win-win.'

'Me? Moan? I think you've got me mixed up with someone else.'

The two friends spent the whole of the thirty-minute drive over to Friary Road nattering about this and that, talking nonsense to stop them talking about anything serious. Still, Jono could feel Hicksy's concern, and he hadn't missed all the casual looks Hicksy had thrown his way either. He knew the worry was coming from a good place, but it was starting to piss Jono off.

'You see? I'm not dead,' Jono said as they parked up outside Christina Osakara's Georgian terrace house.

'Don't get too cocky,' Hicksy said. 'There's still time for it to all go horribly wrong.'

Jono looked out of his window at the block of flats. Two uniforms stood guard outside a ground floor flat cordoned off by blue and white police tape, its entrance covered by a white awning. The SOCO van was parked further along the street. 'This looks like a right grot hole.'

'Good to see your powers of observation haven't gone tits up,' Hicksy said. 'And I can safely say the flats look even worse on the inside.'

Jono peered past Hicksy at the Georgian buildings opposite. 'Talk about night and day. It's only in London where you find million-pound houses five metres away from squats.'

'I think you meant to say "multi-million-pound houses",' Hicksy replied. 'These have got to be worth at least ten big ones.'

'If I'd known I was going somewhere posh, I would've worn my good suit.'

'Or at least not slept in the one you got on.'

'Alright, Mr. GQ,' Jono said. 'Let's go talk to the good woman of the house.'

'What's her name?'

'Christina Something-Unpronounceable.'

Hicksy raised an eyebrow. 'Seriously?'

Jono shrugged. 'You know what I'm like with these foreign names.'

'You're bloody useless.'

'And that's why you love me.'

'Only because you make me look good.'

They both got out. Going from the car's warmth straight into the bollock-freezing wind got Jono coughing like a mad man. He doubled up, trying to catch his breath, but nothing was working. Even coughing felt like choking.

Hicksy moved quickly, opening up the car again and grabbing a bottle of water from the door pocket. Jono took it from him between hacks, and spilt half of it as he tried getting the bottle to his lips. It tasted rank as he gulped it down, but it did the trick, calming his lungs enough for him to catch his breath.

'Fuck,' he gasped. When he looked up, he saw Hicksy had that look on his face, the look Jono hated, the one everyone had around him these days. The pity look. 'Pack it in.'

'Pack what in?' Hicksy said, feigning innocence.

'Watching me like you think I'm about to fall over at any minute and pop my clogs.' Jono shook his head. 'I told you, I'm alright.'

'I know. I know. It's just there's alright and there's alright. I just wanna make sure you're the right sort of alright,' Hicksy replied.

Jono stared at Hicksy. The man had lost his mind. 'What the bloody hell does that even mean?'

'You know what it means,' Hicksy said, his eyebrows furrowed.

'No, I don't. Christ, have you always talked such nonsense?' Jono stropped over to Christina Osakara's front door. He was grateful for the anger. It almost stopped him from acknowledging how weak he felt. How useless. 'Or is this a new personality flaw you've developed while I was off sick?'

Hicksy held up his hands. 'Okay. Forget I said anything.'

'Good.' Jono rang the buzzer, still gulping air, his legs as weak as a newborn colt's.

A beautiful Japanese woman in activewear answered the door. 'Yes?' Her accent was more Borden than Tokyo and she had the look of someone using every trick of modern science to stay looking as young as possible. She looked around forty years old, but she could just as easily have been sixty.

Jono gave her his best smile and held up his warrant card. 'Hello. My name's Detective Sergeant Gray and this is DS Hicks,' Jono said, showing his warrant card. 'Are you Christina?'

'Yes, Ms. Christina Osakara,' the woman said, emphasising her surname, but all that did was make Jono even more afraid to try to say it. She looked like the sort of person who'd lose their shit if he didn't get it right.

He smiled instead. 'You said you had some Ring footage for us to see?'

'Yes, of course. Come this way.' She stepped aside to allow both men in, closed the door and led them down a corridor to a large kitchen at the rear of the house. There was a laptop open on the island. 'I've downloaded all the footage from early Wednesday morning.'

'You weren't here at the time?' Jono asked. The kitchen was spotless, from the white marble flooring to the countertops and appliances. In fact, if someone had said it had been installed the day before and no one else had stepped inside it until just then, he would've believed it. He glanced down at his natty, worn out, scuffed leather shoes and wondered if he should've taken them off at the front door. Then again, his socks weren't really fit for public consumption.

'We had spent a few days at our place in Deal,' Christina replied. 'We only got back this morning and saw all the fuss across the road. Then I found your DS Markham's note. It's a good job we weren't away longer. Everything gets recorded over every forty-eight hours.'

Hicksy pointed at the laptop. 'May we have a look?'

'Is there a time in particular you'd like to see?' Christina asked. 'Or just the whole night?'

'Can we start at 4 a.m?' Hicksy said. 'Depending on what's there then, we can move backwards or forwards as necessary.'

'Certainly.' Christina played around with the laptop's trackpad. Once she had a window with the camera footage up, she moved the timer bar along until it read 0400. She then stepped out of the way to let the two detectives have a closer look.

The video was dark and grainy, but its viewpoint couldn't have been better. It covered the Friary to the right and, to the left, all the flats opposite up to the stairwell.

Hicksy jabbed a finger on the screen, pointing out the flat in the centre of the picture. 'That's the victim's.'

Unlike most of the block, Cameron Nketiam's place had all its lights on, so it looked like someone was wide awake in there despite the time of night. There was no movement at all outside, though, with only the odd car driving past.

That changed when the time stamp clicked over to 0405. The

door to Cameron's flat opened and what appeared to be a man came out, dressed in black with a hood over his head, and clutching a sports bag. He ran to one of the parked cars. As he opened the door, he looked straight at the camera. He then jumped into the car and sped off.

Hicksy rewound the film and froze the video on the clearest shot of the hooded man. 'That's him isn't it? The same bloke who burnt the car at the Maywood?'

'Looks like it to me.' Jono stared at the picture. 'The question I want to know is who's that?' He pointed at the stairwell. There was a man hiding in the shadows, if he wasn't mistaken.

Hicksy hit play again. The hooded man jumped in the car and sped off, but both Jono and Hicksy weren't watching him this time. Their eyes were on mystery person number two.

The figure approached Cameron's flat, taking their time and looking in every direction. At one point, they looked straight at the camera, providing a perfect view of their face in case there was any doubt to their identity.

'Fuck a duck,' Hicksy said. 'I know him.'

'Ahem,' Christina said from behind them.

Hicksy grimaced and looked over his shoulder. 'Sorry about that.'

'Hicksy,' Jono said, patting him on the shoulder. 'The video.'

His friend turned his attention back to the computer just as the man paused by the front door to Cameron's flat. He then entered. A minute passed before he came out again, clutching his stomach, and the two detectives watched him run straight back to the stairwell and up the stairs.

'Who is he?' Jono asked.

'I'll tell you when we're outside,' Hicksy said. He then looked over at Christina. 'I'm going to need to take a copy of this film.'

Five minutes later, they were back at the car. 'So, who's our mystery man?' Jono asked, as he pulled his coat tighter against the wind.

'A man called Leon Tomoral,' Hicksy said, peering over at the flats. 'He lives right above the victim's flat. He's the one who called

999. Leon claimed he discovered the body when he heard a fight and came to investigate, but he was adamant that he didn't go inside.'

'Well, we know that's not true,' Jono said. 'Reckon we should go nick him, then?'

Hicksy got out his phone. 'Let me call the governor first.'

18

Hannah was, at least, starting to feel almost human by the time she left Kennington with Wise to go and see Yusuf Ozdemir. Two lots of Neurofen, a bottle of water, three coffees and a cheese sandwich had managed to counteract some of the alcohol sloshing through her system and her headache had downgraded itself from DEFCON One to a three or a four on the armageddon scale.

She was still angry with herself, though, for getting in that state, especially on a weeknight. Hannah needed all her wits about her if she was going to do her job properly. She'd seen enough officers in the Met with drink problems to know she didn't want to become one of them.

But did getting rat-arsed once mean she had something to worry about? Or was getting drunk just a symptom of other things? Yeah, Hannah was stressed about work, but tracking down the killer of a drug dealer was nothing compared to hunting a serial killer of homeless children.

Hannah had enjoyed hanging out at the Gazelle chatting up Nikki but, the truth was, she'd done more ogling than chatting. She was also smart enough to realise that any flirting on Nikki's part was probably down to her being a smart bartender after more business instead of any romantic interest in Hannah. And how attractive had Hannah looked when she'd stumbled out of the bar to go home anyway?

The reality was simply that Hannah had not wanted to go home and see Emma. Everything else had just been her way of justifying staying away from another night of awkward conversation over a Netflix show she had no interest in.

With that in mind, Hannah had done a good job of letting Emma know things weren't right with them — if the glares and all the slamming of doors in their flat were anything to go by. At the time, with her head imploding, Hannah had been grateful that there'd been no screaming but, thinking about it now, maybe getting yelled at this morning might've been better than what aggro was still to come.

Anyway, that was all stuff to worry about later. She was on her way to meet a very dangerous man and she needed to focus on that.

Thankfully, it hadn't been too hard to track down Ozdemir. According to his police file, he worked out of offices above one of his more legitimate businesses, a strip club called Diamond Nights in Bermondsey, down near Southwark Park.

One phone call later, Hannah had confirmed Ozdemir was at the club and she'd arranged to have an informal interview with him there.

It was, more or less, a straight run to get there from Kennington, via the A201, up Tower Bridge Road then right onto Grange Road. Wise hadn't said much on the way, lost in his own thoughts, and no doubt pissed off that she'd turned up to work stinking like a brewery. She'd nearly apologised a half dozen times as her guilt got to her but, in the end, she'd said nothing.

The club was in another part of London stuck between what it was — a pretty run-down neighbourhood of council flats, low-cost housing and shops that were long since passed their best — and what it wanted to be, a gentrified up-and-coming area full of ultra-modern apartments and restaurants that covered the whole international culinary experience. Nearly every other building had scaffolding as they were renovated for new owners who had cash in their pockets, as opposed to people who needed dole cheques to pay their rents.

Diamond Nights itself was located at the back end of Southwark Park Road, the lone business still operating among a parade of shuttered-up shops with signs begging for new tenants. Posters on either side of the club door promised 'adult entertainment for the discerning gentleman' and proclaimed 'Smart dress only. No jeans allowed.' The pictures of the dancers on display were covered with stars and black bars to protect their modesty but left little to the imagination.

'Looks charming,' Hannah said, peering through the passenger window of the Mondeo.

Wise took in the run-down entrance. 'Whatever turns you on, I suppose.'

He parked the Mondeo in a spot next to an old school that had been converted long ago into low-cost housing. One wing was covered in flags of St George, showing their support for the England team. No doubt more would be displayed before Saturday's World Cup quarter-final match against the French.

Hannah had never really been into sports and couldn't understand how the whole country could go so football crazy, especially now when there were wars going on and everyone was feeling the pinch money-wise. But maybe that was the point? Entertainment for the masses to help them forget the mess of everyday life.

Wise and Hannah left the Mondeo and strolled back towards the strip club. It was still bitterly cold, but the rain had stopped for about the first time that month. However, the rolling grey clouds overhead promised that would only be a brief respite.

An old man in a blue boiler suit opened the doors to the club as they approached. 'You the coppers?'

'Good guess,' Wise said. 'What gave us away?'

The man sneered, showing off a few nicotine-stained teeth. 'I can smell the filth a mile away.' Holding the door open, he pointed down the corridor. 'The boss is in the bar that way.'

The inside looked as sad as the exterior. The reek of stale beer did nothing for Hannah's hangover and the whole place looked like it was overdue a makeover ten years ago. They walked past the ticket booth and cloakroom and down the corridor lined with mirrored walls, and more posters showing off dancers with names like Trixie, Stardust and Vixen. At the far end, under a sign that said, "No touching," black velvet curtains blocked off the view of the bar itself. Somehow though, Hannah knew she wasn't going to be impressed when she saw the interior.

She had to blink as she stepped through the curtains, with Wise following behind her. The house lights were on, illuminating everything so brightly that she could see a multitude of stains on the vulgar paisley-patterned carpet. There was a main stage off to the left with three smaller podiums scattered around, each with its own pole for dancers to gyrate around.

Ozdemir was sitting at the bar, his back to the entrance. He looked like a bald bear perched on a stool far too small for his bulk. His white shirt strained and stretched as he leaned on the bar. He had another man in a suit beside him and both were looking intently at the computer screen on the countertop. Two heavily muscled men loitered behind the bar, ostensibly stocking and cleaning the bar area, but Hannah couldn't help but think they were more likely bodyguards than bar staff.

One of them looked over as Hannah and Wise headed towards them. 'Boss,' he said, putting down the glass he'd been polishing. His hands stayed out of sight behind the bar counter.

Ozdemir turned slowly in his seat, then nearly fell off it in shock. 'What the fuck you doing here?' he said, getting to his feet, fists bunched. 'We had an agreement.'

Hannah held up her warrant card. 'Mister Ozdemir? I'm DS Markham. I spoke to one of your associates earlier. We're here to—'

'I'm not talking to you,' Ozdemir spat, his face going red. 'I'm talking to HIM!' He jabbed a finger towards Wise. 'Walking in here with a cop doesn't make it alright. You've got fucking nerve. But if you want to start a war, let's—'

'I don't know who you think I am but I'm not him.' Wise produced his own warrant card and held it up. 'My name's Detective Inspector Simon Wise.'

'Like fuck,' Ozdemir said. 'I know who you are. You come closer, you dead man.'

Hannah didn't have a clue what was going on, but she knew no one was pissing about. She and Wise were in serious trouble. One of the heavies had come out from behind the bar, a baseball bat in his hand, and more muscle appeared from a door in the far corner of the club and from the curtain behind them. One of them had his hand tucked into his jacket and Hannah had a horrible feeling he was carrying a gun.

She slipped her hand into her own coat pocket where she kept her retractable baton. It wouldn't do any good against a pistol, but it was better than nothing.

Only Wise stood where he was, as he didn't have a care in the world, still holding out his identification. 'Take a look for yourself. I'm not him.'

That got Hannah's attention. Who the hell was Wise referring to?

The man in the suit, who'd been all but hiding behind Ozdemir, poked his head over his boss' shoulder. 'Maybe I should have a look?'

'Go,' Ozdemir said, without taking his eyes off Wise.

The man in the suit scuttled out from behind his boss and slowly made his way over to Wise, getting close enough only to take the warrant card from her governor's hand. The moment he had it, he quickly shuffled a safe distance away. Only then did he have a look at the card. 'It looks real.'

'That's because it is real,' Wise said.

Ozdemir stuck out a hand towards the man in the suit and clicked his fingers. A second later, he had Wise's ID and was checking it for himself.

'What the fuck is going on?' Hannah whispered to Wise.

'I'll tell you later,' he said.

Ozdemir looked at the warrant card, then up at Wise, then back again. 'Simon Wise?' He said eventually.

Wise nodded. 'Detective Inspector Wise.'

'And you're not —'

'No.'

Ozdemir looked at the card again, still not trusting what he was seeing. 'You look exactly like—'

'I know,' Wise said. 'But I'm not him.'

'If you're lying to me ...' Ozdemir said.

'I'm not.'

'This could be fake.'

'It's not.'

Still, no one moved.

'I can always make a call and bring a couple of truckloads of officers down here, arrest you and tear this place apart,' Wise said, 'if that'll help convince you that I am who I say I am.'

Ozdemir glanced over at the man in the suit, who shrugged. 'I think he's telling the truth.'

The Turk had his dark eyes fixed on Wise and, for a heartbeat, Hannah thought he was going to tell his men to kill them both, but then he started laughing as if the whole thing had been the funniest joke ever told. Straight away, the tension in the room evaporated. The men who'd appeared out of nowhere disappeared back to where they'd come from and the barman with the baseball bat returned behind the counter.

'Bloody hell,' Hannah said as she let out a breath.

Ozdemir pointed to a table. 'We chat here.'

Wise and Hannah sat down with the Turk and the man in the suit, who held a hand to shake. 'I'm Saliah Elmals, Mister Ozdemir's solicitor.'

Wise and Hannah both shook the offered hand. After the tension of only moments before, it all felt rather surreal to be doing something so ordinary.

'So, Inspector,' Ozdemir said. 'What we do for you?'

19

Wise kept his face impassive, but inside he was reeling with what had just happened. Ozdemir had obviously thought he was Tom when he'd walked into the club, and it was clear the two men weren't friends. What made the whole situation even worse was the fact the whole conversation had taken place in front of Hannah. How was he going to explain what had just happened? Christ, the Turk's men had looked like they had been on the verge of murdering the pair of them a minute ago.

If he'd realised that Tom and Ozdemir knew each other, he'd have thought of a different way of meeting with the man. Was this going to become an issue with every gangster in London going forward? How far did Tom's reach go?

Wise need to speak to DCI Heer again. He needed to—

'Inspector?' Elmals said, interrupting Wise from his thoughts. 'Do you have any questions for my client?'

Wise smiled, trying to hide his discomfort. 'Yes. Yes, I do.' He looked straight at Ozdemir. 'Do you mind telling me where you were on Tuesday night and early Wednesday morning?'

Ozdemir shrugged. 'I was here until 1, maybe 2. Then I go home and sleep.'

'Can anyone corroborate that?'

'A few hundred people here, then my wife when I get home. I try not to wake her up but, she say I'm always noisy. She wake up and tell me off.'

'What time was that?'

'I don't know. 2? 2:30? It was late, but not too late. I am getting old. I need sleep.'

Wise nodded. The man seemed to be telling the truth. If he'd been guilty of something, Wise would've expected Elmals to stop him from saying anything or have a more detailed alibi. The guilty always over-compensated in their lies. 'And how long were you at home for?'

'Until maybe midday and, yes, my wife, she confirm this. Plus, my cook also. She make me *sucuklu yumurta* for breakfast. That's a Turkish dish. It is eggs with sausage but so much more.' Ozdemir looked from Wise to Hannah and back again, looking genuinely puzzled by the questions. 'What is this about?'

'Do you know a Cameron Nketiam?' Wise asked.

The Turk shook his head. 'No. Who he?'

'He was a drug dealer,' Wise said.

'So? You think I know every drug dealer in London?' Ozdemir replied.

Elmals held up a hand. 'That was a joke. Mister Ozdemir doesn't know any drug dealers, or anyone engaged in any sort of unlawful activity to the best of his knowledge.'

'I'm sure he doesn't,' Wise said. 'But we're curious why we found Mister Ozdemir's fingerprints on two beer bottles in Mister Nketiam's flat.'

'And this drug dealer ... this Nketiam ... he is dead?' Ozdemir said.

'That's right.'

Realisation dawned across Ozdemir's face. He wagged a finger at Wise. 'And you think I kill him.'

'No,' Wise replied. 'But I do want to know why you were having a drink with him in his home.'

Ozdemir sat back and held out his hands. 'But I didn't.'

'Your fingerprints say otherwise.'

The Turk looked over to the bar. 'Zeki! Bring me a bottle of beer.'

The barman, who'd been ready to attack Wise and Hannah with a baseball bat earlier, grabbed a Heineken from the fridge behind the bar, and quickly brought it over to Ozdemir, placing it on the table.

'*Sağol,*' Ozdemir said, and the barman left once more. The Turk then picked up the bottle, making a show of touching it everywhere, before passing it to Wise. 'Here. Take this back to your station. My fingerprints will still be on it but that does not mean I am in your station.'

'So, you're saying the bottles were planted?' Wise said.

'I am saying nothing, but I touch many beer bottles. Once I drink them, I don't know what happened to them. Maybe someone collect it from garbage.'

'How often do you drink Luz Solars?' Hannah asked.

'Luz Solars?' The Turk repeated.

'That's right,' Hannah said.

'That tequila beer, right?' Ozdemir grimaced. 'I have that last week. It not good. I try it once but never again.'

'Where did you drink it last week?' Wise asked.

'It was new restaurant. Fancy. The Brandon Grill. Wednesday or maybe Thursday of last week,' Ozdemir said.

'That's right,' Elmals said. 'I was there too. It's in Peckham. The restaurant was terribly overhyped and the chef wasn't as good as he thought he was.'

Wise caught Hannah's eye, who nodded. Neither of them thought Ozdemir was lying. 'Alright,' Wise said. 'Thank you for talking to us. We'll be in touch if we have any other questions.'

'Always a pleasure,' Ozdemir said. Wise went to stand up, but Ozdemir grabbed his arm, forcing him to remain sitting. 'You know you look like him. Exactly like him.'

Wise met the Turk's eyes. 'But I'm not him.'

There was a pause, then the Turk released Wise's arm. 'Don't take this wrong way but I hope we don't meet again. Mistakes could be made. Mistakes one of us might not walk away from.'

Hannah sat forward. 'Are you threatening—'

Wise put up a hand to stop her. 'If I need to see you, I'll give you plenty of warning — or I'll come mob-handed so there's no mistaking who I am.'

The Turk nodded. 'Perhaps, when you find who put these bottles in the dead man's house, you can let me know? I would like to talk to him myself.'

'I don't think so.' Wise smiled. 'We'll see ourselves out.'

This time Ozdemir didn't stop Wise from getting to his feet. Wise waited for Hannah to get up from her seat and then they both walked out of the club. Wise took his time, though, trying to work out what he could say to Hannah to explain the mix up that could've cost them both their lives — without revealing the truth about Tom.

Whatever sunlight had managed to appear earlier was long gone by the time they stepped outside. Now, there was only the cold, wet darkness to greet them.

'Do you think he was telling the truth?' Hannah asked as they walked over to the Mondeo.

'I do,' Wise replied, unlocking the car. 'He didn't have a clue what we were talking about.'

Hannah looked at Wise over the top of the car. 'So, someone planted the bottles there?'

'Someone like the Turk isn't going to pop over for a beer with a low-level dealer like Cameron.' Wise climbed into the Mondeo, grateful to be out of the rain. Hannah got in a second later. 'Maybe whoever Cameron sold for is one of the Turk's business rivals and our killer knew that. It would make sense then to try and point the finger of blame at Ozdemir and stop them looking within their own crew.'

'You reckon it's an inside job then?'

'If the motive was robbery, then yeah. Or at least, it's someone familiar enough with Cameron's business that he knew Cameron had enough drugs or cash in his flat to make it worth killing him for — and knows the drug world well enough to think framing the Turk was a good idea.'

'Do you want to check out this Brandon Grill place?' Hannah asked. 'Work out how the bottles got from there to Friary Road?'

'Sounds good to me.' Wise turned on the engine — just as his phone rang. He answered it and Hicksy's voice came out of the hands-free speakers.

'Guv, you got a minute?'

'Yeah. Hannah and I are in the car,' Wise said.

'Me and Jono went to see this woman on Friary Road,' Hicksy replied. 'She lives opposite Cameron's place. Hannah had left her a card, asking if she had any CCTV footage.'

'And?' Wise said, feeling a bubble of excitement.

'She did and it's good. Very good. We've got footage of our Civic driver going into the victim's flat, then coming out twenty minutes later and driving off like the clappers.'

'That's good. Any sign of Yusuf Ozdemir?'

'Nah — but our mate from upstairs is on there and he did more than peek through the window. He definitely goes into the flat and stays there for about five minutes before hotfooting it home.'

'Now, that is interesting.'

'Do you want me and Jono to nick him?' Hicksy asked.

'I won't ask why Jono is with you and not in Kennington safely behind his desk,' Wise said. 'Get a Risk Assessment done first, then coordinate things with Helen Kelly and the Territorial Support Group. The TSG can arrest Tomoral for you, and then the SOCOs can move straight in to have a look around.'

'He's just a poncy kid, Guv,' Hicksy said. 'Me and Jono can handle picking him up. We don't need the heavy mob.'

'Just do it by the book, Hicksy. Who knows? Maybe he'll pull a machete out on you if you're on your own. There's no need to take any risks.'

Hicksy sighed. 'You can be a right spoilsport sometimes, Guv.'

'Sorry, mate. It's part of my job,' Wise said. 'But well done. I'll catch up with you properly back at the nick.'

'See you later,' Hicksy said and ended the call.

Wise put the car into gear and moved off. 'What did you make of that?' he said, happy to talk about anything other than the incident with the Turk earlier. Hopefully, Hannah would forget all about it, if he was lucky.

'I don't know,' Hannah said. 'Maybe Tomoral went in to see if Cameron was dead and just didn't want to get too involved by telling us. Or he went in, found him unconscious and cut his throat because he wanted to steal something himself.'

'Or he found him dead and robbed something himself,' Wise said.

'So, on a scale of how much shit Tomoral could be in, he's got the whole thing covered from minor to major.'

'That just about sums it up.'

They drove straight down Ilderton Road, past old out-of-use factories and new construction sites, across the Old Kent Road and then down Pomeroy Street. The rain grew heavier and the night darker. Oppressive.

Neither Wise nor Hannah spoke, the tension building between them, filling the car, suffocating the mood. Wise shifted in his seat, rolling his shoulders, trying to find some space to breathe, some comfort in the cramped Mondeo.

The scrap metal merchants on Evelina Road had gone all out on their Christmas decorations, covering everything in twinkling lights and marking their entrance with a worn-out tree which, in turn, was guarded by an inflatable Santa. For some reason, it just made Wise feel sad as he passed. A reminder that a bit of fake happiness couldn't hide the decay behind it all.

From there it was onto Nunhead Lane and a straight run to the restaurant, past more houses, more blocks of flats. There were flashes of decorations and lights through windows but otherwise the darkness seemed determined to smother everything in sight, aided by far too much rain.

They were five minutes away from the restaurant when Hannah finally cracked. 'Guv?'

'Yeah?' Wise said, keeping his eyes fixed firmly on the road.

'When we walked into that strip club ...' Hannah paused,

obviously hoping Wise would pick up the rest of the question and answer it.

Instead, Wise said nothing, still unsure of what answer to give. The truth wasn't an option.

Or was it?

'Ozdemir seemed to think you were someone else,' Hannah continued. 'Someone dangerous. I thought they were going to kill us for a moment.'

Wise took a deep breath. 'SCO10 came to see me just after we arrested David Smythe. They wanted to show me a picture of a man. A man who was waging a war against some of London's gangs in an attempt to take them all over.'

He could feel her looking at him now. Waiting for the rest.

'He looked exactly like me.'

Wise had to stop the Mondeo at a set of temporary traffic lights, where roadworks had reduced the traffic down to a single lane. He glanced out the window at the cordoned off area. There was a gaping hole where the tarmac had been but, of course, there was no sign of anyone actually working.

He turned to look at Hannah. 'So much so, they thought it might even be me.'

20

Hannah stared at Wise all wide-eyed and open-mouthed. 'What do you mean? They thought you were out murdering people?'

Wise nodded. 'In short, yeah.' The temporary lights turned green and Wise drove off once more.

'That's insane,' Hannah said.

'Let's just say I was very happy to tell them that I was in Birmingham with you when the picture of the man was taken.'

'And you reckon Ozdemir thought you were this ... doppelgänger when we walked into his club?'

'That's the only explanation.'

'Wow. That's ... that's fucked up,' Hannah said, trying to wrap her mind around what Wise had said. But there was something else bothering her. She couldn't help but feel there was more to the story that Wise wasn't telling her. 'Do they have any idea who he is?'

'I've tried finding out but it's obviously an ongoing investigation, so they're keeping it all tight to their chests.'

'Even so, surely you have a right to know. I mean, do you need protection? What if someone else thinks you're this ... this killer and doesn't want to check your ID before coming after you?'

'It's not me I'm worried about.'

'Well, don't worry about me. I can take care of myself,' Hannah said, trying to lighten the mood, but she didn't need to be a detective to know Wise wasn't talking about her.

'There's the restaurant,' Wise said. It was on the right-hand side of Nunhead Lane, squatting on the corner where it met Old James Street. Parking was non-existent, so Wise stopped the Mondeo on the double yellow lines in front of the restaurant.

They both got out, pulling their coats tighter as the rain attacked them, and headed straight to the front door. The place had a 'closed' sign up, but Wise gave the door a good hammering to let anyone inside know they were there. His face gave the impression he'd quite happily the kick the door in if someone didn't answer quickly enough.

Luckily, a chef came hurrying through the restaurant, wiping his hands on a kitchen cloth. 'We're shut,' he called out, but Wise just pounded the door some more, rattling its hinges.

The chef stopped on the other side of the door and glared at the two detectives. Hannah had to wonder whether he was trying to muster the courage to actually open the door and confront Wise. If she was being honest, she'd be in two minds about letting in someone who looked as big and as angry as Wise did. Still, it was too wet and cold to piss about, so she stepped forward and held her warrant card up to the door's window.

The chef did a double-take, then deflated his puffed-out chest and unlocked the door. Wise and Hannah entered the restaurant and Hannah had to do her best not to shake the rain off her like a dog. As she looked around, she had to admit the restaurant had a certain glamour to it, with rich wooden panelling set off against burgundy-painted walls of raw concrete. Pendant lights dangled over tables, all set up with gleaming glassware and spotless cutlery. It said casual, yet expensive, and was definitely out of Hannah's budget.

'Can I help you?' the chef asked, taking a step back from the two police officers.

Wise showed his own warrant card. 'I'm Detective Inspector Wise and this Detective Sergeant Markham. We're investigating a murder and we're hoping someone here could help us with our enquiries.'

'A murder?' The chef's face went white.

'Don't worry. It wasn't the food that killed them,' Wise said.

'Well, that's a bloody relief,' the chef said, not looking relieved at all. 'What do you want to know?'

'You sell Luz Solars here,' Hannah said.

'Yeah. It's not a great beer but it sells.'

'Apparently last Wednesday or Thursday, a customer came here for dinner,' Wise said, 'and he drank Luz Solars.'

The chef shrugged. 'Well, we are a restaurant. That's kind of why we sell it.'

'He says it's the only time he's drunk Luz Solars.'

'As I said, it's not much of a beer.'

'Well, somehow, the bottles ended up in a flat around the corner, keeping a dead man company,' Wise said, stepping closer to the chef.

'Shit.' The chef looked scared now.

'I want to know what magic made that happen.'

'How the hell am I supposed to know?' The chef took another step back, his eyes going from Wise to Hannah. Sweat popped out across his brow. 'Maybe someone took them from our empties?'

'I don't think so.' Wise seemed to grow bigger in size somehow, towering over the poor cook. 'I think someone who works here or maybe a customer took them.'

'Yeah? Well, how am I supposed to know who that could be?'

'Is there anyone else we can speak to who might know?' Hannah asked.

'The kitchen staff are prepping dinner in the back, but the front of house crew don't arrive for another hour,' the chef said.

Wise pointed to the kitchen doors. 'Let's go speak to them.'

'We are busy, you know,' the chef said, trying for one last act of defiance.

Wise loomed over him. 'Best we get on with it, then.'

The chef tutted and shook his head. But he knew he'd lost the fight. 'This way.'

They followed him down the restaurant and through the double doors to the kitchen. It was at least half the size of the front of house. Three women and one man, all in chef whites, were busy cutting and chopping. They looked up, startled to see Hannah and Wise walk in.

'Everyone! Can you gather around for a moment?' the first chef said. Immediately, his team downed their knives and came over, wiping hands on aprons. 'These two detectives want to ask you some questions.'

'Someone took two used bottles of Luz Solars from here last week,' Wise said, 'and left them at a murder scene. Anyone have any idea how that happened?'

Hannah watched the young chefs and their reactions. The three women looked genuinely confused. The man, though — well, he looked like he'd crapped his pants.

'Guv,' Hannah said. 'Let's start with talking to this chap.' She pointed to the nervous young man.

As Wise turned his attention to the young chef, the man's lips began to wobble.

He held up both hands. 'I didn't think there was any harm in it.'

'Perhaps we can have a chat with you out front in private?' Hannah said.

'You fucking numpty, Darren,' the head chef growled. 'Go on, then. Do as they say.'

The young man scuttled off through the double doors into the restaurant and Wise and Hannah followed.

'Well spotted,' Wise whispered.

Hannah smiled, grateful for the praise after her hangover misstep that morning.

Wise pointed to the furthest empty table from the kitchen. 'Park yourself there.'

'Am I in trouble?' the chef said, sitting down.

'It depends,' Wise replied, taking the chair opposite him. Hannah remained standing. 'Let's start with your name.'

'Darren. It's Darren,' the chef said. 'Darren Benton.' Hannah tried to work out how old he was. Early twenties, maybe, but he still had acne on his chin so he could've been even younger.

'Alright, Darren. Tell me about these bottles you moved,' Wise said.

'I didn't move them. Honest,' Darren said. 'Well, I did but I only took them from the waitress' tray and gave them to someone else. That's all.'

'Who did you give them to?'

'I don't want to get into any trouble.'

'Who?' Wise growled, placing both of his hands on the table. They looked big enough to squash Darren into a pulp.

The chef's head fell. 'My dealer.'

'Your drug dealer,' Wise clarified.

'Yes.' It came out in a whisper. When Darren looked up, there were tears in his eyes. Hannah almost felt sorry for the kid. 'He was dropping off a gramme for me and he saw this geezer eating out front. He got all excited and said I could have the coke for free if I got him the bloke's empties off his table.'

Wise glanced up at Hannah and gave her a quick wink before turning back to poor Darren. 'Your dealer—what's his name?'

'Beanz.'

'Beans?' Wise repeated.

'With a zed,' Darren clarified. 'I don't know his real name.'

'You got a number for Beanz?' Hannah asked.

The chef nodded. 'In my phone. It's in the kitchen.'

'Go and get it then,' Wise said. The kid didn't need telling twice. He was up like a shot and bolted back towards the kitchen.

Hannah watched him go. 'He won't do a runner, will he?'

'He's too scared to do that,' Wise said.

Sure enough, a minute later, Darren came bustling through the doors, clutching his phone in one hand like it was the Olympic torch. 'Here it is.'

Wise stood up as Hannah took the phone off Darren. She noted down the number. 'How do you normally contact him?'

'I send him a WhatsApp message,' Darren said.

'How quickly does he normally take to reply?'

'Straight away most times. If he's free, he'll deliver about half an hour later.'

Hannah handed the phone back. 'I've got your number too. If you tell Beanz we're looking for him, we'll find out, and you'll be in a cell next to him before you know what's hit you. Got it?'

Darren nodded furiously. 'I won't. I promise.'

'And maybe give up the drugs,' Wise said.

'I will. I will.' The kid actually looked like he meant it too.

'Thank you,' Hannah said. 'You've been a big help.'

'You better get back to work,' Wise added, pointing to the kitchen.

For a second time, the kid ran off as fast as his legs would take him.

'We've got a name,' Hannah said.

'Yeah,' Wise said. 'But what sort of name, though, is Beanz?'

'With a zed no less.'

'Let's go back to Kennington and find out,' Wise said.

21

It was gone 5 by the time Wise and Hannah walked back in through the doors of MIR-One. There'd been no more chat about Wise's doppelgänger on the way back and Wise was damn happy about that. They'd called Sarah on the way and given her Beanz' name and phone number to dig into. Judging by the happy faces waiting for them, there was lots to talk about.

Wise nodded at Jono. 'Good to see you got back okay.'

'You know me, Guv. I always take it easy,' Jono replied. He didn't look well though. He was pale and his cheeks were drawn.

'I know it's boring but stick to bloody desk duty,' Wise said. 'Or I'm going to have to send you home and you can rest there.'

Jono held up both hands. 'Okay. Okay. Hicksy's been giving me enough grief about it already.'

'I told him he was a fucking idiot, Guv, for wanting to go out,' Hicksy added.

'For once, you're not wrong.' Wise said.

'Well, I never said I wasn't an idiot,' Jono said. 'I heard a rumour my mother dropped me on my head once when I was a baby.'

'Ah, your mum's lying. She definitely dropped you more than once,' Hicksy added. 'And you know what? I don't blame her either. A pain in the arse like you needs dropping on their head every now and then.'

Wise smiled. 'Alright. Let's get everyone together and we can work out what we've got to do next.'

Jono nodded. 'You're the boss.'

Wise left his coat draped over an empty desk and headed to the front of the whiteboards. He clapped his hands. 'I know you're all eager to get home, but let's share what we've all found out before you head off to the pub or your homes or wherever you lot go when you're not here.'

Hicksy stuck up his hand like he was at school. 'Start with us. We brought a movie.'

Wise indicated the TV by the whiteboards with a wave of his hand. 'The screen's all yours.'

'Sarah, can you do your techno mumbo-jumbo?' Hicksy asked.

Sarah shook her head in exasperation but tapped her keyboard and a video came up on the screen. The time stamp in the corner said 0345.

'We got this from a lovely lady called Christina Something-or-other,' Jono said. 'As you can see, she lives right opposite the victim's house and her Ring security camera has a perfect view.'

Sarah hit play and the film came to life. A car pulled up outside Cameron's flat. 'This is the Honda Civic arriving,' Hicksy said. 'And here's our person of interest getting out.' A man dressed in black with his hood up got out of the car. He walked straight over to Cameron's flat, with something tucked under his arm. He knocked on the door, which was quickly opened, and he entered.

'Now, he stays in there for twenty minutes,' Hicksy said. 'The next time something happens is at five past four.'

Sarah wound the tape forward and they all watched the man come out of Cameron's flat clutching a sports bag, run over to the Civic, look straight at the camera, jump in and speed off. Sarah stopped the tape and rewound it back to the shot of the man's face.

'Hello,' Wise said. 'That's definitely the same man who burnt the car a little later.'

'And, thanks to you, Guv, we have a name for him,' Brains said.

'Is that our friend, Beanz?' Wise asked.

'Yeah. AKA Jordan Hines,' Brains said.

Hicksy laughed. 'Beanz means Hines? Not the most imaginative of nicknames.'

'You're not exactly known for your originality and wit when it comes to inventing those,' Hannah said.

'Alright, Diversity. Keep your knickers on,' Hicksy shot back.

Wise held up a finger. 'Hicksy. Watch it.'

The detective shook his head. 'Sure. Whatever.'

Wise turned back to Brains. 'You were telling us about Jordan Hines.'

'Yeah, right. Well, he's a member of the Peckham Lads gang. He's only twenty-one, but he has a long list of previous, including possession, possession with intent, carrying a concealed weapon, a bit of GBH and ABH, and so on,' Brains said.

'Do we know who runs the Peckham Lads?' Wise asked. 'We need to find out who Beanz works for. Cameron too. Maybe they're from rival gangs.'

Sarah stepped forward. 'We don't know yet, but I've got queries out with the squads who investigate the Organised Crime Groups.'

'Good. Keep the pressure on them to give us that intelligence,' Wise said. 'Any joy on the phone number?'

'Yep!' Brains said, smiling. 'Would you believe it's still in use? I've got the phone company gathering his phone history of who he's been calling and they're triangulating his location for us.'

'I can't believe he didn't dump his phone,' Hannah said.

'Thankfully, the David Smythes of this world are few and far between,' Wise said. Before they'd nicked him, he'd led Wise and the others on a merry chase with false clues and random murders to hide his real motives. He was as clever and as calculating as they got.

Wise turned back to Brains. 'Let's see if he kept his phone with him when he went to visit Cameron. I want as many things as possible tying Beanz to this murder.'

'There's someone else to look at, Guv,' Hicksy said. 'Sarah, buzz the film back to when he comes out of the house.'

Sarah did as she was asked.

Jono walked up to the screen and pointed to the stairwell. 'If you look closely, you can see someone lurking here.' He stepped away and Sarah hit play. The team watched the figure wait for Beanz to drive off and then scoot over to Cameron's flat. After a brief pause, he entered the flat for a few minutes, before running out, clutching his stomach. 'That's Leon Tomoral.'

'He's in a hurry to leave Cameron's,' Hannah said. 'It looks like he's taken something and stuck it up his jumper.'

'Play it again,' Wise said. The film jumped back into life, and they watched Leon enter Cameron's flat again, then come running out. 'He's in there for two and a half minutes exactly. It's not long.'

'You don't need that long to cut someone's throat,' Hicksy said.

'Unless you need to work up the courage to do it,' Wise said. 'Leon would have to be pretty damn cold to walk in there, bash Cameron over the head, cut his throat and rob him in two and a half minutes.'

'Cameron could've already been unconscious,' Hannah said. 'All Leon has to do then is grab a knife, do the deed and hotfoot it.'

'Still, it doesn't feel right. The kid was a wreck when we went to see him.' Wise looked over at Hicksy. 'Did you get a risk assessment done?'

'Yeah. No one's worried too much. The TSG are going to grab him early doors tomorrow. We'll do him for perverting the course of justice to start off with. Helen Kelly said she'll have her SOCOS ready to go in the moment we take him out. Hopefully, we can find something before we start talking to him.'

'Who's going with the TSG?'

'Me, Donut and School Boy.'

'Do you need me to come too?'

Hicksy shook his head. 'No, Guv. You can have a lie in. We've got this.'

'Sounds good.' Wise looked over at Jono. 'You better not be planning on going.'

Jono held up his hands in surrender. 'I know where I'm not wanted.'

'Good,' Wise said. 'Now, any progress on the phones we took from Cameron's?'

'Digital Forensics said we should have something from them tomorrow morning,' Brains said.

'Great. Keep chasing them. I don't want tomorrow to become next week,' Wise said. 'Alright, let's call it a night. We've made excellent progress over the last forty-eight hours. Tomorrow, while we have Leon in for a chat, I want Beanz located and, ideally, in our custody too.'

'We'll find him,' Sarah said. 'You can count on us.'

22

Tyrell Lewis sat in the back of the Uber, wondering how he'd got himself mixed up in all this shit. It was bad enough that Beanz was staying in his flat with a bag full of drugs, without getting Tyrell involved more than he was. He should've said no when Beanz had asked him to take the samples to his buyer in Streatham. But no, Tyrell had to agree like the idiot he was.

Then again, if the Feds turned up at his flat, Tyrell was in a world of shit, no matter what the truth was. There was no way the cops would believe Tyrell wasn't involved in whatever Beanz had going on. Not if they found three big bricks of cocaine and heroin in his crib. So, it was in his favour to help get rid of the stuff before the police found them. Still, it didn't make him feel any better about it all.

'We're here, mate,' the driver said.

Shit. Tyrell hadn't even noticed the car had stopped. 'Cheers, man.'

'You give me good rating,' the driver replied. 'Five stars.'

'Sure,' Tyrell said, opening the door and climbing out. Like fuck he would, though. The bloke just wanted a tip on top of the fifteen quid the journey had already cost. But Tyrell wasn't made of money. Not in the slightest.

In fact, getting an Uber was an expense Tyrell could've done without, but there was no way he was going to take public transport with drugs on him. Common sense said it was unlikely he'd be stopped by the police, but he was still a black kid in London. The Feds didn't need any excuse to stop and search someone like Tyrell. All it would take was a copper in a bad mood and Tyrell would be facing a wall with his hands and feet spread. Getting arrested for drugs would mean expulsion from university and the end of any hopes he had of being a doctor. There was no way Tyrell was going to let that happen—hence the Uber.

In fact, the only reason he was helping Beanz out in the first place was because he was so skint. Beanz might be a mate and all, but Tyrell had made a point of not getting involved in all that gang shit and he definitely didn't do drugs, let alone sell them. But Beanz had turned up, needing a place to stay and had offered to pay Tyrell ten grand once everything was over and done with. The way things were for Tyrell right then, ten thousand pounds was life-changing money. He'd have enough cash to get through the rest of the school year and graduate in the summer. There might, maybe, even be enough left over to help his mother out with her rent too.

First, though, he had to get this next bit out of the way. Apparently, Beanz' buyer wanted to test the drugs to make sure they were good quality before he bought them. Beanz reckoned he couldn't show his face anywhere, so he'd persuaded Tyrell to act as messenger. According to Beanz, all he had to do was hand over the envelope with the samples and then get the fuck out of Dodge as quick as he could.

Of course, nothing ever was as easy as it seemed. For starters, it looked like the bastard Uber driver had dropped him off in the wrong bloody street. He was supposed to be meeting this Errol bloke in a car repair garage he owned but, Tyrell couldn't see any workshop. There was a dry cleaner a few yards back, next to a fancy coffee shop, but there was no yard in sight.

Great.

He got his phone out and checked the address that Beanz had

given him in Google maps. However, according to that, he was in the right place and the garage was only a few metres away. It didn't make any sense.

Tyrell walked down the road, alternating between looking at his phone and looking around him. It didn't help that it was pitch black without a streetlight in sight. Not only that, but there was no one around either whom he could ask for directions.

Then Tyrell spotted a break in the pavement. There was a driveway where the bottom of a house should be, leading through to garages at the back. The reason he hadn't spotted it was because there was a top half of the house still there, bridging the gap across the drive. Tyrell stood there for a moment, wondering how the upstairs was being held up with nothing beneath it. It just didn't look safe.

Still, the garages at the back were what he was after, according to the sign that someone had painted across the garage's iron shutters: Streatham A1 Motor Repairs.

Tyrell spotted a door that was cut into the metal gates, but he had to take a breath before he could knock. In fact, he was so scared, he was surprised his knees weren't doing the knocking. Tyrell just wasn't cut out for the gangster life. Every bit of common sense he had told him to turn around and walk away. Tyrell looked back towards the road. He could do it. Beanz would be pissed, but that wasn't his problem.

But he needed the money.

He really needed the cash.

Tyrell took a deep breath, finding what little courage he had, and knocked. Someone must've been waiting on just the other side of the door because they opened it a heartbeat later, spilling light into the driveway.

A white lad stood in the doorway, scowling under his buzz cut. He wasn't that much older than Tyrell but he looked a hundred times tougher. 'Who the fuck are you?'

Tyrell forced the words out of his mouth. 'B... Beanz sent me.'

The bloke looked Tyrell up and down like he stunk something rancid. 'Beanz was supposed to come himself.'

Tyrell reached into his jacket and pulled out the envelope. 'He asked me to drop this off.'

'Did he?' The bloke made no attempt to take the envelope.

'Y... yes.'

The bloke stepped out of the doorway, giving Tyrell room to enter. 'You better give that to the boss, then.'

Tyrell didn't move. 'Can't you give it to him?'

'Yeah, right.' The bloke grinned. It was a cruel and nasty smile. Like a shark's. If sharks smiled. 'This way.'

Maybe if Tyrell was smarter, he'd know how to get himself out of entering the garage, but Tyrell was feeling pretty out of his depth right then. Then again, if he'd been cleverer, he'd not have said yes to Beanz and been there in the first place. So, Tyrell stepped through the doorway into the garage.

It stank of oil, grease and dirt but otherwise the place looked spotless, with space enough for two cars at any one time—not that there were any motors in there as far as Tyrell could tell. The lights were only on in the front of the workshop, leaving the rear in shadow.

'The office is in the back,' the lad said. 'Up the stairs.'

Tyrell nodded. Of course it was. He almost asked the lad to come with him, because he was scared to go there on his own, but stopped himself in time. Instead, he trudged off into the darkness, trying not to wet himself.

The doorway up was easy enough to find and he was thankful that overhead lights came on the moment he stepped into the stairwell. His feet made a clanging sound on the dirty, metal steps, raising his anxiety another notch.

A small sensible voice in the back of his head told him to turn around and get the fuck out of there, but he was way past the point of that even being a possibility.

The door to the office was closed, so Tyrell knocked without thinking.

'Come in.' The man's voice sounded like he'd been gargling concrete.

Tyrell opened the door and walked in. The office was pretty basic.

There was a sofa in one corner, a fridge with a kettle and some mugs on top of it, a few filing cabinets, a window that overlooked the workshop, and a desk with two empty chairs in front of it and a big, scary white guy sitting behind it.

'Are you... Errol?' Tyrell asked, despite the fact it was obviously him.

'I am, but you're not Beanz,' the man growled. A faded scar ran down one side of his face from hairline to jawline and Tyrell shivered at the thought of how it got there. 'I was expecting Beanz.'

'No. Beanz asked me to drop this off for him.' Tyrell held up the envelope, despite the fact there was still a metre of space still between him and the desk.

'Did he?'

'Yes.'

'And who the fuck are you?'

'No one.'

Mad Errol shifted in his seat and the whole office seemed to groan with the movement. 'You ain't no one, boy. You're someone if Beanz trusts you to bring me that envelope.'

'He... he paid me. Fifty quid to drop it off,' Tyrell said. 'That's all.'

Errol nodded at his desk. 'Go on, then. Drop it off.'

Tyrell shuffled forward, trying not to crap himself, and placed the envelope on the tabletop. 'Cheers,' he said, managing a weak smile, and turned to leave.

'Where do you think you're going?' Errol said.

Tyrell glanced back over his shoulder. 'I was going to go home.'

'Sit down,' Errol commanded. 'You're not going anywhere until I've tested what's in that envelope.'

'But that's got nothing to do with me. I was just supposed to drop it off.'

'Oh, no. If you're going to play messenger, Mr. No One, then you play messenger. I do my tests and then you can tell Beanz if he's rich or if he's a dead man for wasting my time. So, park your arse and we'll tell you when you can fuck off. Okay?'

Tyrell hesitated for a moment and then sat in one of the empty chairs. He hated being so close to the big man. It felt like Tyrell was more likely to get squashed now that he was in reach of the gangster's hands.

Keeping his beady eyes fixed on Tyrell, Errol picked up his desk phone, pressed a button with a podgy finger and then lifted the receiver to his ear. 'Come up.'

He placed the phone back in its cradle and they both listened to running footsteps up the stairs. The lad who'd let Tyrell into the garage came through the door. 'Yeah?'

'Get your chemistry kit out, Dougie,' Errol said.

Dougie went over to the fridge and opened it up. He took out a black bag and brought it over to the desk. He quickly unzipped it and produced two test tubes with a clear liquid inside and a small stand for both. After slotting them into the stand, he picked up the envelope and tore it open, shaking the contents onto the desk. Two plastic baggies fell out. One had brown powder in it, the other white.

Dougie unscrewed one test tube, selected a baggie, opened that and then sprinkled some of the contents into the test tube. When that was done, he repeated the process with the second test tube and bag. Immediately, the liquids in each began to change colour.

'The cocaine makes the liquid go orange,' Dougie said. 'The brighter the colour, the purer the gear. If it looks like piss, then it's not worth piss. Same with the H. That turns the liquid green.'

Tyrell watched nervously, his heart hammering away and his mouth dry, as the liquids swirled away, praying the right colours appeared. Both looked pretty weak and washed out, though, and for a moment, Tyrell thought that was going to be it. He could feel the fear building inside him, dreading what Errol would do if the drugs turned out to be crap.

But the liquid inside the test tubes continued to grow in vibrancy. The cocaine went from a weak yellow to straw-coloured to tangerine, while the heroin looked like pea soup. Thank God for that.

Errol was clearly happy too. Grinning away. Revealing a gold tooth on the right-hand side of his mouth. 'Lovely. Very lovely indeed.' He picked up the baggie with the coke in it and dabbed a finger inside, then snorted what was on it. He winked at Tyrell. 'I used to be right into the marching powder when I was younger, but I keep it as a rare treat these days. But I only ever do a little. Too much and I go crazy and want to start stomping on heads.'

Tyrell didn't know what to say. He just wanted to get out of there and get home.

Errol leaned back in his chair. 'Now, Dougie will go with you to pick up the rest of the gear from Beanz and give him his money.'

Tyrell might not get the gangster life, but alarm bells went off inside his head when Errol said that. He glanced over at Dougie and saw the feral look in his eyes. Saw murder in them. 'Er... I don't know where Beanz is. He said he'd call me later to give me the money he owes me.'

'Don't bullshit me, boy,' Errol said.

'I'm not. I'm not. I just don't know where Beanz is, so I can't take you to him. I can give you his number if you need that, though.'

'I've got his number.'

'Good. That's good,' Tyrell said. He stood up. 'Anyway, I'd better go. It's getting late and my mum's expecting me.'

He turned to leave but Dougie was there, in his face, blocking his way, eyeballing him, daring him to try and get past.

It was a miracle Tyrell didn't piss his pants.

'Let him go,' Errol said from behind him. 'We can't keep his mother waiting.'

Dougie very slowly stepped aside but he didn't take his eyes off Tyrell.

Tyrell, on the other hand, was off like a shot the moment he could, legging it down those metal stairs, not caring about the racket he made. He sprinted across the workshop, fumbled with the door handle until finally it opened and he all but fell out into the driveway.

He ran out onto the street and down the road, past the dry cleaners, past the fancy coffee shop. Tyrell took a right by a pub, painted all blue and white, not knowing where he was, just running, his chest burning, heart pounding, scared shitless, desperate to get away as fast as he could.

He stopped only when he couldn't run any more. Bending over double, Tyrell puked all over his kicks, retching up all the fear from earlier, trying to gulp down air at the same time, only to vomit some more.

When his stomach was empty and he could breathe some more, Tyrell got out his phone and opened his Uber app. A car was nearby. Three minutes. Thank God for that. He typed in his booking and hit confirm.

Tyrell couldn't wait to get home, to be safe.

He just needed his Uber to arrive.

Friday 9th December

23

It was 8 a.m. and Wise had another night's fitful sleep, made worse, no doubt, by Jean not speaking to him all the previous evening. At least the arrest of Leon Tomoral earlier had happened without incident and now the man was in a holding cell in Brixton Police Station, waiting to be interviewed.

For now, though, Wise sat in Doctor Shaw's office for his weekly meeting with the psychiatrist.

'How are you, Simon?' Doctor Shaw asked, her voice as soothing as ever. They faced each other, sitting in armchairs in front of her desk, her Persian rug underfoot.

Wise took a sip of his Starbucks. 'I'm okay. Not great. Not bad though. Well, not terrible.'

'How's everything at home?' Shaw looked at him, glasses perched on the end of her nose, eyes shining bright despite the early start and the miserable weather outside.

'The kids are good. Claire's causing chaos and Ed is working hard at school. Both are excited for Christmas,' Wise replied.

'And Jean?' Up popped that eyebrow of Shaw's that always sensed when Wise was avoiding things.

He shrugged. 'It's not good at the moment. It's pretty bad, in fact.'

'In what way?'

'We've got a few problems with Tom that are causing even more problems between Jean and I.'

'I didn't know you were in contact with your brother again.'

'I'm not, really. I bumped into him a few months back when he was leaving my father's house, but that's it really.' Wise paused and took another gulp of coffee. 'But he's come up in the day job in quite a big way.'

'Ah,' Shaw said.

'Quite.'

'Is it bad?'

That question got a chuckle out of Wise. 'You could say that. He's the subject of a very serious investigation. When I found out about that, I did some digging of my own. Tom found out I was nosing around and rang me up to warn me off. He made some indirect threats against my family in the process. Now Jean's worried that the kids and her are in danger.'

'Are they?'

'No. Yes. Maybe.' Wise glanced over at the window as it got battered by the rain. 'I hope not, but who knows? It turns out I don't know my brother at all. I don't know what he's capable of. If half of what I've heard is true, he's a very dangerous man.'

'So, Jean's fears are justified?'

'They are but ... she's talking about going to stay at her mother's for Christmas with the kids.'

'And you're not invited?'

'No.'

'And how do you feel about that?'

'Guilty. Angry. Frustrated. Let down. Helpless. Responsible. Resentful. The list goes on,' Wise said. 'She's right to feel scared. She's right to want to protect the kids and herself. I can understand why she wants to get away. But I don't want to lose my family and I don't want to lose my job because of Tom.'

'Is losing your job a possibility too?' Shaw asked.

'Yeah. Very much so. I never told anyone at work about Tom or his criminal history. I lied on my application form all those years ago and I've kept him secret ever since.'

'Is his criminal history why you fell out twenty years ago?'

'It was more to do with why and how he got that history,' Wise said. 'And my part in that.'

Shaw nodded. 'Do you want to talk about it?'

Wise had been seeing Shaw for five months and had always avoided going into details about what happened that night so long ago. 'Not talking about it has always been my default approach to what happened. I've spent my life trying to bury it and move on.'

'It doesn't feel like the past wants you to do that yet,' Shaw said. 'Maybe acknowledging it will allow you to go forward in the right way.'

Wise finished his coffee. He knew Shaw was right, but that didn't make it any easier to open up to her. Not about this. He'd never spoken to anyone about that night. Not even to his father.

'Whatever you say will stay between us,' Shaw said. 'You know that. This room is a safe place. There are no judgements.'

Wise sighed, puffing out his cheeks. His hands were shaking and he flexed his fingers to try and get them back under control. Why was he so scared about the past?

Wise took a breath and then told Shaw about the day of the Spurs match, about the violence before the game and Mad Errol's challenge to the brothers to prove themselves, finishing with the fight in the pub, Tom killing Brian Sellers, the arrival of the police and his brother's arrest.

'Tom told the police that he didn't know the person with him and he stuck to that even when he was sent down. But that didn't mean he was alright with it. He said I should've dragged him out of there, that I just ran to save myself and left him to get arrested. He refused to speak to me after that. I tried seeing him once, when he was in Feltham. I went along with my dad but Tom... Tom attacked me. The guards had to drag him off me and he got banned from having any visitors for four months.'

'And how do you feel about what happened?' Shaw asked.

Wise reached for his coffee, then realised that he'd finished it. 'I've spent my life wondering if I could've done more to get him out of that pub in time. Maybe I should've handed myself in as well, but I was scared and I was only a kid really. Looking back now, though, there's a part of me that's glad it happened. It was the wakeup call I needed. I doubt I would've become a police officer if not for that night and I've spent my whole career trying to make amends for what happened.

'Tom, on the other hand... well, in another life, I'm sure I'd be right next to him doing whatever he's doing.'

'You're not the person your brother is, Simon,' Shaw said. 'Give yourself some credit.'

Wise shook his head. 'I don't know. There's a part of me that still enjoys violence. A part of me that's still dangerous.'

'The fact you recognise this dark side of you ... It's something for you to be proud about and a good reason why you shouldn't worry about who you are,' Shaw said. 'We all have dark sides — you only have to look at people's search histories on their computers to know that — but what makes us different from the criminals you deal with is the fact that we don't act on those impulses, because we understand what's right and what's wrong.'

An alarm beeped. It was the end of the session. Shaw smiled sympathetically. 'I'm sorry we have to stop for now, but we can take this back up again next week.' She stood up.

Wise got to his feet. 'If you think that's best.' He wasn't sure he wanted to carry on talking about what had happened, though. He felt raw and vulnerable from the session, as if he'd just ripped the scab off a horrible wound that had never properly healed.

As he left, he couldn't shake off the image stuck in his head, of Tom and him together. A pair of proper villains.

24

An hour and a half later, Wise was in one of Brixton Police Station's observation rooms with Hicksy beside him and a half-decent coffee in his hand. They watched two monitors connected to one of the interview suites, where Leon Tomoral was being interviewed by Jono and Hannah.

Wise hated not being in the interview room himself, but it was better for him to watch and listen. Besides, Jono and Hannah were better than he was at getting people to open up. Maybe in the old days it helped having a six-foot two bruiser in with the suspect, but not now. Jono had that whole 'kind old man' vibe going on, whereas Hannah was Miss Efficiency. It was a combination that felt right when he'd suggested it. Hicksy had bristled at not being involved, but even he had to admit Jono and Hannah had good chemistry in the room.

The interview was being conducted at Brixton because Kennington was a purely administrative building now. It didn't have any officers to staff custody suites and the interview rooms had been decommissioned. As the nearest station, Brixton got the honour of hosting anyone Wise's team arrested or wanted to talk to.

In the interview room, Leon Tomoral, looking even more like the stereotypical student, was nervously playing with his hands and fidgeting in his seat. He'd had a couple of sips of the coffee that Jono had given him but, by the looks of things, he'd quickly decided the hot liquid from the station canteen wasn't fit for human consumption. At least that proved he was of sound mind and body. If Leon had happily drunk that muck, they would've called the police psychologist in to check his mental wellbeing.

So far, the interview was all very cordial. Leon, after turning down the offer of a solicitor, had gone over his statement from Wednesday and hadn't deviated from his early recollection of events.

'It must have been very traumatic for you,' Jono said, in that rasping smoker's voice of his as he leaned back in his chair. The veteran detective looked like everyone's favourite grandfather, albeit in need of a haircut. His long, grey hair didn't do him any favours. 'We really appreciate you calling 999 so quickly.'

'I just wanted to help,' Leon said, eyes flicking from Jono to Hannah and back again.

'Not many people do these days,' Hannah said, smiling.

'There's just a couple of things we need to clear up first,' Jono said. 'Before we can let you nip off back home.'

'Okay,' Leon said. 'Of course.' He reached for the coffee cup, then must've thought better of it as he pulled his arm back and clasped his hands once more.

Hannah made a show of looking at her notes, then looked up and gave Leon a big, beaming smile. 'You said you didn't enter the downstairs flat when you went to investigate after you…' Another look at her notes. 'After you heard the "fight."'

The note of incredibility Hannah put on the word fight made Leon straighten up like he'd been slapped. 'I did. I mean, I didn't. I didn't go in, but I did hear a fight.'

'How close to the flat did you go, then?' Hannah said. 'To see the body?'

'I was on the street. I could see him through the window. Two metres away maybe.'

'And you didn't go in to check if he was still breathing, or anything like that?'

'No. Absolutely not. I was too scared. I just rang 999.' Leon attempted a smile of his own but all he produced was a kind of awkward wince.

'Are you sure?' Jono said. 'I mean, it must've been traumatic seeing the body lying there. All that blood, the knife. I could imagine it's easy to get confused.'

'No. No, I didn't go in,' Leon said. 'I remember very clearly. Like I said.'

'That's good.' Jono scratched his nose, screwing his face up as he did so. 'Now humour me for a moment, because I'm just a bit confused. If you didn't go in and you just stayed on the deck like you say, then how come we found your fingerprints on the door handle to Cameron's flat?'

'My what?'

'Your fingerprints.' Jono nodded at Leon's hands. 'There're at the end of your fingers.'

'That's impossible,' Leon said. 'There must be some kind of mistake.'

'I would've thought that too,' Jono said, leaning forward. 'Except our forensics team don't do mistakes, especially not with fingerprints. How to take fingerprint impressions properly is the first thing they learn to do. And our computer matched the ones we found with yours. But we all know computers can make mistakes, so just to be extra double positive they were yours, we had two experts, who do nothing but check fingerprints all day long, have a look too. Now, they confirmed the fingerprints we found on the door are yours as well.'

'But I didn't touch the door,' Leon said. 'I didn't.'

'Okay,' Hannah said. 'We believe you. They're all wrong. It can happen. Now we've cleared that up, we'd just like to show you a video clip from a CCTV camera.'

Hannah turned her laptop around so Leon could see the screen. The video from Christina Osakara's Ring camera was on it, paused just after Beanz had fled the scene and Leon had just appeared by the stairwell.

'Do you recognise this location?' Jono asked.

Leon nodded. 'Yes.'

'Where is it?'

'It's Wilmsden Terrace.'

Jono pointed to the figure that they believed was Leon. 'And do you recognise this person?'

Leon peered at the screen. 'I don't know. It's dark.'

'We think that's you, Leon,' Hannah said.

'Me?'

'You.'

'But it's not.'

'Perhaps,' Jono said. 'It is dark, as you say. But you'll note the time and date of the film. It's when the murder took place. You just confirmed in your statement that you came downstairs to investigate the noises you heard. So, with that in mind, this scene matches exactly what you told us — unless there was another person with you? Perhaps this figure could be them?'

'Was there anyone with you, Leon?' Hannah asked.

'No,' the lad replied. 'I was on my own.'

Jono smiled. 'Okay then, if I hit play, we should see you — I mean this figure — walk over to Cameron's flat, peer through the window and then leave. After which you call 999. That sound about right?'

Even through the monitor, Wise could see the fear on Leon's face now that his lie was about to be exposed.

When Leon spoke, his voice came out in a squeak. 'Yes.'

'Shall we watch, then?' Jon asked.

Leon just stared at the screen as his leg bounced up and down twice as fast.

Jono hit play and the people in the interview suite watched Leon approach the flat, open the door, enter, then leave a few minutes later.

'As you can see, Leon, this film shows you touching the door where we found your fingerprints, confirming it is you and we didn't make a mistake.' Jono leaned back in his chair and crossed his arms.

'So, maybe it was you that made the mistake when you told us you didn't enter the flat.'

'I did. I did make a mistake,' Leon said. 'I misremembered. I was in shock.'

'You're saying you did go into the flat?'

'Yes — I went in, saw the body, then left.'

'You were in there for two and a half minutes, Leon,' Hannah said.

The lad looked up as if startled. 'Was I? I don't know. I was in shock.'

'And all you did was stare at the body,' Jono said. 'You didn't do anything else.'

'No.'

'I was wondering if you noticed the cash lying on the floor, by any chance, when you were staring at the body?'

'Cash?' Leon sounded like he didn't even know what the word meant.

'Yes, cash. Did you see it? Did you take any?' Hannah asked.

'No one would blame you if you did,' Jono added. 'I mean, you're only human. We all are. I'm sure it was tempting, with Cameron being dead and all. And that money lying on the ground. If I was in your shoes, I'd help myself.'

'I ... I ...' Leon gulped. 'No. No, I didn't. No.'

'It's just that our Scene Of Crime officers been having a look in your flat, Leon, while you've been here,' Hannah said.

'They have?' Even watching through the monitors, Wise could feel Leon's anxiety levels go through the roof.

'They have,' Hannah confirmed. 'And they found two thousand pounds tucked away in your sock drawer.'

'And our Scene of Crimes Officers said they weren't very nice-looking bank notes either,' Jono added. 'Not like you'd get from the bank or the cash your dad might give you to go buy a meal or something. These were ...' He looked over at Hannah. 'How did the SOCOs describe them?'

Hannah looked down at her notes again. 'Crumpled. Filthy. Like they'd been nicked from a drug dealer. Apparently, some even had blood on them.'

'There you go,' Jono said, holding up your hands. 'Now, we're going to be doing some tests on them. More fingerprinting, a bit of DNA testing. All that science bollocks. By the time we're done, we'll know everyone who's ever touched them.'

'Everyone,' Hannah said.

'So, while we do that,' Jono said, 'is there anything else you want to tell us? Like where you got this grubby wad of cash from?'

In the monitor room, Hicksy chuckled. 'Got him good and proper.'

'I still don't see him as our killer,' Wise said, eyes fixed on the screens.

In the interview room, Leon's head had dropped. Even his leg had stopped twitching. 'He was dead already. I promise you that. And I did go down to help.'

'But there wasn't a fight, Leon. No shouting,' Hannah said.

'I was out in the hallway, having a smoke,' Leon said. 'And I heard this crash, like something falling. It sounded bad, so I went down to have a look. That's when I saw the geezer running out of Cameron's flat. He looked well dodgy, so I thought I should see if Cameron was okay.'

Hannah leaned forward. 'Did you know Cameron before the night he was killed?'

Leon nodded. 'I'd buy a bit of gear from him now and then.'

'You knew he was a drug dealer?'

'Yes.' Leon looked up and wiped a tear from his eyes. 'But he was dead, and I saw this money lying there. Unwanted like you said. So, I took it.'

Watching, Wise almost felt sorry for the kid. He'd been dumb, but Wise could see how he'd been tempted. A moment of weakness and now Leon was in a world of shit.

'This doesn't look good for you, Leon,' Jono said. 'Not good at all.'

'You should've been honest with us from the beginning,' Hannah said. 'You've wasted a lot of our time. That's a crime.'

'I didn't mean to. I just didn't know what to do after I took the money and, once I'd started lying, I didn't know how to stop.'

'Did you get a good look at the man who'd been in Cameron's flat before you?' Hannah asked.

'No. I only saw the back of his head,' Leon replied.

'And you only took the money? Nothing else?' Jono added.

'Just the money.'

Jono glanced over at Hannah, who nodded. 'Alright. We're going to terminate the interview for now, Leon, while we go and have a chat with our governor. Then we'll probably want to talk to you again.'

'Am I in trouble?' Tears fell freely down Leon's cheeks.

'We'll see,' Hannah said. 'But it's good that you stopped lying to us.'

After recording the time, Hannah switched off the tapes and both detectives stood up. 'Someone will take you back to your custody suite.'

'Fucking hell,' Hicksy said next to Wise. 'I still cringe when anyone says "custody suite." It's a bloody cell that doesn't even have a toilet and the only thing you have to sit on is a blue plastic mattress that some tramp probably pissed on the night before. No amount of PC terminology makes that anything but what it is.'

Wise glanced over at the detective. 'You've got to move with the times, my friend. We're the friendly face of policing now.'

'No wonder the criminals aren't scared of us anymore,' Hicksy replied.

The door to the observation room opened and Jono and Hannah walked in. 'What do you think, Guv?' Jono said.

'Well done, you two,' Wise replied. 'That was expertly handled.'

'I wouldn't say "expertly",' mumbled Hicksy.

'I thought dear old Leon was going to shit himself when we showed him the video,' Jono said.

'I think he's telling the truth now, though,' Hannah said. 'He's not our killer.'

'I agree.' Wise puffed out his cheeks. 'It certainly looks like Beanz is our man. We just need to find him.'

25

Beanz peaked through the curtains at the street below. For the thousandth time, he checked the cars parked along both sides of the street as best he could, trying to spot any Feds lurking, but saw none.

There were only civilians out and about as best he could tell; a couple arguing while they pushed a kid in a stroller, two old girls having a natter at the bus stop, an Amazon delivery man dropping a box off three doors down, and some kids in hoods vaping on the corner. None of them looked like undercover cops to him. Even better than that, though, was the fact that none of them looked like fucking gangsters. And he was especially happy to see that none of them looked like Ollie Konza.

Beanz was safe for now.

He let the net curtain fall back into place and mooched back to the sofa, pushing his sleeping bag to one side before sitting down. He thought about rolling a spliff and having a smoke but quickly decided against it. Getting high didn't feel right. He needed to be sharp. He needed to be on his game.

That was easier said than done, though. It'd been three days since he'd done Cam and nicked his gear. Since then, he'd been lying low, holed up in Tyrell's flat. Going stir-crazy. Getting paranoid. A million thoughts rattling through his brain. A billion fears.

Beanz glanced down at the sports bag beside the sofa and thought of the drugs inside. Cam's drugs once, now his. Drugs he wanted rid of as quickly as possible.

Sitting up, he opened up the bag and had a look inside. Seeing the wrapped-up bricks of gear was enough to calm him down and make him smile. Two bricks of heroin and one of cocaine, each one weighing a kilo. Together, they were worth three hundred grand easy. And ten times that once everything was all cut up and diluted down.

God only knew why Cam had been showing off that he had so much gear in his place, telling Beanz how much it was all worth, playing the Big Man. He'd wanted Beanz and his crew to sell it for him, making pennies while Cam raked in the serious cheddar. But Beanz was no idiot. He might've flunked out of school, but he could add up and he knew it was better to have all the drugs than flog a few bags here and there for someone else.

He might not have no education, but he had ambition. And, in his book, killing a man for three hundred K was a good day's work. Except the drugs weren't actually Cam's to begin with. He was merely the middleman for Ollie Konza and all the money in the world wasn't worth having that mad fucker coming after him. In fact, the last fool to steal from Konza had ended up tied to a lamppost with a burning tyre hung around his neck.

But then Beanz had spotted The Turk eating in that fancy restaurant when he'd gone to give the chef his coke. And, just like that, Beanz saw how he could get away with it.

Everyone knew that The Turk hated Konza. And he was definitely the sort of man who'd have the balls to steal from Konza and not worry about retaliation.

One free gramme had been enough to get The Turk's empty bottles of beer. Bottles that had his fingerprints all over it and a tonne of DNA no doubt.

Beanz had given it a bit of a wipe before he dumped it at Cameron's. After all, he didn't want to make it too easy for the Pigs, but he left enough for them to find something and send them running off in completely the wrong direction.

And, of course, Konza had enough cops in his pocket to find out the moment the Feds thought The Turk had slotted Cam.

No one would suspect it was Beanz who'd done the deed.

Or so he'd thought at the time. Now, three days on, Beanz wasn't feeling so clever. In fact, he was starting to think he might've been pretty dumb to risk his neck for three hundred K.

Especially since Mad Errol hadn't been in touch to pick up his gear and give Beanz his money. He wasn't answering his phone either and that never happened.

Shit.

Beanz got up and went over to the window, hoping that he wouldn't see a mad fucker with a tyre in his hand walking down the street.

'You looking out that window again?' Tyrell said, coming out of his bedroom.

'Why hasn't Errol called me?' Beanz said.

His friend shrugged. 'I don't know. He was happy when I left him. Maybe too happy.'

'You should've brought his boy back here with you like he wanted. We'd be rid of the gear and have our dosh.'

'I told you why I didn't do that,' Tyrell said. 'I thought they were going to rob us — or worse.'

Beanz laughed. 'Why would they do that? Me and Mad Errol have a deal. They're going to make a fortune from these drugs I nicked.'

Tyrell gave him a look. 'They'll make even more money if they don't have to pay us for them in the first place.'

His friend had a point, but Beanz wasn't going to tell him that. 'How about you go back to the garage and see what's going on?'

'How about I don't?' Tyrell plopped himself onto the sofa. 'I thought I was going to get slotted last night. I ain't going back. No way.'

'But Errol's not answering his phone and we need to get paid.'

'What if he don't have the cash? That's even more reason why he'd wanna rob you.'

Beanz put his hands over his face. 'Fuuuuuuck!' Why couldn't anything ever be simple?

'What if he don't come through?' Tyrell asked. 'Is there anyone else you could sell the gear to?'

'You don't get it, do you?' Beanz said, trying not to sound panicked. 'I stole this gear from Ollie Konza. He's fucking big time. There ain't that many players that'll take him on. There's The Turk and there's Mad Errol. I don't know no one else. And I've already framed The Turk for the robbery. So, there's no way I can go up to him now and ask him if he wants to buy a load of stolen drugs from me.'

'What about selling it ourselves? You know, cut it up and bag it up and flog it in the clubs and pubs?'

Christ. Tyrell just didn't get it. 'First of all, we'd need a table about the size of this flat to dump the contents of just one bag out on,' Beanz said. 'Then we'd need ten times that amount of baby formula or whatever to mix into it. That process alone will take us days, if not weeks, if we're doing it ourselves. Then we have to bag it up and start selling it. Now, seems to me, Ollie Konza would notice if me and you are suddenly in his clubs and pubs, flogging gear we didn't buy from him. We'd be dead within a day.'

'Shit,' Tyrell said.

'Yeah, shit.' Beanz checked the window again, looking for Feds and dodgy geezers. Nothing. 'Our only hope is to flog it all at once, get paid and then disappear until people forget we even existed.'

Tyrell looked up with those sad puppy dog eyes of his. 'I wish you'd never brought it here, man. This shit is dangerous.'

'You'll get paid when I do.'

'Ten grand ain't worth getting killed over. I think you should go somewhere else.'

That wasn't what Beanz wanted to hear. 'Look. Let's not panic, alright? I'm sure Errol will come through and look — how about I give you thirty gees instead? For being a good mate.'

'Still don't want to get killed for thirty thousand,' Tyrell said.

Beanz shook his head. Maybe his boy wasn't such an innocent. 'What about fifty and I promise you won't get killed.'

'Fifty works.'

'You robbing me, man,' Beanz said, his eye drifting back to the window. Fifty was a lot to give away even if Tyrell was his mate. But it was all just meaningless numbers unless Mad Errol turned up with the cash.

Beanz sighed and then got out his phone again. He found the man's number and hit the call button. He listened to the dial tone and prayed this time Errol would pick up.

26

'Guv! Guv!' Brains waved at Wise the moment he walked into MIR-One. 'We've got him.'

Wise walked over to Brains' desk. 'Who have we got?'

'Jordan Hines. Beanz. The idiot is still using his phone.' Brains tapped away at his keyboard and a street map came up on his screen. 'We've cell-sited his mobile and it's in Western Towers in Bibury Close.'

'That's where Sarah tracked him to, right after he'd burned the Honda Civic,' Wise said.

'Yeah, we're definitely not dealing with a master criminal here.'

'Do we know what flat he's in?'

Brains grinned. 'Funny you should say that, Guv. I've been doing a bit of research into Beanz. Known associates, etcetera. Trying to work out where he might be. Then I went through his socials, checking his friends and followers and all that good stuff.'

'And?'

'A while back Beanz posted a screen shot on Instagram from a video game he was playing. That had his Xbox username — which is rather imaginatively "BeanzKillz." From there, I checked out his mutuals.'

'Alright,' Wise said. 'I haven't got a clue what you're talking about, but go on.'

'Well, he plays a lot with someone called TurboT1000, so I looked into him.'

'Right ...'

Brains tapped away again, and an Instagram account came up on screen. 'This is Tyrell "TurboT1000" Lewis. He went to school with Beanz back in the day and is now studying to be a doctor. And guess where Tyrell lives?'

'Western Towers?'

'Bingo. Flat on the fifth floor.'

'Tyrell have any previous?'

'None. He's squeaky clean.'

'Not in any gangs or anything like that?'

'The kid is at medical school. He wants to be a doctor,' Brains said. 'He's not in the game.'

Now Wise was grinning too. 'That makes him a perfect person to lay low with.'

'If you weren't an idiot who doesn't have the sense to dump your phone,' Brains replied. 'There's more too. I've got Beanz' call details. He's in regular contact with Cameron's burner phone right up until the murder, but then he doesn't call him once afterwards.'

'Because he knows he's dead.'

'Exactly. And his phone travels towards Friary Road on Wednesday morning, but it gets switched off at 0340, and then turned on again after the Civic gets torched.'

Wise laughed. 'He might as well have posted a message saying "I'm committing a crime right now".'

Brains shrugged. 'What can I say? The boy's an idiot. Case in point number three — he's been calling one number pretty frequently since the murder and only one number.' Brains clicked away and a mug shot appeared on his screen. 'Unlike Tyrell, Mad Errol Gallagher has more form than Ronnie and Reggie.'

Wise took a step back. Seeing that squat face, with its beady eyes and a scar running down one side was like being punched in the face by a ghost from long ago. Christ, he'd only been talking about him that morning with Doctor Shaw. About that day — that night — in April, Two Thousand and Four.

Wise looked down for a moment, sucking on his cheeks, trying to calm his thoughts, telling himself that it was only a coincidence and it had always just been a matter of time before he ran into someone from the bad old days. 'What's Mad Errol's crime of choice?'

'Drugs, drugs and more drugs, but he's not been busted for anything in the last six years.'

'I doubt he's gone straight,' Wise said. 'Maybe he bought whatever Beanz stole from Cameron.'

'I don't think the deal's done yet,' Brains said. 'He's been calling Mad Errol non-stop without any joy. In fact, the last call was at 11:30 this morning and your man here didn't pick up.'

'Interesting.' Wise looked over his shoulder. 'Sarah, can you come here for a sec?'

The petite detective rose from her desk and joined Wise at Brains' desk. 'Everything okay?'

'Brains has tracked down Beanz to a flat in Western Towers,' Wise said. 'Can you go down there with Hannah and see who answers when you knock on the door? Don't let on you're police. Just pretend you're Jehovah's or something.'

'Western Towers?' Sarah said. 'That place has a bad reputation.'

'I know. But you'll be okay during the day and the pair of you will do a better job of keeping a low profile than Hicksy and Donut would.'

Sarah glanced over at Donut sitting in the corner. 'You've got a point.'

'I want you to check out the door while you're there and take some pictures if you can. It'll be good to know if it's reinforced or if it has serious locks for when we come calling officially. I doubt it will, though. The place is rented out to a medical student.'

'I'll give Hannah a call and head over,' Sarah said.

'She's still over at Brixton, but she should be all wrapped up by now.'

'Beanz is our man, then?' Sarah asked.

'Yeah. Looks very much like it,' Wise replied.

Sarah pulled her phone out of her pocket. 'I'll call Hannah now.'

'Cheers, Sarah.' Wise watched Sarah head back to her desk, grateful as ever that she was on his team. The woman was the backbone of the department, keeping everything and everyone on track at all times. He'd be lost without her.

27

Hannah parked her Ducati in the car park at Kennington and saw that Sarah was already waiting for her by the main doors to the station, smoking furiously as ever.

'The governor decided to let you out of the office again?' Hannah said, walking over.

Sarah took a long hard drag of her cigarette. 'I know. Twice in two days. Lucky me.'

Hannah waved her helmet. 'Let me put this somewhere safe and I'll be right with you.'

'No rush,' Sarah replied. 'I'll be here, freezing my tits off.'

'I would've thought all that cigarette smoke would keep you warm.'

'Not as much as I'd like.'

'I'm sure you'll do your best,' Hannah said and jogged inside. As she was on her own, she used the station lift to go up to the third floor where MIR-One was situated. The incident room was buzzing when she walked in.

She saluted Wise with a finger to her brow as she passed him talking with Brains.

'Everything okay?' he asked.

'All good,' Hannah replied. 'Just dropping my helmet off. Sarah's waiting for me downstairs.'

'Good. Take it easy over there. Don't get carried away and try to arrest them by yourselves. Beanz might look like a scrotty kid but he cut a man's throat a few days ago.'

'Got it. I might have to restrain Sarah, though. She loves kicking in doors.'

Wise chuckled. 'Yeah, she can be a handful. Let me know how you get on.'

'See you in a bit.' Hannah took the stairs down and found Sarah working hard on another cigarette.

Bibury Close was only a twenty minute drive from the station but Sarah attacked the traffic like she was on an offensive driving course. To say the petite woman was fast and aggressive was, in fact, quite the understatement.

'Jesus,' Hannah said, after they'd only just avoided being sideswiped by a bus. 'Can we get there in one piece, please?'

'Oh, don't overreact,' Sarah said, accelerating down a bus lane. 'I know what I'm doing.'

'You sure?' Hannah reached up and grabbed the hand grip above her door, as if that would keep her safe.

'Oh, don't be such a coward.' Sarah reached down for a pack of cigarettes in the centre console pocket.

'What are you doing?' Hannah asked, horrified.

'Getting a cigarette. Why?'

'Not with me in the car, you're not. Keep your hands on the steering wheel.'

Sarah dropped the pack. 'You are no fun today.'

'I just don't want to die.'

Needless to say, the atmosphere in the car wasn't great for the rest of the journey. Sarah took out her frustration at not being able to smoke by driving even more aggressively, and that didn't help.

By the time they pulled up at Western Towers, Hannah was feeling both nauseous and very grateful to still be alive. That said, Sarah was out the car and had a cigarette in her mouth before

Hannah had even managed to get her seatbelt off. By the time Hannah joined her out in the cold, Sarah had gone through half of the cigarette already. Hannah had no doubt that if smoking ever became an Olympic sport, her colleague would be a shoo-in for a gold medal.

Western Towers was actually a set of three blocks of flats connected by walkways and a circular, glass-fronted tower. Each block consisted of eight floors and the ground floor flats came with small private gardens walled off from the street by red iron gates. A few residents had made an effort with their plot of land, but most appeared to use the extra space for dumping miscellaneous crap like old prams and dead fridges, aided and abetted no doubt by any passersby with anything they needed to get rid of.

Hannah looked up at the building. It was made of that reddish brick that Hannah associated with anything constructed in the sixties or seventies, when no one apparently gave a shit what their homes looked like. In fact, Western Towers was the sort of place the people who were vital to the running of every part of London life got put, so they could be out of sight and forgotten about by the ones who employed them. It was the sort of place Hannah knew only too well because she'd grown up in an estate just like it.

Hannah had been lucky though. She'd had two hard-working parents who always made her feel loved, safe and wanted no matter how tough things were. The same couldn't be said of a lot of her friends at the time. Too many were now in prison, addicted to substances or plain dead.

It was fair to say Hannah was more than happy that she'd didn't still live in a place like Western Towers.

Sarah wasn't impressed with the place either. 'What a shithole.'

Hannah bristled at the comment. 'That's because it's cheap — for London anyway. You don't get looks without paying for it.'

'What floor is our man on?'

'Fifth.'

'Please tell me there's a working lift.'

'Let's go find out.' Hannah waited while Sarah took one last drag of her cigarette and chucked it onto the ground, then headed into the central tower. The interior wasn't anything fancy but Hannah was pleasantly surprised that it was relatively clean and didn't smell of piss.

There were two lifts side by side and, when Sarah pressed the call button, one stirred into life immediately and the doors opened.

They stepped inside. The steel interior was brightly lit, and Hannah could still see some faded graffiti here and there, despite someone's best efforts to remove it all. But no one had used it as a toilet, and it started to go up when she pressed the button for the fifth floor, so all in all things were looking good.

Sarah reached into her handbag and pulled out some leaflets. 'The governor said we should claim to be Jehovah's Witnesses, so I picked up some copies of *The Watchtower* from their place in Padfield Road.'

'They didn't try and get you in for a chat while you were there?' Hannah asked.

'I think they saw that I'm beyond saving,' Sarah replied. There was something in her voice, though, that made Hannah think there was something behind the joke.

'Hey. Sorry about earlier in the car,' Hannah said. 'Didn't mean to piss you off.'

'You didn't,' Sarah replied.

'Is everything else okay?'

'Couldn't be better.' Sarah kept her eyes on the floor numbers above the doors.

'You sure?'

The lift shuddered to a halt on the fifth floor and the doors opened. 'We're here,' Sarah said, walking quickly out onto the landing. Hannah followed her out, putting whatever problems Sarah might have out of her mind. After all, she had enough of her own.

Emma had stopped being pissed off about Hannah's bender the other night and had, instead, decided to overcompensate with attention and affection. All that had succeeded in doing was irritating

Hannah further and it had taken all her willpower not to storm out of the flat the previous night.

She knew the relationship was dying, but also knew neither of them had the money to move out and start somewhere new by themselves. So, for now, Hannah just had to grin and bear it, and fake that all was well, no matter how frustrated she was.

'This is the one,' Sarah said.

Tyrell Lewis's flat had a plain white door that didn't look strong enough to withstand a good kick from Hannah's motorbike boots. All the same, she took some quick sneaky pictures of the locks and hinges with her phone for when they did the risk assessment later.

'You ready?' Sarah asked, clutching her copies of *The Watchtower*.

'As I'll ever be,' Hannah replied.

Sarah pressed the doorbell and Hannah put on her best Happy Clapper smile just in case anyone had a peak out of a window.

No one came to answer the door though.

Sarah pressed the button again as Hannah tried to listen if there were any noises coming from inside. It all seemed quiet.

'Maybe they're out,' Hannah said.

'They better not be,' Sarah said. She didn't bother with the doorbell again, though. She knocked on the door, putting some force behind it to make it really echo through the flat.

'Fucking hell, Sarah,' Hannah hissed. 'We might as well show our warrant cards if you're going to knock like a copper.'

Sarah gave Hannah a 'whatever' glower, but it had done the trick. The door opened a crack before anything else could be said.

A young black man peered through the gap. Hannah recognised him as Tyrell from his social media pictures. 'What do you want?'

'Hello,' Sarah said. 'We're Jehovah's Witnesses. We were wondering if—'

'Fuck off,' Tyrell said and slammed the door shut once more.

'Charming,' Hannah said.

Sarah arched an eyebrow. 'Well, at least we know he's home.'

'Should we knock on a few other doors in case he's suspicious?'

'No. It's too cold to piss about.'

They headed back to the lift and returned to the ground floor. Hannah got out her phone and sent the pictures of Tyrell's door to Wise. He called her a second later.

'How did you get on?' Wise asked.

'All good. Tyrell's there but we didn't see anyone else there. He slammed the door in our faces the moment he heard we were Jehovah's Witnesses,' Hannah replied.

'Fair enough,' Wise said. 'He won't get a chance to do that when we come calling in the morning.'

'It's definitely on, then?'

'Yeah. Unless there's a problem with the risk assessment but I can't see that happening. You coming back to the station?'

Hannah looked over at Sarah, who was standing by her car, talking on the phone while smoking yet another cigarette. 'Yeah, we're on our way back now.'

'Excellent. We can catch up then.' Wise ended the call and Hannah slipped her phone back in her pocket. She walked over to Sarah, who, on seeing Hannah approaching, ended her own call and threw her cigarette on the ground.

'You ... er ... ready to go?' Sarah said.

'Sure — as long as you promise not to kill me on the way back,' Hannah replied.

Something passed over Sarah's face, like an unpleasant thought or a bad memory. She opened her car door, not meeting Hannah's eye. 'Let's go.'

28

The meeting with the Risk Assessment team and the Territorial Support Group had gone very well. They would move in on Beanz at 5 a.m. the next morning. They'd decided that they didn't need Armed Response with them as neither Beanz nor his friend, Tyrell, had a history of using guns and the TSG were more than capable of handling anything else. However, because of where they were going, they'd doubled up on the officers they'd normally take to an arrest. One team would pick up Beanz and Tyrell while a second team would wait downstairs in case the neighbours got rowdy in any way.

No one wanted a repeat of what happened in the summer when a simple call out to a domestic in the estate had escalated into a mass brawl in the street. His boss, Detective Chief Inspector Anne Roberts, would have Wise's balls if this operation went tits up like that.

With that in mind, it was time Wise updated her on what was going on before he headed home.

Wise took the stairs down to the second floor and headed straight to Roberts' office. In her late forties, Roberts oversaw the four Murder Investigation Teams that worked out of Kennington. He'd always thought her a good boss but, lately, he wasn't so sure. She'd been struggling with the politics that had crept into The Job and the endless demands to get better and better results with less and less resources from the higher ups and the politicians. Wise used to believe that she'd have his back when it mattered, but now? He'd come to realise she'd happily leave him up shit creek without a paddle if it meant saving her own skin.

Still, she was his boss.

He knocked on her door.

'Come in,' she called out.

Her office was twice the size of Wise's, which meant that it was just about big enough for all her paperwork and files. Which was a lot. Wise couldn't remember a time when Roberts wasn't struggling to go through all the reports that came her way.

She looked up as he entered, reading glasses perched on the end of her nose, her silver hair cropped shorter than ever. She didn't smile but, then again, Roberts never did. 'Simon.'

'Boss. How are you?'

'Bloody dandy,' she muttered as she took off her glasses and pointed at a chair opposite. 'What can I do for you?'

Wise sat down. 'Just wanted to fill you in on the Friary Road murder.'

She threw her glasses on her desk. 'Don't tell me you've uncovered another serial killer.'

'No. Not yet. In fact, this one looks pretty straightforward. The victim, Cameron Nketiam, was a drug dealer and we think he was killed because someone wanted to steal his stash. We have CCTV of a Jordan Hines arriving at Cameron's flat in a stolen car, then fleeing the scene. We also have footage of him torching the same car.'

'Seriously?'

'That's not all. He's continued using his own phone, so we've managed to cell-site his location and Brains did his magic to get the address of where he's hiding. We're heading out with the TSG to pick him up tomorrow morning. The only dicey thing is the location.'

'Where is it?'

'The flats in Bibury Close,' Wise said.

'Shit. Is that where the riot was back in the summer?' Roberts asked.

'That's the one. I'm hoping we can be in and out without anyone noticing but, if someone does spot us, that the miserable weather will keep them inside and stop them from causing problems. We're taking an extra TSG team just in case, though.'

'Okay, but try not to get too carried away with things,' Roberts said. 'My budget's running on fumes until the new year.'

'I'll do my best.' Wise stood up. 'I'll let you know how we get on.'

'And Simon,' Roberts said as he opened the door. He stopped and looked back. 'I wasn't joking about finding another serial killer. Keep this one simple, eh?'

'I don't think life does simple anymore,' Wise said.

As he headed down the stairs, Wise tried not to let the conversation with Roberts annoy him. It was all about money these days with her. And as for the serial killer cracks? She should've been happy his team had got results with both the Motorbike Killer case and the Green Anorak Man murders. Christ, Wise could've easily have got killed in the tube tunnels when he went after George Bartholomew. Even though, looking back now, he'd been stupid chasing Bartholomew on his own, Roberts should be giving him a medal instead of a bollocking.

The cold and rain slapped him in the face as he stepped outside. Wise pulled his coat tight as he ran to his Mondeo. If the traffic was kind to him, he'd be home in time to eat with Jean and the kids and hang out with them. He only hoped Jean would be in a better mood. She'd not spoken to him since she'd announced her plans for Christmas. After the day he'd had, he didn't fancy World War Three when he walked through the door.

Wise was halfway down the Wandsworth Road when his phone rang. The caller ID said it was his father.

'Dad! How are you?' Wise said on answering.

'Not too bad, son. Ticking on,' his father replied, his voice coming out over the car's speakers. 'What are you up to?'

'Not much. Just heading home. I've barely seen the kids all week, so I'm hoping I'll get back in time to hang out with them. Everything okay with you?'

'Yeah, you know me. Looking forward to the England game tomorrow.'

Wise chuckled. 'I'd forgotten it was on. What time's kickoff?'

'7 p.m. our time. That's ten o'clock in Qatar.'

'Good job you're not playing,' Wise said. 'That's past your bedtime.'

'I'm surprised Gareth Southgate hasn't been on the phone to me, actually,' his dad said. 'Even at my age, I reckon I could do a better job than that Jordan Henderson. I can certainly run faster.'

'What do you expect? He's Liverpool,' Wise said. Like any true-blue Chelsea fan, he had no love for the scousers, even when they played for England. 'Where are you going to be watching the game?'

'Probably at home. The pub gets too rowdy for me, and I spend half my time trying to see around some idiot who thinks it's a good idea to stand in front of me. And, of course, I can go to the toilet whenever I want at home without having to queue up. That's important when you get old like me.'

'I think you're doing alright, Dad. You're about as fit and strong as a man your age can be.'

'Are you thinking about watching?' His dad asked. 'I could do with some company if you are.'

'I'd love to watch the game with you, Dad. It's just ... well, me and Jean are having a few problems at the moment.'

'Nothing serious, I hope.'

'She's talking about going to spend Christmas with the kids at her parents.'

'Without you?'

Wise sighed. 'That's her plan.'

'Bloody hell,' his dad said. 'What's brought that on? You been a dickhead again?'

Wise didn't know what to say. He couldn't tell his father that Jean was scared of Tom, and what he might do to her and the kids. His old man had enough to worry about without that burden. 'Just life stuff. You know how it is.'

'Well, it can't be easy being married to you.' It wasn't the best joke his dad had ever made, but Wise appreciated the attempt.

'You're not wrong about that.'

Silence filled the car as Wise passed Nine Elms tube station.

'Look, whatever it is, I hope you can sort it out. She's a good 'un and worth fighting for,' his dad said eventually, his voice full of emotion. 'Listen to what she has to say and don't just dismiss it. Us Wise men aren't known for being that good when it comes to understanding women. Believe me, I know — I used to drive your mum mad.'

'I always thought you two were the perfect couple.'

His dad laughed. 'That's because you were too young to know any better. Don't get me wrong, I loved your mother, but she could be a right ball buster when she wanted to be. And sometimes that was a lot.'

'Didn't she chase Tom around the garden once with a bottle of bleach because he swore at her?'

'I don't think the poor kid even knew what the words meant,' his dad said. 'He was probably just repeating what I'd said more than once. He climbed up on top of the garden shed to get away from her and refused to come down for hours.'

'I found it really funny at the time,' Wise said as more memories came back to him. 'I remember when I'd done something wrong, I was expected to apologise before she counted to three. I'd try and front it out, but I'd always give in before she did.'

His dad was really laughing now. 'You were such a stubborn so-and so. Your poor mum would be standing there, counting, "two and a third", "two and a half", "two and three-quarters", so she didn't have to get to three and wallop you, and you'd be giving it the full Billy Big Boots act until you couldn't hold out any longer.'

'They were happy days, Dad,' Wise said, laughing himself.

'Yeah, they were. Life seemed a lot simpler back then. Sometimes,

I think the whole world's gone mad now. Anyways, I'd best let you go. Give my love to the family,' his dad said.

'I will. I love you, Dad.'

'Love you too, son.'

'No matter what happens, I'll call you during the game,' Wise said. 'We can at least cry over our beers together.'

'You don't think we'll get through then?' his dad asked.

'Not a chance.'

'Yeah, me neither — but you've got to live in hope, eh?' His dad ended the call, leaving Wise alone with his thoughts and memories. Of simpler days, when the only worry was getting home in time for tea. Of being in their own little gang, of him, Tom, Mum and Dad.

He knew he'd never appreciated how lucky he'd been at the time. He just took it all for granted like any other kid. In fact, it was only when he became a parent himself that he really appreciated the hard work his mum and dad had put into looking after him and Tom.

There'd been many a time now when he could imagine his mum laughing her head off as he tried to deal with whatever nonsense his own kids were up to. A few times, he'd even wished he could ring her up and apologise for being such a pain in the backside when he'd been little, especially when it was taking all his self-control not to strangle Ed or Claire. When their antics were mere echoes of what he and Tom had done.

Of course, thinking about the past now only made Wise feel even sadder about what had become of them all. And he knew the worst was still to come.

He only hoped they could all survive what the future brought.

Saturday 10th December

29

Wise followed the Territorial Support Group carrier up Commercial Way. He wished he'd had time for another coffee before they'd set off from Brixton Police Station. Hopefully, his adrenaline would kick in when they got to Western Towers and blow away the fog in his brain.

At least Wise had had a good evening at home. Jean had actually relaxed a bit and was talking to him again. In the end, they'd shared a pizza and scoffed popcorn with the kids while watching a movie. He'd gone to bed at a reasonable time too, as he had to be up by 3:30 a.m. to meet the team at Brixton for 4:20.

However, Wise hadn't slept much once he'd got into bed. For a change though, it hadn't been The Dream keeping him awake. Instead, he'd watched the clock tick around, doing his best not to wake Jean, as thoughts of what could go wrong on the raid ran through his mind.

It was always the same before an op. He couldn't help going over and over everything. His old partner used to call him a worrier. 'It'll be alright on the night,' Andy would say, but when did anything ever go to plan? In Wise's experience, he could probably count on one hand the times that happened.

So, instead of sleeping, Wise would spend the night picking his operation apart, gaming out in his head the different scenarios that he and his team might encounter. Once that was done, he'd work out what he'd do to deal with each situation. It might cost him some sleep, but Wise saw it as preparation as vital as anything else they did before a raid — especially if there was a chance things could get nasty.

Still, today should be pretty straightforward. All in all, the Cameron Nketiam murder had been easy to solve. And, after everything his team had been through recently, he was happy to have a simple case for once.

Hannah shifted in her seat next to him, wriggling in her stab-proof vest. 'I hate these bloody things. I feel like I can't breathe.' On her lap was a printout with the picture and history of their target that morning.

'Better to have it and not need it, than need it and not have it,' Wise said. He glanced in the rearview mirror. Hicksy and Jono were in the vehicle behind, with another TSG carrier taking up the rear. Wise hadn't been impressed when he'd seen Jono waiting for them at Brixton but the man had promised to not get involved if everything went off plan. Wise had reluctantly agreed to let him come along as he didn't want to delay things by arguing. However, the two men would have words later.

'What's happening with Leon?' Hannah asked.

'We've charged him with perverting the course of justice, wasting police time and a few other things. Serves the idiot right. As if no one would notice if he nicked a dead man's money?' Wise took pressure off the accelerator as their little convoy slowed. They were passing the Maywood estate and both sides of the street were packed almost bumper to bumper with cars and vans, reducing the width of the road down to single lane traffic. It made navigating the warren-like estate hard work. 'At least he came clean and admitted everything. That'll count in his favour when the time comes. Besides, it's young Jordan Hines we really want.'

'Don't you mean Beanz?' Hannah emphasised the zed at the end of his name, so she sounded like a bee buzzing. 'How can he be a serious gangster with a name like that?'

'I think getting arrested for murder is as serious as it gets. Beanz has graduated to the big time.'

'Yeah, well,' Hannah said, 'I'm not sure big-time villains allow themselves to be captured on half the city's CCTV cameras fleeing the crime scene. I mean, he could've at least worn a mask when he committed murder.'

Wise chuckled. 'I don't think he's going to win this year's criminal mastermind competition. He might get a runner's up prize of twenty years to life, though.'

'What? The one that comes with an all expenses stay at a maximum security hotel? Lucky boy,' Hannah said.

Wise didn't reply. They had arrived at Bibury Close.

He watched the TSG carrier stop by a load of green recycling bins lined up along the side of the flats and pulled in behind it. A team of eight uniformed officers climbed out of the carrier, all dressed to impress and ready to play, with stab vests over their blue jumpsuits and visored helmets to go along with their riot shields. Each had an X2 taser holstered on their hip, capable of firing two shots into a suspect if they believed there was a threat to life at any point. The suspect would then receive a nice little shock of twelve hundred volts, more than enough to incapacitate anyone short of the Incredible Hulk.

Wise and Hannah climbed out of the Mondeo to join the TSGs. Wise shivered at the change in temperature now he was out of his nice warm car and pulled his overcoat over his vest as the last two vehicles stopped behind his Mondeo.

'Fancy meeting you here,' Wise said as Hicksy and Jono came to join them.

'You know me, Guv, I only go to the best places,' Jono said, rubbing his hands together. 'It's proper brass monkey weather, isn't it?'

'I told you to eat your Ready Brek before you came out,' Hicksy said.

Jono winced. 'Do they even make that disgusting stuff anymore?'

'What? It was lovely. A proper breakfast,' Hicksy said. 'I'm not having any of this Coco Pop nonsense.'

Wise smiled, but his attention was back on the block of flats on the other side of the shrubbery bush. With any luck, they'd have Beanz in custody within the next ten to fifteen minutes and they could all head back to Brixton nick and have a well-earned breakfast.

Peter Brett, the sergeant leading the TSG team, walked over. 'We're ready to go in, if you're happy.'

'Yeah, we're good,' Wise said, feeling that lovely kick of adrenaline. This was it. 'Go. Go. Go.'

As the uniforms headed up the path to the central tower, Wise turned to Jono and Hicksy. 'You two stay down here in case there are any surprises. I doubt Beanz will attempt to jump out of a fifth-floor window, but you never know. And, if he does, let the TSGs nick him. I don't want you getting involved in any fisticuffs, Jono.'

'I'm not even here, Guv,' Jono said.

'Don't even get me started on that,' Wise said. 'You've got a weird idea of what constitutes desk duty.'

'We'll be okay, Guv,' Hicksy said. 'I'll keep him safe.'

'I hope so.' With that, Wise headed into Western Towers, Hannah by his side. He was glad to see that the TSGs were using the stairwell to reach Tyrell's floor, instead of trying to cram into the lift. They moved quickly up the stairs with well-practised precision. The approach and method of entry had all been mapped out beforehand using the information Hannah and Sarah had gathered in their visit the day before. That's why the lead officer carried a battering ram that was affectionately known as The Big Red Key among police officers. It was sixteen kilos of hardened steel would have no trouble defeating the door Beanz was hiding behind.

Risk Assessment might have decided there was no need for Armed Response Officers to attend the arrest, but no one was taking any chances either. Especially in that neighbourhood. Eight TSG officers should be enough to handle anything Beanz tried on, though. If they weren't, they were all in trouble.

Wise was halfway up the stairs from the fourth floor when he heard the TSGs smash Tyrell's door in. The crash echoed around the stairwell and Wise couldn't help but think they'd probably woken up most of Western Towers as well.

'Police with taser,' an officer shouted. 'Police with taser. Come to the door now.'

As Wise reached the top of the stairs, he saw three uniforms lined up around the broken doorway, sheltering behind their shields and with their tasers aimed into the flat.

'Police with taser. Come to the door now,' the officer shouted again. There was a pause but there was no response from anyone inside the flat.

'Going in. Going in,' another officer shouted. Again, the team moved as one, fast and aggressive, shouting at the tops of their voices to frighten the crap out of anyone inside. 'Police with taser. Show us your hands. Police with taser. Show us your hands.'

Wise listened to the shouting from the corridor with Hannah and the TSG Sergeant. He knew it wasn't a big flat with only the one bedroom. There wouldn't be that many places for Beanz to hide. Surely—

The shouting stopped. That wasn't a good sign. If they'd found Beanz, they would be telling him to get down and show his hands. There'd be more noise. More shouts.

Not silence.

A TSG appeared at the door and called his senior officer over. 'Sarge. You need to see this.'

Shit. Wise exchanged looks with Hannah. This really wasn't good. They followed Brett into the flat, stepping over bits of broken door into a narrow corridor. Two TSGs waited at the far end by a door to another room, tasers holstered and their shields hanging limply in their hands. An overhead light cast everything in a sickly hue.

'Urgh. What's that smell?' Hannah said.

Wise didn't reply. But he knew. He'd been in the murder game long enough to recognise that type of stench didn't come from rotten eggs.

At the end of the corridor, the uniforms stepped aside to allow Wise to see what the fuss was all about.

Beanz was sat on the sofa, as dead as could be.

His trousers were around his ankles and his once white boxer shorts were soaked in blood, as was everything around him. Something had been shoved in his mouth, forcing it open to an unnatural degree, and more blood stained his chin.

'Looks like someone's fed Beanz his balls,' the TSG sergeant said.

'Christ,' Hannah said before turning away. Wise didn't blame her. He'd not seen anything this grisly in a long time. In all the scenarios he'd imagined as outcomes for today's raid, this wasn't one of them.

'There's a second body in the bedroom,' another TSG said.

Wise left the living room and headed into the room across the hallway. Sure enough, another man was in the bed. He'd been sitting propped up against some pillows when he'd been shot in the head. Wise recognised him from their intelligence. 'Tyrell.'

'At least this one died quickly,' Brett said from behind him.

'Alright, let's get everyone out,' Wise said. 'This is now a crime scene. We need to get forensics down here immediately and get whoever the pathologist is on call right now.'

'Come on, you heard the man,' the sergeant said, clapping his hands.

As the TSGs filed out, Wise went back to take another look at the body of Jordan 'Beanz' Hines. It was hard to tell with all the blood and mess but it looked like Beanz had been beaten up pretty badly before he'd had his balls cut off.

Wise shook his head. The lad had made a play for the big time with the murder of Cameron Nketiam but someone had shown Beanz it didn't matter how tough you thought you were, there was always someone bigger and meaner.

So much for it being an easy case.

Wise left the flat, dread building in his gut. He had a horrible feeling that things were only going to get worse.

Hannah was waiting for him in the corridor, ashen faced. 'Sorry,

Guv. It was just ...' She put a hand to her mouth as if she was about to be sick.

'It's okay,' Wise said. 'Go down and tell the others what's happened. I'll join you in a minute.'

As Hannah headed back down the stairs, Wise walked to the balcony overlooking the estate. Lights were coming on in houses and apartments up and down the street. They'd soon have a crowd to deal with on top of everything else, all with their phones out, hoping to capture something to share on social media, making the police's job a hundred times harder.

He pulled his own phone out of his pocket. He might as well wake up the boss and tell her the bad news. The time on the screen said it was 5:15 a.m. Wise shook his head. The sun wasn't even up and already the day had gone to shit.

30

An hour later, the whole circus had gathered at Bibury Close. Helen Kelly was there with her SOCOs, Harmet Singh had arrived to check the bodies, and Wise had called his team and a load of uniforms in to knock on doors and see if anyone had seen anything that could help the officers track down who had murdered and mutilated Beanz and shot Tyrell. He'd also had to call in even more uniforms on top of that, as the police presence in the cul-de-sac and in the building had drawn more and more of the residents out to see what was going on. As the crowd had grown, it had become more and more unruly, with many happy to throw insults, threats and the odd lump of shit at the police. If they weren't careful, things would get really out of hand.

Wise had sent Brains to Kennington to get an update on Beanz' phone use and Tyrell's too. Beanz had been in hiding, after all. He might not have been the brightest spark, but Wise doubted he'd publicised where he was staying. So, logic said the killer had to be someone he was in touch with and given his address to.

Someone like Mad Errol.

Wise hadn't seen or heard about the man for twenty years, but he had no doubt he was more than capable of murdering someone or have someone else do it for him. He'd asked Brains to track down an address for the man as well, but he wasn't sure whether he should pay him a visit just yet.

Sarah was back at Kennington too, gathering what CCTV footage she could. It'd be hard, though. Whoever had done it wouldn't have turned up with a flashing sign above their car and Western Towers had to have a good few hundred residents. Many of whom, no doubt, were working all hours. They couldn't assume someone was a suspect just because someone turned up at Western Towers in the middle of the night.

A black Audi S3 Sedan pulled up, drawing Wise's eye. It stopped. The door opened and DCI Roberts stepped out, looking grimmer than the weather.

'Boss,' Wise said, walking over. 'Sorry to ruin your Saturday.'

'So much for keeping it fucking simple, Simon,' Roberts said, looking at the army gathered around Western Towers. 'I suppose everyone's on bloody overtime as well.'

'Budgets aren't my prerogative,' Wise said. 'I just deal with the crimes.'

'Cute. I should use that line when Walling is tearing me a new one on Monday for blowing what little money we had left.'

Wise shook his head. 'What do you suggest we do then? Email all of London's low-lives and tell them to not commit any more crimes until January because we can't afford to investigate anything?'

They stared at each other for a few moments, the argument continuing unspoken. Wise wasn't going to back down, though. He'd had enough of this bullshit. Maybe Roberts saw that, because she took a deep breath and blew it out in a plume of mist, deflating as she did so, the fight leaving her. 'Sorry. I shouldn't go off at you. It's not your fault. I know you're doing your best.'

'We all are.'

'How bad is it in there?' She nodded towards Western Towers.

'As bad as it gets. Someone executed Tyrell with a single shot to the head. Beanz wasn't so lucky. He had his balls cut off and shoved in his mouth. It wasn't pretty. It wasn't quick.'

'Sounds like a message.'

'Maybe. If he nicked drugs from Cameron Nketiam, then they had to come from somewhere. Cameron was only ever a middleman. It could be the original owner isn't happy about being robbed. Or whoever Beanz was trying to sell the gear to didn't want to fork out any cash for them.'

'Do we know who Nketiam worked for?'

'We've not been able to find out yet. He was part of a gang called The Peckham Lads, though. We're trying to track down who runs them,' Wise replied. 'But we do know he was trying to get hold of Errol Gallagher for the past few days. He's a face on the South London drug scene.'

'I've heard of him. Do we have an address?'

'Brains is on that now.'

'The moment you know, go see him and take a crew of AROs with you,' Roberts said. 'Let him know we're not pissing around.'

Wise raised an eyebrow. 'What about your budget?'

Roberts' mouth twitched. It was almost a smile. 'The whole country's in debt. Why should we be any different?'

'You're the boss.' Wise smiled. 'Do you want to go up and have a look at the crime scene?'

'It's okay. I think there are more than enough people getting in the way,' Roberts replied. 'Keep me updated on any progress you make.'

'I will.'

'Good luck.' Roberts climbed into her Audi, turned on the engine with a roar and then quickly backed out of Bibury Close.

'Guv.' He turned around and saw Hannah walking towards him, a paper cup in each hand. She held one out for him. 'Thought you might want a coffee?'

'You lifesaver.' He took the cup from her and had a sip. It was hot and strong enough to wake the dead. It was exactly what he needed.

'I'm sorry about earlier,' Hannah said. 'I've just never seen anything like that before.'

'Nor have I,' Wise replied. 'It was pretty horrific.'

'You were right when you said this case wasn't going to be easy.'

'Yeah, well. I wish I'd remembered that myself. I was feeling all too smug about today's arrest and "getting our man". I should've known better.'

'I can't help thinking me and Sarah should've nicked them both yesterday when we were here.'

'Don't think that. You did the right thing. You did what I asked you to do,' Wise said. 'We do things by the book. Always. It keeps us safe and it stops any smart-arse solicitor from getting a guilty person off on a technicality.'

'I know, but Tyrell Lewis was alive then. We could've stopped this from happening.'

'Hey,' Wise said. 'Who knows what could have happened if the pair of you had gone into that flat? You could've ended up dead, not them. So, stop double-guessing yourself. We go on. Our job now is to find Tyrell and Beanz's killers. That's it.'

'Okay,' Hannah replied, but Wise could tell she wasn't going to let go of her guilt that easily. But what more could he say? He was hardly a role model when it came to brooding. Wise had more baggage than Heathrow.

He took a gulp of coffee, enjoying its warmth. 'Have you seen Donut?'

'He was knocking on doors with some uniforms,' Hannah replied.

'Can you call him? Get him down here. And Hicksy and Jono too.'

'No problem.' Hannah pulled out her phone and scrolled through her contacts for Donut's number.

In the meantime, Wise saw Helen Kelly coming out of Western Towers. She pulled her hood off and gasped in the cold, morning air. He walked over to join her. 'How are you getting on in there?'

Helen puffed out her cheeks. 'I think that one's going on my list of horrible deaths. What a way to go.'

'It was nasty. Any sign of the drugs Beanz stole in there?'

Helen shook her head. 'Nope. There are a few smoked joints in an ashtray, but that's about it so far. No Class As yet.'

'No calling card with the killer's name and address?'

'Unfortunately not.' Helen smiled. 'The bathroom's interesting though. It looks like whoever did it washed their hands in there afterwards. There's blood on the soap and on the towel and in the sink. I presume most of that belongs to the victim, but it would suggest the killer wasn't wearing gloves. We're taking samples of everything. Maybe we'll find the assailant's DNA or fingerprints amongst it all.'

'That would be marvellous,' Wise said.

Helen held up her hands. 'No promises.'

'Can you ask the lab to rush everything through?'

'I'll do my best, but it is a Saturday and there's a certain football match on tonight.'

'I'd forgotten all about that. It'll be a miracle getting anything done.'

'You never know, maybe there's a geek in a lab coat who hates football just waiting to help us out.'

Wise sighed. 'The way my day's going? I doubt it.'

'Keep your chin up,' Helen replied. 'It could be worse — just ask your victims in the flat upstairs.'

Wise's phone rang. The caller ID said it was Brains. 'Excuse me, I've got to take this.'

'No problem,' Helen replied. 'No doubt we'll speak more.'

As the SOCO headed back towards the stairs, Wise answered his phone. 'Brains. What've you got?'

'For starters, Beanz had a ten-minute chat with Mad Errol's phone last night at five past eight,' Brains said.

'So, he could've easily given him his address,' Wise replied.

'Yeah, but according to Mad Errol's phone, he didn't leave his house all night after that. Nor was it switched off.'

'Did he make any calls?'

'No.'

'Maybe he left his phone at home and came here.'

'Yeah, but I haven't got any proof yet that says he did that.'

'Anything on the CCTV?'

'Sarah's just starting on that.'

'Okay. If there's anything to find, she'll find it. Now, Roberts wants us to go around to Errol's hard and heavy, so I'm going to come back to MIR-One in a minute. Can you get word out that we need to do another risk assessment? I'd imagine we'll need Armed Response, and who knows what else.'

'I'll get on it now,' Brains replied.

'And text me the address. I'm going to send some bodies over to keep an eye on Errol while we rustle up the troops.'

'Sent.'

Wise heard the ping of the information arriving. 'See you soon.' Wise ended the call and checked the address. East Sheen. Errol had done well for himself, if he was living in that neighbourhood. Who said crime didn't pay?

He had to admit, though, that calling on Mad Errol was the last thing he wanted to do. He just couldn't see any other way forward with the case. At the moment, Errol Gallagher was their only lead.

But there was something that just didn't fit in his mind. Yes, Errol was violent, he was a thug, a hooligan, but Wise found it hard to see Errol committing the atrocity he saw upstairs. Perhaps if both men had been shot, he wouldn't be so unsure, but the castration of Beanz was an unnecessary act. The killer or killers weren't simply robbing Beanz of whatever he had. They'd wanted him to suffer. They wanted to make an example of him.

But who would do that?

That's what Wise had to work out.

Looking up, he spotted Donut, Hicksy and Jono coming out of the flats to join Hannah. He headed over, his mind in a million different places.

'Hello, Guv. What's occurring?' Jono asked.

'Good to see you're still holding up,' Wise said. 'Have you had any luck with the door-to-doors?'

'Fuck no,' Hicksy replied. 'You'd think we'd fed Beanz his balls ourselves if the residents around here are anything to go by. They do not like the police. Not one bit.'

'I'm not surprised, but it's a pity.' Wise turned to Donut. 'When you went to see Cameron's widow, are you sure she didn't say anything about who he worked for?'

'I don't know, Guv,' Donut said. 'I didn't go in. Sarah saw her on her own. She left me out in the corridor.'

That surprised Wise. 'Really? She didn't mention that.'

'She was in a bit of a mood that day,' Donut said. 'And that's putting it mildly.'

'Okay. Can you go back and have a chat with her? Take Hicksy with you,' Wise said. 'She must know something. You don't live with someone as long as she did without knowing the ins and outs of his business.'

'Do you want us to bring her in?' Hicksy asked.

'No. In fact, stress that she's not in any trouble,' Wise replied. 'Maybe that will help her open up.'

'What about me?' Jono said.

'How are you feeling?'

'Never better.'

'Are you sure you don't need to go home? It's been a long day already.'

'Behave yourself. You'll be wrapping me up in cotton wool next. I'm fine. What do you need me to do?'

'Okay. Can you head over to Errol's place in East Sheen, then, and keep an eye on the place? I don't want you to go in or do anything stupid. Just sit in your car. If Errol comes out, call us, and follow him to wherever he goes but you don't get out the car no matter what. Okay?'

'Got it. My arse will stay firmly in my seat.' He held up his fingers in a boy scout salute. 'You have my word.'

31

Leon Tomoral got off the bus and walked towards Wilmsden Terrace, cursing his luck every step of the way. The police had finally let him out on bail, with the promise of plenty of court dates to come. The solicitor they'd given him said there was a good chance Leon would get community service and not have to do time, but Leon couldn't help but fear the worst.

With his hood up and head down, Leon hugged himself, trying to keep warm as the rain pelted down. He'd asked the Feds to drive him home, but they'd just laughed like he was the funniest man alive.

Bastards.

Of course, Leon knew really that he had no one but himself to blame for the mess he was in. He should've minded his own business the other night. He should've stayed in his flat and not gone to have a look in that dead geezer's place. But he had and he'd seen all that cash lying there. Cash that the dead guy didn't need anymore, and he did.

How was he supposed to know the old bag across the road had a camera recording everything? There should be laws against that. It was an invasion of privacy or something. He told his brief that, but the man had shaken his head. It wasn't like it was on TV. He couldn't get the evidence thrown out on a technicality. Besides, Leon had confessed to everything after the Feds had found all that money in his sock drawer. The solicitor said Leon should've stayed all 'No comment' during his interview but, now Leon had admitted to everything, there wasn't much he could do.

Talk about a useless man.

The police still had tape up around the dead man's flat and there was a uniformed officer in his high-viz jacket standing guard outside. Leon was tempted to give him the finger as he passed but, knowing his luck, the copper would nick him, and he'd end up in even more trouble. Instead, he gave the woman opposite the finger and smiled at the thought of her watching the footage later. If she watched, that is. He couldn't imagine the rich bitch spent her nights watching her security videos instead of Netflix. Feeling stupid now, he picked up his pace and all but ran to the stairwell.

The wet made it stink even worse than before, a horrible mix of damp, mould, piss and skunk. Maybe a bit of puke too. Leon hated living in Wilmsden Terrace, but it was cheap for London and he couldn't afford anything better. It was going to be a happy day, though, when he could get away from there and live somewhere clean, where leaving the house didn't involve walking past a neighbourhood full of pimps, prostitutes, dealers and road men.

His mum kept going on about coming up for a visit, but he'd been putting her off. There was no way he was going to let her see the dump he lived in. She'd have a heart attack and then start hassling him about moving.

She wouldn't be wrong though and, right then, he could do with a bit of his mum's nagging and fussing. At least Leon knew she loved him.

He trudged along to his front door, feeling more and more miserable. Maybe he should bunk off college for a bit. It was nearly the holidays anyway. No one would care. He could go home early, see his parents, get spoiled and cared for. Sleep in a warm bed, eat as much food as he wanted. No working. No worrying. Just hide away.

Yeah, that sounded good. He could pretend none of this shit existed while he was there. He could pretend everything was alright.

Leon got his key out to open the front door, then noticed it was slightly ajar. One of his flatmates must've forgotten to shut it. The wankers. How long had it been like that? Were they in the flat or had they left it unlocked when they were going out?

Christ, he hoped no one had come in and robbed the place. There was no way he could afford to replace his Mac if it got pinched. Without that, he could kiss his college degree goodbye.

Shit.

He walked inside. 'Daryl! Mischa!'

No answer. His flatmates must be out.

The living room was a mess, but it always was. It was a shame the coppers couldn't have tidied up after they'd searched the place. At least the TV was still there and the PS4 so, maybe, the gaff hadn't been robbed.

'Daryl! Mischa!' he called out again, but they definitely weren't home. He hurried to his bedroom, hoping that his kit was still there, dreading that it wasn't.

He flung the door open and then stopped, suddenly very scared.

A man sat on his bed. His hood was up, hiding his face in shadow, but his cold eyes shone out. He made a clicking sound with his mouth and grinned. 'About time you made it back.'

'Who... who are you?' Leon managed to say but he really didn't want to know. He took a step back, everything telling him to run. He just needed to get back into the hallway. Then to the door.

'Uh-huh,' the man said. 'Don't move.'

Leon froze. He knew he should keep moving but the fear he felt overruled his mind. Especially when he saw the knife in the man's hand.

'Now, to answer your question,' the intruder said, standing up. 'Who am I? Well, I'm the man who's going to teach you a lesson. Didn't anyone tell you it was wrong to steal from people?'

32

In MIR-One, Sarah stared at her monitor and wanted to be sick.

What had she done?

She'd got two people killed, that's what.

She cursed Andy again for getting her involved with the bastard. She could hear him now, selling his betrayal like it was nothing at all. *'No one will get hurt. No one innocent at least. And who cares about the scumbags, eh?'*

She should've punched him then or reported him or just told him to fuck off because, it turned out, she did care about the scumbags. She cared a lot.

Sarah didn't want anyone's blood on her hands. Getting people killed wasn't why she'd become a cop.

Of course, she hadn't become a police officer to be skint either. How did they expect her to live off thirty-five grand in London? Even with her husband's income, there wasn't enough left over after they'd paid the bills and half filled the fridge.

When was the last time she'd had a holiday or bought something nice for herself? Or went for a meal out? The truth was, buying anything that wasn't an absolute necessity was only possible when she made a bit of extra cash on the side. Over the years, she'd sold the odd story to the press but that had become less lucrative lately. The public didn't care about ordinary crimes. They only wanted information on the ghastly and sleazy cases.

It was no wonder her morals had gone out the window when the bastard put that bag of cash in her hands. And to think, most of it went on paying off her credit card and the fucking heating bill. That's all. There was no expensive jewellery tucked away, no Rolls-Royce parked in the garage.

No, she just had a credit card with no crippling debt piling up more and more each month. A card she'd cut up after she'd paid it off.

And now? Now, she was at that bastard's mercy.

Shit. Shit. Shit.

She'd tried calling him ever since she'd heard the news about Beanz being fed his balls, but he wasn't picking up. Of course he wasn't. He only got in touch when he wanted.

She sat back in her chair and glanced over at Brains, who was busy beavering away. She'd heard him update Wise on what he'd found out. So far, no one had connected Cameron to Ollie Konza but it was only a matter of time.

And the moment that happened?

She was fucked.

Brains looked up and caught her eye. 'How are you getting on? Any luck with the CCTV yet?'

'Not yet,' she replied. How could she find anything? She'd not even bothered looking. Her mind was too caught up with the mess she was in.

'I bet your husband wasn't happy about you getting called in,' Brains blathered away. 'My wife went berserk. She reckoned I was just trying to get out of looking after the kids for the day. I told her that it didn't work like that. It's not as if I planned on that little scrote bag getting his balls cut off, is it? I —'

'Brains!' Sarah snapped, cutting him off. 'I'm trying to work.'

'Sorry. I was just trying to pass the time. I mean, it's only you and me here at the moment and I —'

'Will you just shut up!'

Brains dropped his head back down behind his monitor and a painful silence filled MIR-One. Despite getting what she wanted, Sarah felt terrible for shouting at him like that. The man hadn't done anything really to deserve it. He hadn't fucked up. She had.

Christ, she needed a cigarette.

'I'm going out for a smoke,' Sarah said, picking up her phone, fags and lighter.

'Okay,' Brains replied, not even daring to look up.

She hesitated for a moment, thinking she should apologise, but what was done was done. So, Sarah marched out of the incident room and headed straight for the lift. By the time she exited it on the ground floor, she had a cigarette in her mouth and her lighter poised to spark it into life the moment she stepped outside.

That's when her phone rang.

The caller ID said 'NAILS.'

Sarah all but ran out the main doors into the car park, her phone shrilling away. She did a mad dash to the gates and then she was out into the street, aware that she didn't have a coat on, despite the drizzle.

Only then did she feel safe enough to answer his call.

'What have you done?' she said as she crossed the road, heading towards Luigi's. Hopefully it wouldn't be full of police on a Saturday, and she could talk in private and be dry.

'Hello yourself,' Tom Wise said. 'Something wrong?'

'Something wrong?' Sarah almost choked on the words. 'You told me you just wanted the drugs back. Not that you were going to kill two people.'

'You better not be taping this,' Tom said in that low growl of his. 'But even if you are, I didn't do anything, and I've got dozens of witnesses who can confirm that. I don't know what's got you so worked up, Detective Constable, but none of it has anything to do with me.'

'For Christ's sake, I gave you Beanz' address.'

'And what have I given you, Sarah? Eh? Do you want me to run through the list here and now? I can do that quite easily. Or shall I just send you pictures?' Tom laughed. 'I know you like watching CCTV, so perhaps you'd prefer me to send you a video or two? Maybe my brother would like to have a look.'

Sarah stopped walking, oblivious to the cold and the rain, the cigarette unlit in her hand. 'You wouldn't.'

'But you know I would. All too easily.'

'You'd implicate yourself.'

'Would I? I just gave money to an officer in need. I think they'd be more worried about you taking it. It'd certainly break Simon's heart, seeing you involved with me. From what I've heard, he's not got over poor Andy yet.'

'It's your fault Andy got killed too.'

'Is it? I thought your lot shot him while he was trying to murder a witness while high on drugs. Again, that had nothing to do with me.'

Sarah didn't know what to say. She knew how it would look for her if the bastard started throwing dirt around. Even if Professional Standards didn't find anything to fire her over, her team would never trust her again.

'You still there, Sarah?' Tom cooed.

'Bastard.'

'Sticks and stones and all that, darling. Now, what with it being a Saturday and all, I'm going to go off and have some fun. But, before I go, I just want you to know that I'm still looking for what was taken. When we popped around to see Eggs and Bacon, someone had relieved them of our gear.'

'What?'

'Yeah, I know. I was surprised, too, to find out that there are other villains in London besides my lot. The big question, though, is who thinks they're clever enough to get one over on me and Ollie? Who do you lot think it could be?'

'Didn't he tell you?'

'Who? Beanz? Nah, he had his mouth full at the time. Anyway, why should I speak to oiks like him when I have more reliable people to talk to — like you.'

Sarah took a breath. Should she tell him about Mad Errol Gallagher? Wise and the others were planning to raid him later that day. No. She couldn't let someone else die. 'I don't know. We haven't got any other suspects.'

The bastard laughed. 'I can always tell when people lie to me, Sarah. It's like a spider-sense going off and, believe me, it's tingling now. Don't piss me about, darling.'

'I'm not —'

'Sarah.' He cut her off, wielding her name like a sword. 'Don't.'

Tears ran down her cheeks, only to be lost in the rain a heartbeat later. 'Why can't you leave me alone?'

'Because life doesn't work that way. Now, who's got my gear?'

'We think Beanz was trying to do a deal with a man called Errol Gallagher.'

'Mad Errol, eh? Yeah, I can see that. Unlike Beanz, the man always had balls. You got an address for him?'

'Please, you can't make me do this.'

'Oh, I can. In for a penny, in for a pound, as they say.'

'He's in East Sheen.' Sarah gave him the address.

The bastard whistled. 'Nice. The boy's done good. Thanks for that, love. Chat soon.'

The line went dead.

God, she wanted to scream. She wanted to cry.

The rain pelted her face, bringing her back to the world outside her nightmare. Her cigarette was soaked through and falling apart, so she chucked it onto the ground and headed back to the police station, her hair plastered all over her face, her clothes drenched.

Knowing her luck, she'd go down with pneumonia if she didn't get some dry clothes on quickly.

Then again, maybe that wouldn't be a bad thing. It was one way to sort out her problems. Maybe she should stand out in the cold and wet even longer. Get really wet. Get really sick.

Maybe she should just fucking die.

33

Hicksy wished Jono was with him. Everything felt alright when he was. Like it always used to be. He certainly didn't like this revolving door of partners thing he had going on right now. Being lumbered with Diversity was bad enough but Donut? Fucking hell. No wonder Sarah got in a right temper when she'd gone out with him. Even dog shit smelt better than Donut.

At least they didn't have far to go. Nadine Ake's place was just off Peckham Park Road, in a block of flats where someone had gone mad with a pot of blue paint until the whole place looked like it was a home away from home for bloody Smurfs.

He climbed out of Donut's old banger and looked at all the blue doors and window frames, and the blue railings and bannisters. 'If I lived here, I'd have to paint my door white as a fuck you to everyone else.'

'Maybe there's a housing association that won't let anyone do that,' Donut said. He had a North Face puffer coat on that swamped the skinny git.

'Which one's Nadine's?' Hicksy asked.

Donut pointed to the entrance to the building. 'It's this way.'

'No shit, Sherlock,' Hicksy muttered as he followed Donut to the double doors. Once inside, they climbed the stairs, which had Hicksy huffing and puffing a bit more than he'd like. Come the new year, he was going to make more of an effort to get in shape. Jono's illness had been enough of a wakeup call to convince him to start looking after himself a bit more. He'd already cut sugar from his tea and swapped his evening beers for a tot or two of whiskey. That way, he still got a buzz without the calories. On a day like today, that was a good thing because he had a feeling he'd need more than a few by the time he was tucked up in front of the telly later.

Donut stopped by one of the blue front doors. 'This is hers.'

'Alright,' Hicksy said. 'Let me do the talking.' He knocked hard on the door and, a few moments later, a short yet curvaceous woman answered the door, a floral headscarf holding her hair up and eyes all but hidden beneath eyelashes so big a jumbo jet could make an emergency landing on them.

'Yes?' she said, not sounding impressed at being disturbed.

Hicksy held up his warrant card. 'I'm Detective Sergeant Roy Hicks, Ms Ake. My colleague and I would like to ask you a few questions if we may.'

Nadine Ake looked up and down the corridor and looked relieved that none of her neighbours were having a nose at what was going on. 'I already talked to someone the other day.'

Hicksy gave her his most charming smile. 'I know. We just have a few follow up questions. We shouldn't take up too much of your time.'

Nadine didn't reply. She just looked him up and down, appraising him. For a moment, Hicksy thought that she was going to tell them to clear off but, from somewhere behind her, a baby started crying. She sighed. 'Come in.'

They followed her through to the living room. The wailing baby was in a playpen by the window, standing up by holding onto the netted sides. A slightly older child, a girl, was playing with some Lego while watching YouTube videos on an iPad. Giant pink headphones covered her ears.

Nadine walked over to the baby and picked it up, settling it on her hip as it wailed away. Then she noticed something else in the pen. She bent down and picked up a large, red Lego brick. When she turned around, she had a face like thunder. 'Maxine! Did you throw this at Esme?'

She waved the Lego brick at her daughter who ignored her completely, her eyes fixed determinedly on YouTube.

'Oi, Maxine. I know you can hear me,' she shouted over the baby's cries, but Maxine didn't even look up from her iPad. In the end, her mother gave up. She pointed towards the kitchen. 'We can talk in there.'

Hicksy and Donut followed her through. Nadine, with the baby parked on her hip, began pouring formula into a bottle. The kitchen was tiny, with a sink and a counter filled with a toaster, kettle and air fryer by the window and an oven, dishwasher and fridge on the other side. Somehow, Nadine had managed to fit in a small table with two chairs and a highchair as well, which left little room to swing a cat, let alone have a conversation.

Hicksy turned to Donut. 'Why don't you wait outside? There's not enough room for the three of us and the baby.'

'Why is it me who always has to wait outside?' Donut said, with a right proper pout of his lips.

'Because I'm your senior officer, that's why,' Hicksy replied. He was never one for pulling his rank on people but there was no way he could sit in that little kitchen with Donut's body odour polluting it. In the end, Donut huffed a bit but he flounced off all the same, like a good little boy doing as he was told.

Nadine gave him a smile as if she knew why he'd done what he'd done, then turned on the kettle and, for a moment, Hicksy thought he was going to be offered a tea or a coffee, which he would've gratefully accepted. But, once it was done boiling, she filled a small bowl with the water. She then placed the baby bottle, with its formula mixed with cold water, into the hot water. She saw Hicksy watching with curiosity. 'Have you never made a baby's bottle before?'

'No,' Hicksy said. 'I haven't.'

'Don't tell me you're one of those Neanderthals who never help out with the kids?'

'I don't have any kids,' Hicksy replied. 'I've never been married.'

'You don't need to be married to have kids. I'd say look at this one, but I was married when I had her — just not to the baby's father.' Nadine laughed. It was a warm, rich sound that automatically made Hicksy smile too. 'But I'm not married now, and I still got two kids to look after.'

'Well, kids aren't really for me.'

'Oh, you're not gay, are you?'

Normally, that sort of question in the wrong place was enough to start a fight but, somehow, Nadine made it sound perfectly harmless.

Hicksy smiled. 'No, I'm not gay. Maybe I just haven't met the right woman.'

'I'm glad to hear that, but a good-looking man like you? You should have no problem finding a little baby mama to keep you warm.' Again, Nadine laughed but Hicksy had a feeling that was because she'd spotted his cheeks going red.

'Can I talk to you about your ex-husband, Ms Ake?' he said, desperate to get the interview back on track.

'Only if you call me Nadine.'

'Nadine,' Hicksy said, surprised that he liked saying it.

Nadine swivelled around, plucked the bottle from the bowl, and squeezed a drop onto the back of her other hand, all while still holding the baby. 'Perfect,' she said and stuck the bottle in the baby's mouth. That done, she lowered herself into the chair opposite Hicksy. 'Ask away.'

'You told my colleague before that you didn't know who your ex-husband worked for,' Hicksy said, 'but did you know any of his old associates? Anyone who might be able to help us narrow down who his boss might've been?'

'Is that what she told you? The woman detective?' Nadine said. 'That I didn't know who Cam worked for?'

'Yeah.'

Nadine watched her baby for a few moments, but Hicksy could

tell something had changed. The humour was gone. The flirtatiousness, if he could call it that. She looked scared now.

'Do you know who his boss was?' Hicksy asked.

Nadine nodded, still concentrating on feeding her baby. 'I told the other police detective.'

'Who is it?'

She looked up then and Hicksy saw the fear in her eyes. 'This can't come back to me. I got kids. Now Cam's dead, I'm all they got.'

'It's alright. It won't.'

'He worked for Ollie Konza.'

'Ollie Konza?' Hicksy repeated.

'That's right.'

Hicksy didn't need to look that name up. He reckoned most of the Met would've known that name. No wonder Nadine was scared. That man was bad news. Why the hell hadn't Sarah told them about him if she knew? It didn't make any sense. 'And he was working for him when he got out of prison?'

'That's right. He reckoned Ollie was setting him up for the big time, that he wouldn't be dealing himself no more. He'd have others to do that for him. That's why he thought I'd take him back. The idiot really thought that would make a difference.' She smiled. 'Then he saw Esme and I didn't have to tell him I wasn't interested. He was off on his heels as quick as you like.'

'Considering what happened, that was a good thing,' Hicksy said.

'You think?'

'I know.' Hicksy smiled. He liked Nadine. 'Do you know where we can find Ollie Konza by any chance?'

'He's got a flat in Peckham somewhere but I don't know where. I never went with Cam when he was doing his pick-ups. I may have been an idiot getting involved with him, but I did have some common sense.'

'I'm sure you have. You've been a great help, Nadine. I'll get out of your hair now. I'm sure you've got better things to do on a Saturday than answer my questions.'

Nadine fluttered her large eyelashes at him. 'Darling, you're the most exciting thing to happen to me today.'

'Then you need to get out more,' Hicksy said, standing up.

Nadine laughed. 'You offering?'

Hicksy went red again. 'Er. No.'

'You didn't even want to think about that for a second?'

'I didn't mean it like that. I ... er, I think you're a very attractive woman ...'

'Go on.'

God, let the ground swallow him up. Hicksy couldn't be more embarrassed if he tried. 'It's just, it's ... it's against the rules. It's not that I don't want to, but I can't.'

'But you do want to?' Nadine grinned, enjoying every second of Hicksy's discomfort.

He pointed to the front door. 'I better be off. My colleague's waiting for me.'

'Goodbye, sergeant. It's been lovely meeting you.'

Hicksy all but ran from Nadine's kitchen, her laughter chasing after him.

Donut was waiting for him outside and, luckily, he was still too pissed off at being kicked out of the flat to notice how flustered Hicksy was. He felt like a fool. A teenage fool. But how long had it been since anyone had shown any sort of interest in him?

'Did you find out anything?' Donut asked when they were halfway down the stairs to the ground floor.

'Yeah. The name of Cameron Nketiam's boss,' Hicksy replied. 'And he's a bad one.'

'How bad?'

'As bad as they fucking come.' Hicksy pushed the blue doors open and marched outside. 'Come on. Hop. Hop. We need to get back and tell the boss.

34

Wise had returned to MIR-One with Hannah, to coordinate the upcoming raid on Mad Errol Gallagher's place in Richmond. Sarah had stuck up pictures of Errol's house on one of the whiteboards — a mixture of images taken from Google Street View and some taken from an estate agent's website from before Errol bought it. She'd even tracked down a layout of the interior rooms.

According to the database, he lived there with his wife of twenty-five years, a woman named Angela. There were two children, but both had left home — the youngest to university in Kent, while the other had gone to work in Hong Kong as a financial analyst.

Standing there, looking at Errol's mugshot and his home, Wise could feel his discomfort growing. Would his presence at the arrest help or hinder the team? Granted, he'd not seen Errol in twenty years but there was no denying the history between them, none of which was good. Wise couldn't help but think of what could be said, what secrets would be spilled.

He should step back and let the team handle the arrest, but what reason could he give to justify it? *I'm worried that he'll mention we used to kick people's heads in together?* Or *I've not seen him since the night my twin brother murdered someone?* It was easy to imagine how well that would go down.

He looked around the gathered team; there were officers from Armed Response who would lead the raid, a TSG team who'd handle the arrest and transportation of Errol back to Brixton, a canine unit whose dog would be used to sniff out any weapons or drugs on the premise, and some uniforms who'd been drafted in to help with a thorough search for evidence on the property afterwards.

From his own team, however, only Hannah and Callum were available to go on the raid. He had absolute faith in Hannah's ability, but he wasn't prepared to send her in with just a trainee DC for company. The trouble was, there wasn't anyone else available to go with her. Everyone was tied up elsewhere.

It was, once again, a reminder at how short-staffed he was and another reason why he had to go on the raid.

'When do you think you'll all be ready to leave?' he asked the group.

'We have to finish checking our weapons and equipment,' the head ARO said. He looked at his watch. 'It's eleven thirty hours now so shall we say twelve hundred?'

There were nods of agreement among the others.

'Okay, good,' Wise said. 'Twelve hundred hours it is then. I'll see you all downstairs.'

As the group broke up, Wise's phone rang. It was Hicksy. 'Guv. We need to talk.'

'Yeah? What's up?' Wise replied.

'Me and Donut have just left Nadine Ake's place. She told me she knew who her ex worked for.'

'And?'

'His boss was Ollie Konza.'

'Konza?' Wise knew that name. He caught Brains' eye and waved him over. 'She's sure?'

'Yeah. One hundred percent. Apparently, Cameron and Ollie go way back. She said Ollie had a place in Peckham somewhere that he uses as his base.'

'You on your way back here?'

'Yeah. Unless you need us elsewhere?'

'Reckon you can be back here before twelve?' Wise asked.

'Should be.'

'Speak to you then.' Wise ended the call and turned to Brains. 'That was Hicksy. He said Cameron worked for Ollie Konza.'

'Fuck. If Beanz nicked Konza's drugs or money, he was even more stupid than I thought,' Brains said. 'If ever there was a man who'd feed you your own balls for crossing him, it's Konza.'

'Yeah. That's what I was thinking.' Suddenly everything started to make sense.

'Do you want to call the Gallagher raid off until we know more?'

'I'm not sure,' Wise said. 'Can you dig up whatever there is on Konza as quick as you can? Previous, known associates, phone numbers, vehicles, addresses — all that stuff?'

'I'll get on it now.'

'We need to find out if he was anywhere near Western Towers last night.'

Hannah came over with Sarah. 'Everything okay?'

'I'm not sure,' Wise replied. 'Hicksy just called. He said that Cameron was dealing on behalf of a nasty piece of work called Ollie Konza.'

Hannah frowned. 'Should I know who that is?'

'Let's put it this way — he makes Yusuf Ozdemir look like a boy scout,' Wise said. 'And he's just the sort of person who'd tear London apart trying to find out who'd stolen from him.'

'Do you think he's the one who killed Beanz?'

Wise didn't even have to think about it. 'Yeah, I do.'

'But that doesn't make sense,' Sarah said. 'How would he even know where Beanz was?'

'Maybe someone talked,' Wise said. 'Maybe someone spotted Beanz or overheard something. The man has a big enough crew working for him.'

'But Beanz was holed up in Tyrell's flat and we know the only person Beanz spoke to was Errol Gallagher. They had a conversation a few hours before he died. Gallagher has to be our man,' Sarah said. 'If we don't go after him now, who knows what could happen? The man could do a runner while we piss about here.'

'It's alright,' Wise said. 'I've got Jono over at Errol's place keeping an eye on things. We'll know if he goes anywhere.'

'You've what?' Sarah took a step back. 'Jono's at Gallagher's?'

'Yeah. Why? Is that a problem?'

'But he's supposed to be on desk duty. He shouldn't be doing surveillance. What if something happens? What if there's trouble?'

Wise glanced over at Hannah, who looked just as confused by Sarah's behaviour as he did. 'Is there something I don't know about?'

'No. No, there isn't,' Sarah replied, clearly trying to compose herself. 'I'm just worried about Jono. He's not as strong as he makes out. Christ, he shouldn't even be working today. Why didn't you send him home?'

'He's just sitting in his car, house watching. He's not going to get involved in anything.'

'Yeah? You sure about that? People are getting fucking killed out there and you send him off on his own? I can't believe it.'

'Sarah,' Wise said, stepping towards her. 'What's —'

Sarah held up a hand. 'Whatever. You're the governor. You make the decisions. I just work here.'

'Sarah,' Wise tried again, confused. She was normally so calm. 'What's wrong?'

She shook her head. 'I'm going for a smoke.' She spun on her heels, marched back to her desk, grabbed her cigarettes and phone, and stormed off out of the incident room.

'Don't forget your coat this time,' Brains called after her. 'You'll catch a death if you're not careful.'

But Sarah was gone, the door slamming shut behind her.

'What the hell was that about?' Wise asked.

'She's been in a strange mood these past few days.' Hannah said. 'I thought there was something wrong when we went to Western Towers yesterday, but she wouldn't say what it was.'

'And she snapped my head off earlier when I asked her if her husband minded her working on a Saturday,' Brains added. 'She stormed out then, too. She came back absolutely soaked through.'

Wise didn't like the sound of any of that. Sarah was always so dependable, so level-headed. She kept everything running for him. 'I'll have a chat with her later.'

'Do you want me to stick Konza's mug shot up on the board?' Brains asked.

'Yeah. If you could.' Wise looked over at the whiteboards as Brains got up, walked over to the printer, and collected the picture of Konza. There were already headshots of Cameron, Beanz, Tyrell, Ozdemir and Mad Errol up there. Tyrell's was the only picture not taken at a police station while in custody. Brains had picked an image from his Instagram account, a selfie of Tyrell in a doctor's coat on a ward. The others all looked like hardened criminals and none more so than Ollie Konza. In his mug shot, he was scowling at the camera, a curl to his top lip. His hair was tied back in cornrows and dangled down to his shoulders.

Wise walked over to the boarded headed *'What do we think?'* He wrote down Cameron's name in the centre, then above his, he added Konza's and put 'BOSS' in brackets next to it. To the side of Cameron's he wrote down 'Beanz' with 'KILLER' next to it and an arrow pointing to Cameron. To the right of Beanz' name, he wrote first Ozdemir's name, then Mad Errol's underneath that.

He stepped back. 'Right. Cameron works for Konza, distributing drugs for him. Beanz comes along and kills him. We think his motive was to steal his drugs because we didn't find anything in Beanz' flat. We do find a bottle of beer with The Turk's fingerprints on it, but Beanz got hold of that from a restaurant where Ozdemir was eating. He leaves it at the crime scene, so we all go running off after the wrong person, while he contacts and, presumably, sells what he's nicked to Mad Errol. We know they spoke last night a few hours before Beanz was murdered himself, while hiding at his friend Tyrell's place.'

'That sounds about right,' Hannah said.

'So why kill Beanz and Tyrell?'

'Tyrell is just in the wrong place at the wrong time. He's a nobody, just putting Beanz up.' Hannah walked over to the board and tapped Errol's picture. 'But this one? He knows Beanz has a load of drugs and wants them. He says he's going to buy them but why fork out a pile of cash when you can just kill the killer? So, he goes over, pops Tyrell, then goes to work on Beanz.'

'Or,' Brains said, 'you're pissed off that someone has had the cheek to steal from you and you want to make an example of Beanz to stop anyone else thinking you're weak.'

'Which brings us back to Konza,' Wise said.

'Is he really that bad?' Hannah asked.

'Yeah, he is,' Wise replied.

'He was first arrested when he was sixteen,' Brains said, 'for knifing another teenager in the heart. He got away with that when every witness recanted their statements — we believe under duress, but we couldn't prove it. Since then, he's got cleverer and more violent. He was running Brixton's drug trade by the time he was eighteen and has dealt with anyone moving in on his territory with utter ruthlessness.'

'Did you hear about a bloke called Mickey Kane?' Wise said. 'He allegedly got into a beef with Konza in a nightclub in Hackney. Just an argument over a woman. Nothing serious. But three nights later, he was found tied to a lamppost with a burning tyre around his neck and his face melted.'

Hannah nodded. 'I think everyone in the Met heard about that.'

'Konza's crew have adopted South American cartel tactics when dealing with anyone who threatens them,' Brains said. 'Whenever we have arrested any of them, we've had witnesses disappear, others mutilated and, if any of his boys looked like they might talk, they end up with their throats cut.'

'Shit,' Hannah said. 'And this is who we might be dealing with?'

'Yeah.' Wise rubbed his face. 'I've got to say I was a bit hesitant to go after Errol as it was. The mutilation of Beanz just isn't his sort of thing. The man's a businessman. I'm not saying he wouldn't kill if there was money in it, but I can't see him castrating someone.'

'Do we call the raid off then?' Hannah asked.

'I think so. For now. We need to do more digging first. Once we—' Wise's phone rang, cutting him off. He took it out of his pocket and saw Jono's name on the caller ID. A sense of dread ran through him as he answered it, putting the call on speaker. 'Jono? Everything okay?'

'I'm at Errol's place, Guv,' Jono said, his words spilling out in a rush. 'A van's just driven through his gate. Four IC3 males have got out and they're armed. I saw a couple of machetes and some pistols.'

'Have they seen you?' Wise asked. 'Are you in any danger?'

'Not yet. But I'm parked down the road. I —' Jono stopped talking and Wise heard the sound of an engine, more like a motorbike than a car. 'Fuck. No —'

They all heard the gunshot.

35

Wise, Hannah and Brains had all stared at the phone in Wise's hand, the silence from the other end petrifying after the loud bark of the gun. Calling Jono's name had got no reply. Trying to reach him on the radio had been equally unsuccessful.

After asking for immediate assistance from the police stations in Wimbledon and Roehampton, Wise drove like a madman down to East Sheen, lights flashing, siren wailing. Hannah was in the seat next to him; Brains and Callum were in the back. They'd diverted Hicksy and Donut from returning to Kennington and told them to get to East Sheen as fast as they bloody could as well, leaving only Sarah behind to man MIR-One.

The ARO van, originally intended for the raid on Errol Gallagher's house, travelled in convey behind Wise's Mondeo as the two vehicles rattled down Nine Elms Lane to Battersea and into Putney. The narrow roads were clogged up with weekend traffic, but most were willing to pull over and allow Wise and the AROs through as quickly as possible.

Still, Wise couldn't shake the dread and fear raging inside him, the sound of that gunshot still ringing in his ears. Why had he sent Jono down to watch Errol's place? He could've got the local police to do that. He should've sent Jono home or insisted he stayed at Kennington. But no, he'd fucked up and sent him alone to die.

Another officer down, another friend lost.

'Jono's going to be okay,' Hannah muttered next to him. No one else in the car replied. All knew what she'd said was a lie. They'd all been in the game too long to hold onto a fool's hope. Even young Callum, still a trainee, knew better.

They were still ten minutes out when the first radio calls came through from the local police. 'This Zero Yankee Bravo. We've arrived at Fife Road. We have an IC1 male in need of urgent medical assistance. Repeat, we need urgent medical assistance at the incident in Fife Road. Gunshot to the head.'

'Roger that, Zero Yankee Bravo. Alerting medical aid now. What is the current situation at the premises? Over,' a voice answered.

'The door to the house is open,' the officer replied, 'but we can't see anyone. No sign of the van that was reported to be here. Should we go in? Over.'

'Negative. Stay where you are until Armed Response units arrive. Repeat, stay where you are. The assailants might still be on the premises.'

Wise gulped for air as he listened, guilt weighing down on him. He'd caused this. This was all his fault.

They were on the Upper Richmond Road, fighting their way forward, through quiet high streets, full of restaurants, cafes, charity shops and estate agents. Christmas decorations flickered in windows and dangled across the street. Neon lit angels blew trumpets against darkening skies. Families with arms full of shopping bags watched the police vehicles whiz by, no doubt wondering what the emergency was, unaware that a good man lay dying or was already dead.

They swung left, down Sheen Lane, past houses that might have only been seven or eight miles from the estates of Bibury Close but, financially, they might as well have on the moon. They raced through suburban streets unused to scream of police sirens.

'This Zero Yankee Bravo. Armed Response have arrived. What's the ETA on the ambulance, over?' the officer at Fife Road radioed in.

'ETA three minutes, Zero Yankee Bravo. Repeat, ETA three minutes,' the dispatcher replied.

'We don't have three minutes. They need to get here now.'

Wise accelerated, wishing time would stop, hoping that Jono was still alive somehow, still holding on, still fighting. The road narrowed, parked cars on either side reducing it to single lane traffic. The houses grew bigger and bigger, hiding everything but their roofs from sight behind walls, fences and bushes.

'Come on,' Wise urged. 'Come on.'

Then they were there. At Mad Errol Gallagher's house. Police cars were everywhere. An Armed Response van, much like the one that had travelled with Wise was on site, plus three ambulances. All had their lights flashing, washing the quiet street in alien blues and reds that promised nothing but horror.

Wise skidded to a halt and was out of the car a second later, leaving his engine running and door open because he'd spotted Jono's Volvo. It was ten metres away from Errol's house, surrounded by police officers and an ambulance crew, its own doors open, blood spattered across the windscreen.

Too much blood.

A police officer came to stop Wise, but he had his warrant card out without breaking stride. 'That's my officer in the car.'

The uniform got herself between Wise and the Volvo, holding up both hands. 'Sir, you can't go over there.'

'Yes, I can.' Wise tried to push past but the woman had him now, wrapping her arms around him, trying to block his view. 'Get out of my —'

Wise stopped. He could see Jono slumped back in his seat, head rolled to the left, a bloody mess on the side of his face. Obviously dead. As Wise knew he would be.

The strength went from his legs, and he was glad of the officer now, holding him back. Holding him up. Wise steadied himself, fighting his emotions, trying to keep his face unmoved, in a mask, burying his guilt, his despair, hiding his heartbreak.

'Oh my God,' Hannah said from behind him.

'I'm sorry, sir,' the officer said.

Wise nodded, stepping back, unable to take his eyes off his dead friend. Only back in the job three days earlier.

Another car stopped outside the house in Fife Road. Wise looked over and saw Hicksy climb out, his eyes wide and full of worry.

'Jono!' he cried and started to run towards them. This time it was Wise's turn to intercept the officer.

'Hicksy. No,' Wise said, grabbing hold of his friend. 'You don't want to go over there. Not now.'

'Get out of my fucking way.' Hicksy tried pushing Wise, but he tightened his grip, fixing his feet.

'Mate,' Wise whispered in his ear. 'There's nothing you can do. He's gone.'

'No, he's not. I don't believe it. He can't be.' Hicksy's voice cracked.

'I'm sorry.'

'No.'

Then Hannah was with them, taking Hicksy from Wise, hugging the officer, and Hicksy began to sob into her shoulder.

Wise stepped away, giving them room, and looked around. Brains, Donut and Callum stood in a tight group, all as shell-shocked as each other. He went over, composing himself, holding his shattered soul together. 'Are you three okay?' It was a pointless thing to say. Inadequate in every way. He could see they weren't.

Brains nodded all the same, giving him permission to leave them.

Wise moved on, heading to the house. Even with the madness around it, it was a beautiful building, just a little shy of a mansion. A waist-high brick wall separated the property from the road with a gravel drive leading from Fife Road to the front door with space for multiple cars to park. At the moment, apart from emergency vehicles, a Porsche Macan and a black Range Rover took up two of the spaces. A black iron gate lay mangled to one side, trampled no doubt by the van Jono had reported.

A man in a long black overcoat saw Wise approaching and came over. 'I'm DCI Nathan Rane from Roehampton. Are you DI Wise?'

'Yes.' Wise almost choked on the word, as if speaking would somehow unleash all the turmoil inside him.

'I'm sorry about your man,' Rane said.

'Yeah. Me too,' Wise replied. He nodded towards the house. 'What's happened in there?'

'Grim stuff,' Rane replied. 'Two dead. A man and a woman. The woman was shot but the man ...' He shook his head.

'Mutilated?'

'That's putting it mildly.'

'How bad?'

'Put it this way, he's going to be singing soprano up in heaven.'

Wise doubted Mad Errol would make it past Saint Peter's pearly gates, but he kept that thought to himself. 'Can I have a look?'

'Yeah but you'll have to be quick,' Rane said. 'We're waiting for the SOCOs to arrive, and you know what they're like about people trampling over their crime scenes.'

'I'll be careful.'

'This way, then.' Rane headed into the house, Wise following close behind.

If the outside looked like a house that wasn't quite a mansion, then whoever had decorated the inside had wanted it to look like a palace. Black and white tiles formed a checker pattern across the floor, while a chandelier, too big for the space, dangled overhead. A large round oak table stood next to the stairs, with a floral display taking up most of its surface. Family photographs in silver frames were scattered around it. Wise wandered over and saw the man he'd once known so well grinning away, alongside with an attractive blonde woman, accompanied by two children who grew in size between pictures. They looked like the perfect happy family.

'The woman's through here,' Rane said, pointing to an open doorway. The living room was just as ostentatious as the hallway and offered views of a beautiful garden and a long swimming pool. But

Wise's attention was quickly drawn to the dead woman sitting in one of the armchairs, a bullet hole in the centre of her forehead.

Wise recognised her from the photographs in the hallway. 'Mrs. Gallagher.'

'It would appear so,' Rane replied.

Wise looked around the room. The drawers to the sideboard were either open or pulled out completely, with their contents lying scattered over the floor. Cushions on the sofa had been cut open and turned inside out. Even DVDs had been taken out from the TV unit and thrown everywhere. 'They were looking for something.'

'Considering how quickly we got here, they still managed to turn the whole place over pretty much and still get away.'

'We believe a quantity of drugs or cash were stolen from a dealer in London a few days back. The man who stole them was murdered last night. Someone had shoved his balls in his mouth.'

'Let me show you the other victim,' Rane said. 'Because it sounds like the work of the same person. He's upstairs.'

Again, Wise followed Rane back out into the hallway and then up the staircase.

Mad Errol Gallagher waited for them in the main bedroom. He sat on the floor with his back to the wall, legs outstretched. His groin, like Beanz's, was a bloody mess, his blood staining the white carpet in a metre wide circumference. Dead eyes stared at Wise, that scar on his cheek vivid against his alabaster skin, his mouth unnaturally open, full of his genitals, dripping more blood down his chin and over his shirt.

'Is that Mr. Gallagher?' Rane asked.

'That's him,' Wise replied. Mad Errol might have done a lot of bad things in his life, but that was no way to die. 'Poor sod.'

There was a safe set into the wall above his head, its door open and empty of any contents.

'I'm not sure they found what they were looking for in there,' Rane said. He pointed to a doorway. 'There's a walk-in wardrobe through there that's been ripped apart and the other bedrooms have been turned over too. I doubt they would have done that before getting him to open the safe.'

Wise nodded. 'Yeah. Why carry on looking if you've got what you were after?'

'Exactly.'

Wise looked down at the man he'd once considered a friend and shook his head. So many people had died, and it wasn't over yet.

36

It was a flurry of activity in Fife Road. The AROs had gone home but there were more uniforms on site, most going from door to door looking for witnesses. Red and white police tape cordoned off the immediate area around Errol Gallagher's house, while blue and white tape blocked off access to the road further down.

Halogen lights blazed away in Errol's driveway, turning the afternoon darkness into daylight once more as SOCOs searched for tyre prints and other evidence. Jono's car had been covered with a forensic tent to protect any evidence in case it started to rain again and to provide the dead officer with some privacy while everyone did their jobs.

Thank God they had too because word had got out to the wider world somehow, perhaps via one of the neighbours who had watched the coming and goings from their windows, and TV crews had turned up to find out what the drama was.

Wise stood on the pavement opposite Errol's house with the rest of his team, feeling more than a little broken. He knew he should send everyone home, but their company was all that was keeping him together right then. Even so, his eyes kept returning to the awning over Jono's car and, each time they did, the pain in his heart grew ever greater.

'When we find whoever did this,' Hicksy growled, 'I'm going to kill them. I'm going to rip their bloody throats out with my bare hands.'

Hannah put her arm around Hicksy's shoulders and pulled him close to her. 'I'm so sorry.'

'He was my best friend,' Hicksy said. 'I can't believe he's dead.'

Callum had tears running down his cheeks as he watched the house, shaking his head. 'I can't believe it. I just can't believe it.'

Car headlights came around the corner of Fife Road, drawing their attention. It pulled to a stop near them and, when the engine was turned off and the lights went out, Wise saw that it was DCI Roberts' black Audi S3 Sedan. When she got out of the car, she looked like she'd aged a hundred years since he'd seen her that morning. But, maybe, they all had.

She walked over, stopping by Hicksy first. She placed her hand on his arm and give it a gentle squeeze. 'I'm so sorry, Hicksy. He was a good man.'

Hicksy nodded. 'The best.'

She looked around at the others. 'How are you all holding up?'

'It's tough to take in,' Hannah said.

'You should all head home,' Roberts said. 'There's nothing you can do here right now. Get a lift off some uniforms if you have to, but go home and be with your loved ones. Try to get some sleep. It's been a terrible shock at the end of an awful day.'

That got nods from everyone. Hannah looked over at Wise. 'You going to be okay, Guv?'

'Yeah,' Wise replied, unable to say any more than that.

'Head home, DS Markham,' Roberts said. 'I'll stay here with Simon.'

'Okay. I'll be in tomorrow,' Hannah said.

'See you how you feel,' Roberts replied. 'Don't feel you have to. Your well-being is more important.'

With one last look towards Wise, she headed off with the others.

Roberts turned to Wise. 'And how are you, Simon?'

Wise shook his head, struggling to formulate words.

'I understand Jono was shot?' she asked.

'Yeah. It was quick, at least.'

'What about inside the house?'

'The wife was shot downstairs. Gallagher was castrated upstairs, like the kid this morning.'

'It's the same people then?'

'Without a doubt. The house had been turned over too, the safe opened. Whoever did it is looking for something. Drugs, most likely. Cash maybe. We still don't know.'

'Do you think they found anything?'

'It's hard to say. Maybe. Maybe not. The SOCOs might be able to tell us if there were any drugs in the house at any point but it'll be hard to say if it's what the killer or killers are after.' Wise sucked his bottom lip for a second. 'My gut says no though. I reckon they'll still be looking. Still hunting.'

'But if they came here, they must think Gallagher had it.'

'Maybe Beanz sold it to him before he got killed last night and they wanted to retrieve it.' Wise shrugged. 'Who knows?'

'By the way, Detective Chief Superintendent Walling is on way down here, Simon,' Roberts said.

'Furious, no doubt, that we've ruined his Saturday.'

'He's upset about Jono, like the rest of us.' Roberts tried a smile. 'And he can handle the media.'

'He's good at that.'

'Have you made any progress on the case since this morning?'

'Just before we came down here, we found out that Cameron Nketiam, the first victim, worked for Ollie Konza. He's young but vicious. He's modelled himself after the Columbian cartels.' Wise glanced back at the house. 'Mutilation is right up his street.'

'Well, if it's him, he's going to have the whole Met after him now,' Roberts said. 'There won't be anywhere in London he'll be able to hide.'

'Hicksy heard he might have a place in Peckham somewhere.'

'I don't care if he's holed up in Buckingham Palace. These gangsters might think they're tough but we're still the biggest gang in town and no one gets away with killing one of ours.'

Another car pulled up by the TV crews. A Mercedes. A tall and very broad man climbed out the back and immediately put on a peaked cap. 'Looks like Walling has arrived,' Wise said.

An officer held the blue and white tape up for Walling to duck under and he walked over to join Wise and Roberts. 'Anne. Simon. A sad business. DS Gray was a fine officer.'

'He was,' Wise said. 'He'll be missed.'

'He was married, wasn't he?' Walling asked.

'To Pat.' Wise puffed out his cheeks, dread building once more, thinking how the news would destroy another life. 'I should go and see her. She's not been told yet.'

'I'll come with you,' Roberts said. 'It's always better to deliver a death notice with someone — especially when it's one of our own.'

'That would be great, if you could,' Wise replied. He and Roberts might not be the best of friends, but he knew he could do with the support. The last time he'd seen Jono's wife was when Jono had been in intensive care with blood clots in his lungs and now, he was going to have to tell her that her husband had been killed on duty.

'I thought DS Gray was on medical leave?' Walling said.

'He was, sir,' Wise said. 'He was being treated for lung cancer. He only came back to work on Thursday.'

Walling took a deep breath and rubbed his face. 'Christ. That's not good. Not good at all.'

'I thought he was supposed to be on desk duty?' Roberts said.

'Yeah, he was — but he wanted to do more and we're short staffed.' Wise looked over at the tent covering Jono's car and thought of his body inside. The hole in his head. 'He was just sitting in the car, watching the house.'

'Okay. We can worry about the rights and the wrongs of that decision for the enquiry,' Walling said. 'I take it this has something to do with the death of the drug dealer the other day?'

'That's right,' Wise said. He went over the events of the last few days and the various leads they'd chased.

'It sounds like this Beanz chap really stirred up a hornet's nest. We need to get this thing under control and Mr. Konza in custody as quickly as possible.' Walling's eyes drifted over towards the press. 'Let's chat in the morning back at Kennington and come up with a plan. In the meantime, you should see DS Gray's widow while I deal with this mob here.'

'Thank you, sir,' Wise said.

'Do you know Jono's address?' Roberts asked.

Wise nodded. 'I have it on my phone. It's over in Hackney.'

'Okay. I'll follow you in my car.'

Walling straightened his uniform and ran a hand down the front of his jacket. 'Good luck and don't worry — we'll get these bastards.'

Wise didn't reply. It was hard to think after what had happened to Jono but there was something really wrong about the whole investigation. He could understand Konza or whoever it was getting the jump on them once? But twice? It should've been impossible.

He headed over to the Mondeo, stewing it over in his mind. If he could work out how the killers were getting their intelligence, maybe he could turn the table on the bastards.

37

Sarah sat in her car in the police station car park, crying her eyes out. She'd heard the news about Jono and what had happened to Errol Gallagher and his wife. Heard what that bastard and his boy, Ollie Konza, had done.

All because she'd given them Gallagher's address.

The rain had started again. It hammered her windscreen and pounded the car roof. Hiding her from view. Hiding her shame.

What had she done?

Christ.

She didn't know what to do. How could she get out of this mess?

Her phone rang. She picked it up and saw the caller ID said NAILS.

It was him.

Sarah rejected the call. She was never speaking to that bastard again. Not unless it was to nick him. But how could she do that without confessing what she'd done and going to prison herself?

She couldn't do time. She couldn't. She'd rather kill herself first.

Her phone rang again. NAILS. Sarah declined the call again.

It rang again. She rejected it again.

Immediately, her phone chirped once more.

'Just fuck off,' she shouted at it. 'Leave me alone.' This time she let it just ring out and go to voice mail. Hopefully, the bastard would get the message.

Her phone pinged again. It was a message this time. She opened it. It was a picture of her husband, taken through a window. He was sitting at home in their lounge, watching TV. He was wearing the clothes he'd had on that morning.

The phone pinged again. Another message. Another picture. It was a selfie of a masked man, holding a gun, standing outside her house, her husband still visible through the window.

'No.'

Dear God. They were going to kill her husband. She had to get home. She had to stop them.

Sarah fumbled her handbag open, searching for the car keys buried under all the crap she dumped in there. She could barely see, the tears falling even more now, her heart racing, the nausea rising.

Bing.

Another message. *Answer the phone, bitch.*

The phone rang again, startling her so much, she dropped it into the footwell on the passenger side. Panicking, she lunged after it, all coordination gone. Sarah snatched it up but her hands were shaking so much, it took three attempts to answer it. 'H... Hell... Hello.'

'About fucking time,' Tom Wise said.

'Please, don't kill my husband. I'll do anything.'

'You know the drill, darling. When I ring, you answer. Do that and everyone stays safe.'

Sarah just sobbed down the phone.

'Pull yourself together, Sarah. People will get suspicious if they see you wailing, and I can't have that. Not yet.'

'You killed ... you killed my friend.'

'Who? Not Mad Errol?'

'There was a police officer in a car outside the house.'

'What? That old geezer with the mangy hair? He was a copper?' The bastard actually sounded surprised.

'He was on my team. He was my friend.'

'Fucking hell. Old Simon's going to upset. That's the second one in a year. People will think he's cursed.'

'Only because of you.'

'Well, them's the breaks. Now, guess what?'

Sarah closed her eyes and prayed to God to save her from this madness. 'What?'

'We didn't find the drugs,' Tom said. 'Unbelievable, I know, but we didn't and old Mad Errol, well, he wasn't that helpful in the end. It turns out he was pissed off that we whacked his missus. And he knew he was dead anyway, so he gave us the finger and let Ollie cut his balls off.'

Sarah couldn't believe what she was hearing, how matter of fact he was about it all, like he was discussing a prang in his car, instead of murdering human beings.

'So, there's a load of drugs out there, somewhere, that belong to me,' Tom continued. 'I want you to find them.'

'What?' Sarah felt like she'd been punched in the head.

'You're the fucking detective. You've got all the tricks and the tools. I want you to find them for me.'

'I can't do that. You know I can't.'

'Oh yes, you can,' Tom said. 'And, if you ever have any doubts, just look at that lovely picture of Mister Choi and think how much you want him to see old age. Should be motivation enough for you.'

'I... I...'

'You have forty-eight hours.'

'What? Forty —'

The line went dead.

Sarah sat back, unable to catch her breath, as her heart hammered away faster than the rain and the inside of the car began to shift in and out of focus. Nausea squeezed her gut and she thought she was going to pass out. In fact, she wanted to. It'd be a blessing. It'd be —

Her phone rang again, the sound sending another wave of panic through her. What did he want now? What fresh horror was he going to ask of her?

But it wasn't him. It was Ken, her husband.

Sarah gulped, trying to catch her breath, sniffing up tears. 'Hel ... hello? Ken?'

'Hey,' her husband replied. 'How are you getting on?'

'Er ... Okay ...'

'It doesn't sound okay. Are you sure you're alright?' God, it hurt so much. His voice was so full of love.

'A colleague died today.'

'Oh my God, who?'

'Jon ... Jono.'

'No wonder you sound so upset. Do you want me to come and pick you up?'

'No ... you just stay where you are. I've still got work to do. I'll ... I'll be home late.'

'Alright, my love,' Ken replied. 'Take it easy on yourself, eh?'

'I'll try,' Sarah said, 'and hey, I love you, Ken Choi.'

'Blimey, now you're really making me worried.' He laughed and, for one brief heartbeat, Sarah almost felt like everything would be okay.

Then she thought of the man outside her house and what he would do if she failed to find the bastard's drugs. All the lives he'd destroy.

38

Wise was shattered by the time he got home. The visit to Pat had left him utterly drained and he could barely remember the drive back, his mind working on auto-pilot. All he wanted to do was crawl into bed and hope that, somehow, he'd be able to sleep and forget the day.

However, as he climbed out of his Mondeo, he was surprised to see his father's car parked outside his house. A thousand thoughts rushed through his head; had he invited him over and forgotten about it? Or was something wrong with him or Jean? Had she called his father over to look after the kids because something had happened to her? Had something happened to the kids?

He sprinted to the door, trying not to think what else could've gone wrong. He opened the door and was met by the sound of laughter, of his dad chuckling away with Jean. They were in the lounge, the fire on, a Stella in his father's hand and a glass of Sauvignon Blanc in Jean's, a World Cup report playing soundless on the TV.

Thank God. Wise swallowed down his panic and tried to look as if nothing was wrong.

'Dad? I didn't expect to see you here,' Wise said as his father got up to hug him.

'I was chatting to Jean earlier and she invited me over for a bit of supper and to watch the football,' his dad said. 'We thought you'd be back in time for the game.'

Wise glanced over at Jean. 'Sorry. I should've called. It's not been a good day.'

'What happened?' Jean asked.

'I lost a man today. Jono. He was shot this afternoon. I've just been to see his wife.'

'He was the chap who had cancer?'

'That's him. He only came back to work on Thursday.'

'Why don't you sit down, son,' his dad said. 'I'll get you a beer.'

Wise allowed himself to be guided to one of the armchairs. As he sat down, he could feel the exhaustion of the day deep in his bones. It'd been a nightmare from start to finish.

'Here you go, Simon,' his dad said, returning with a cold Stella in his hand. 'Have a gulp of that.'

Wise took the bottle and drank, savouring the chilled liquid. Then he noticed Jean hadn't moved. She stood to one side, her arms wrapped around herself, her face full of sadness. 'Are you alright, love?'

'I was just thinking of Jono's wife, and what she must be going through right now,' Jean said. 'It's what we all dread — that knock on the door, strangers on the other side of it, waiting to tell you your loved one is dead.'

'I know. It was hard telling her, especially after everything she's already been through lately.'

'Is it worth it, Simon?'

'What do you mean?'

'Is *The Job* worth dying for?' Jean managed to fill the words with utter contempt. 'Is it worth risking your life every day to chase villains around? You've got two kids upstairs who want their dad around to see them grow up.'

Wise noticed she didn't include herself in that statement. 'Getting killed on duty hardly ever happens. The Job's not as dangerous as it seems.'

'No?' Jean spat back. 'Tell that to Andy's wife and kids. Tell that to your brother the next time he threatens to kill you. Tell —'

'Whoa, whoa, whoa,' Wise's father said. 'What do you mean by that? What's happened? Has Tom said something to you, Simon?'

'It's nothing, Dad. Don't worry about it.' Wise shot Jean a glare, warning her not to say any more.

Jean wasn't having any of it, though. 'What do you mean, nothing? Haven't you told your dad that Tom's a murdering gangster? That he threatened you, me and the kids?'

Wise's father stood up, his face white, confusion in his eyes. He looked at Wise. 'What's she saying, Si?'

Wise went over to his father, seeing his pain. 'It's nothing worth worrying about now, Dad. Tom might have got himself into a bit of bother, that's all. I was looking into it, and he got angry when he found out. He said a few things in the heat of the moment.'

'A bit of bother?' Jean repeated. 'They told you he was waging a war, killing people.'

'Jean!' Wise snapped, his father in his arms, wanting nothing more than to protect his old man from the realities of the world and the cruelty of Jean's words. 'This isn't the time or the place.'

'When is it then?' Jean said. 'Would our funerals be more appropriate? I'm sorry, Sam. I really am, but Simon needs to tell you the truth about Tom.' She turned on her tail then and stormed out of the living room. Wise listened to the sound of her feet stamping their way up the stairs and the bedroom door slamming shut.

'What's going on, Si?' his dad asked, his eyes wide with worry.

'Sit down, Dad,' Wise said as gently as he could. He helped lower the man into an armchair, aware of how frail his father was now, the years having chipped away at the superman who'd raised him, and hoped his heart was strong enough for what Wise had to say. 'I'm sorry you had to hear that. I told you things between me and Jean were a bit ropey.'

'I know, but what's that got to do with Tom?'

Wise picked up his beer and had another swig, buying himself a few seconds, knowing that, once he started talking, everything was going to change, from his relationship with his father, his father's with Tom and so on. He was also aware that, depending on what his dad said to Tom next time they saw each other, Jean's little truth bomb might very well provoke Tom to act on his threats.

'Back in the summer, I was visited by a couple of detectives working for a special unit. They were investigating a war that had started up across organised crime in London. Apparently, there was a new player who was trying to take over. They had a picture to show me of the person they thought was responsible. A picture of a man they thought was me.'

'You?'

Wise nodded. 'When I saw the picture, I wasn't surprised they thought that. The man was identical to me in every way. It was Tom.'

'Tom.'

'Yeah. I didn't tell them that, though. I claimed ignorance at the time because I couldn't believe it myself. But then I started to look into things myself. Nothing serious, just a little nosing about here and there, but Tom found out and he called me up. He implied that, if I didn't back off, bad things could happen to Jean and the kids.'

His dad shook his head. 'No. He didn't mean that. He wouldn't hurt them. You must've misunderstood what he said.'

'I wish I had, Dad. I wish I had.'

'I don't believe it. There's a mix-up somewhere. It's not Tom. I mean, he screwed up when he was younger but he's getting his life back now. Building something good.'

'He's not. Far from it.'

His dad stood up, pushing Wise's hands away. 'Look, I don't know what's going on between you and Jean, but don't blame it on Tom. And if your ... your colleagues think Tom's up to no good, you should be fighting to prove they're wrong — not side with them against your own family.' He walked to the front door and snatched his coat off the hook.

Wise went over. 'Dad, this is the last thing I ever wanted, believe me.'

His dad pulled his coat on, not meeting Wise's eyes. 'I'm really disappointed in you, son. I never thought I'd ever say that, but I am.'

'Dad —'

His father opened the door. 'Thank Jean for the food and tell the kids I love them.'

'Dad, please —'

But his father wasn't listening. He was off down their little path and out the gate to his car. He didn't look back as he unlocked the car, nor did he when he got in. Wise went after him, calling his name, begging for him not to go, but his father kept his eyes fixed firmly on the road as he started the engine, and he was off down the street a second later.

Wise stayed standing by his front gate long after his father's car lights had disappeared in the distance, feeling lost, feeling broken.

It was the cold that brought him to his senses. Its cruel bite snapping him out of his melancholy. None of this was Wise's doing. It was Tom causing all this chaos. Tom's actions that were upsetting everyone and screwing up his life.

The solution was still the same: Tom had to be stopped.

Once that was done, they could all get on with rebuilding the damage he'd done.

As he walked back into the house, Wise thought yet again about what had happened that day. More importantly, he thought about how it had happened.

He didn't care if Konza was the world's greatest gangster, there was no way he could've got the jump on Wise and his team twice in one day like that.

Not without help.

The man was getting the same intelligence Wise was at the same time. And there was only one way that could happen.

Sunday 11th December

39

8 a.m. Sunday morning and Wise was in Walling's office. Roberts was also there, as well as DCI Rane from Roehampton. Everyone was seated around Walling's desk, armed with teas and coffees. Wise was the only one in a suit, though. He didn't care that it was the weekend. He needed the strength it gave him, his armour to go into battle.

He'd spent the night going over everything, looking for areas where his team might've gone wrong or avenues of enquiries he might've missed, and from there, he'd pondered over how they were going to catch Ollie Konza.

'I spoke to the commissioner last night and he said that we can have whatever resources we need to put this Ollie Konza behind bars,' Walling said. He looked strange out of uniform, despite the formality of the white shirt and round-collared jumper he had on. 'At this moment, extra officers and support staff are being notified that they are now part of Operation Anthem, and they will report to this station tomorrow. They will now be at your disposal for this investigation.'

'Thank you, sir,' Wise replied. 'It'll make a massive difference.'

'DCI Roberts will be the SIO, assisted by yourself and DCI Rane here,' Walling continued. 'That's no reflection on the job you've done so far, Simon. Far from it. I went over the case last night and you've done an excellent job. What happened yesterday couldn't have been foreseen with the information you had available.'

'I appreciate that,' Wise said, even though it didn't make him feel any better about what had happened.

'Now, what are your thoughts on next steps?'

'There are three avenues I feel that we need to explore,' Wise said. 'First of all, we need to find Ollie Konza. To do that, we need to go after his known associates, his businesses, ideally get hold of his phone or phones, identify and track down his vehicles, get into his financials and crawl over every other millimetre of his life. We also need hard, physical evidence that can link him to our crime scenes, so that means digging up whatever forensics, witnesses, video footage and any other data we can find that can put him in Western Towers and Fife Road at the time of the murders — or, even better, in the room with the victims.'

'I agree,' Roberts said. 'No matter how clever he thinks he is, he'll have slipped up somewhere. No one's perfect.'

'I also don't think Konza has found the drugs or whatever it was that Beanz stole from him,' Wise continued. 'Both Western Towers and Fife Road had been ransacked by the killer or killers. Maybe they found something in the end, but I don't think so.'

'As we said yesterday, you don't rip a place apart like that if you've got what you came for,' Rane said. 'No, the drugs are still out there.'

'If that's the case, then Konza is still going to be looking for them,' Wise said. 'If we can find them first, that might give us a chance to get ahead of Konza for once. Maybe we can even use them to lure him out of hiding and into handcuffs.'

'Konza must've believed that Gallagher had bought the drugs from Beanz,' Roberts said. 'That would explain why he went after him.'

'If that's the case, where would Gallagher have stashed them if they weren't at his house?' Walling asked.

'That's what we need to find out, sir,' Wise said.

The super nodded. 'You said there were three avenues.'

Wise winced. 'I'm not sure how to say this.'

'Why?'

'I spent all last night trying to work out how Konza has been able to stay ahead of us.' Wise took a sip of his coffee. 'Beanz was in hiding. The only person he was communicating with was Gallagher. We only tracked him down because Brains followed some digital breadcrumbs after we cell-sited Beanz's mobile. So how did Konza know where he was?'

Wise let that question sink in for a moment before continuing. 'Now, maybe Beanz talked before he died and told Konza that he'd given the drugs to Gallagher. But, if he had, why wait until the afternoon to go around to Gallagher's home to retrieve them? Why not go to Gallagher's immediately after killing Beanz?'

'Because he didn't know where Gallagher lived?' Rane replied.

'Exactly,' Wise said. 'But, somehow, he managed to find out while we were getting ready to go around there and beat us to it by half an hour. That's just a tad too convenient for my liking.'

Walling leaned forward in his seat, the leather creaking at the shift in weight. 'What are you suggesting, Simon?'

'The only thing I can think of is that Konza has someone telling him what we learn in real time. He then acts on that information while we are getting ready to move.' Wise looked from Walling to Roberts to Rane. 'I think one of my team is working for Konza.'

Roberts nearly dropped her cup of tea. 'You're joking.'

'I wish I was,' Wise said, 'but it's the only explanation that I can think of. Beanz was an idiot, but he knew who he was dealing with. He was hiding at Tyrell's for a reason. Yeah, he should've dumped his mobile, but Konza can't track phones — only we can.'

'Oh my God. An inside man?' Roberts said, shaking her head. 'This is the last thing we need.'

'I think he's got a point, though, as unpleasant as it is,' Rane added. 'I've been a police officer too long to believe in coincidences of any kind.'

'If you're right, we'll have to take your team off the investigation,' Walling said. 'And let Professional Standards know.'

'Perhaps there's another alternative,' Wise said.

Walling raised an eyebrow. 'And that is?'

'We keep them in place.'

'But whoever is feeding Konza information will continue to do so. We'll never catch him if that continues.'

'It may seem like that, but we didn't know they were doing that before. Now, we do.' Wise paused for a moment. 'What if we use that to our advantage?'

'How?' Roberts asked.

'If we find out where the drugs are, Konza's spy will tell him. If that's the case, we can be there waiting to nick Konza the moment he shows his face.'

'Do you have any idea who the officer is?' Rane asked.

Wise took another gulp of coffee. 'I don't think there's a long list of possibilities. Hicksy — that's DS Roy Hicks — was Jono's best friend and partner. If he knew Konza was going to Gallagher's, he could easily have come up with an excuse to get him out of there, so I think we can eliminate him as a possible. I'd rule out Callum Chabolah as well. He's still a trainee and has little access to valuable information. So, that leaves DS Hannah Markham, DC Ian Vollers, DC Sarah Choi or DC Alan Park as our insider.'

'Hannah's new,' Roberts said.

'I know,' Wise replied, 'but she only transferred in from Brixton, so it's not impossible for her to know the local OCGs, and she did request to join my team specifically. But my gut says no.'

Walling glowered at him from under his thick eyebrows. 'Your gut's been wrong before.'

Any other day, Wise would've been upset by that jab, but not that morning. 'That's why I'm not ruling her out, sir.'

'I'm not sure DC Vollers has got the mental capacity to be an inside man,' Roberts said. 'Sometimes, I'm amazed he gets his shoes on by himself, let alone on the correct feet.'

'I don't think it's him either,' Wise agreed.

'That leaves Choi and Park.' Roberts rubbed her face. 'I can't believe it's either of them.'

'Have any of them been acting strangely since the case began?' Rane asked.

Wise took a deep breath before answering. 'Yeah. Sarah Choi. She's had a few emotional outbursts that are really out of character and she got quite agitated yesterday when I mentioned Jono was at Gallagher's.' Wise held up a hand. 'But as Detective Chief Superintendent Walling mentioned, I've got things very wrong before.'

'Sarah's one of our most dependable officers,' Roberts said.

Wise nodded. 'She's the heart of my team, keeps us all on target and a genius when it comes to searching through CCTV. Most of all though, she's a friend. Even suspecting her breaks my heart. Especially after what happened to Andy.'

'She has access to all the information, though,' Roberts said.

'More than anyone else on the team.'

'And you still don't want to pull her out?' Walling asked.

Wise sat back. 'I think we have to watch all of them until we're sure who's leaking our intelligence. Once we know who the insider is, we can use that knowledge to get to Konza.'

'I agree,' Rane said. 'We need to let this play out.'

'Okay,' Walling replied. 'We'll do it your way. Just make sure we get the right result — and quickly.'

'We will,' Wise said.

Roberts stood up. 'Let's get to work, then.'

40

Wise walked into MIR-One, flanked by Roberts and Rane. Despite everything, he felt stronger than he had for a long time and ready to deal with what lay ahead. The idea that he had another bent officer on his team had stirred up a fury that left no room for grief. He'd mourn Jono later. Justice had to come first.

What was left of his team had all come in. Even Hicksy was there, looking like he'd spent the night drinking and crying. Hannah had a rather shell-shocked expression, as if she wasn't really taking anything in. Brains was safely behind his monitor, no doubt finding some comfort in the Matrix. Callum was scrolling through his phone in that way people do when they aren't thinking about anything and Donut was sitting at his desk, waiting, as ever, for something to happen or someone to tell him what to do. And then there was Sarah, staring at her screen from under her fringe, her face set in grim determination.

Was Wise wrong about her?

Dear God, he really wished he was. More than anything.

'Good to see you all,' he said, moving to the whiteboards. 'I hope some of you managed to get some sleep last night because we have a lot of work ahead of us. I've just come from Detective Chief Superintendent Walling's office, and from tomorrow, we'll have more than enough officers helping us. The boss — DCI Roberts — will be leading what is now designated Operation Anthem, assisted by DCI Rane from Roehampton, who most of you met yesterday, and myself.'

Roberts looked around the room. 'If any of you feel like you'd rather be at home today to help deal with yesterday's events, please do so. No one will think any the less of you for doing so. You all know more than any of us that Jono was a great friend and colleague and his loss hurts.'

A few eyes glanced over at Hicksy.

'I'm not going anywhere,' he growled. 'I want to catch the bastard responsible and I ain't stopping until that happens.'

'I wouldn't expect anything else from you, mate,' Wise said.

'Okay, that's good,' Roberts added. 'As Simon said, we've got more support arriving tomorrow but, for now, we need to focus on yesterday's crime scenes. The killer or killers didn't magically appear out of nowhere. Jono reported a van turning up at Fife Road and Simon said he also heard a motorbike. DCI Rane's team are going door-to-door, looking for either witnesses or private CCTV footage, but let's start going over the road cams and see what we can find both there and around Bibury Close.'

'I'm working on that now,' Sarah said.

'Thank you,' Roberts replied. 'I take it we didn't have any luck with witnesses at Western Towers yesterday?'

'They don't like the police down there,' Donut said.

'Right. Well, let's —' Roberts was cut off by the sound of Wise's phone ringing.

He checked the screen and didn't recognise the number. Ordinarily, he'd reject the call, but something told him that would be a mistake. Heading into his office, he answered it. 'Detective Inspector Wise.'

'Hello, sir. This is PC Hayes,' a woman said. 'I'm guarding the scene at Friary Road.'

'Has something happened?' Wise asked.

'Yes, sir. In the flat upstairs. Leon Tomoral's been murdered, sir. His flatmates got back from a night away a few moments ago and found his body,' Hayes replied.

'Shit. How was he killed?'

'He's been stabbed multiple times, sir.'

'Right, thanks for letting me know. I'll be down shortly with the cavalry,' Wise said. 'Keep the scene safe until we get there.'

'Yes, sir.'

Wise ended the call and headed back out into the incident room.

'Everything okay?' Roberts asked.

'There's been another murder,' Wise said and updated them all about Leon.

'Jesus Christ,' Roberts said. 'We only let him out yesterday.'

'It doesn't look good, does it?' Wise replied. 'I said we'd head over straight away — if that's okay with you.'

Roberts nodded. 'I'll go and get my coat.'

'Sarah,' Wise called out. 'Can you arrange for the SOCOs to go over and get some uniforms down there to help as well? The PC I spoke to is supposed to be guarding Cameron's flat downstairs. She needs help quickly.'

'Of ... of course,' Sarah replied, looking more shaken up than anyone. 'I'll call the pathologist as well.'

'Hicksy, Donut, I want you down there as well,' Wise said. 'The others can stay here and work on the other murders.'

'I'm going to head back to Fife Road,' Rane said, 'and help the troops there. Let me know if anything else happens, otherwise I'll see you back here tomorrow.'

'Thank you, Nathan,' Roberts said. 'It's good to have you onboard.'

Hannah wandered over to Wise. 'Don't you want me to come with you?' she asked, keeping her voice low.

For a moment, Wise considered taking her to his office and telling her his fears about Sarah, but a tiny voice at the back of his head whispered *what if she's the insider?* 'I'd rather you stayed here and keep an eye on things. Maybe go over everything and see if there's anything we've missed.'

'Okay.' Hannah looked disappointed.

'Look,' Wise said. 'This case ... it's spiralling, and we're being pulled in a hundred different directions. If something comes up while I'm over at Friary Road, I know you can deal with it.'

'Sure,' Hannah replied.

'Just keep me updated if you uncover anything — And call me before you do anything. Okay?'

'I will.'

'Good. I'll catch you in a bit, then.' Wise returned to his office, retrieved his coat and keys, then paused. He'd not spoken to his wife since the argument the night before. He knew he should call her, but what would he say? A part of him was still angry that she'd told his dad about Tom in the way that she did, furious at her brutality, the way she used his father's feelings and vulnerability to hurt Wise.

No. He wasn't in the mood to speak to Jean. It was better they each had some space from the other and a chance to cool off. Another fight wouldn't do either of them any good.

The trouble was they'd spent so much time these past few months giving each other more and more space that, now, there was so much distance between them, Wise wasn't sure if he could even see a way back to the way things were.

Christ, how had things come to this?

There was a knock on his door, then Hicksy stuck his head in. 'You ready, Guv?'

'Yeah. Let's go.'

41

Hannah sat in MIR-One, unsure of how she felt. There was something behind Wise asking her to stay behind but she wasn't sure what it was. Was he unhappy with her performance, perhaps? Or was he trying to protect her somehow after everything that had happened?

Jono's death had really upset her. Despite her initial misgivings about the man, she'd soon come to realise the man had a good heart and a lot of his gruffness had been more of an act than anything else. She'd admired his courage in fighting his cancer and was impressed when he'd come back to work.

And now he was dead. Shot on what should've been a harmless stakeout. What a way to go.

Her phone beeped. It was a message from Emma. Hannah dropped the phone back on her desk without opening it.

'Hannah?' It was Brains. 'Can you come here for a second?'

'Sure.' She got up from her desk and went over. 'What is it?'

'I was having a nose through Tyrell's banking over the last week or so. There's not much going on. A few food deliveries, that sort of stuff,' Brains said, pointing at some data on his screen.

'Okay,' Hannah replied. 'And?'

'Well, on Thursday night, young Tyrell took two Uber journeys, a half hour apart from each other.'

'He did?'

Brains nodded. 'He did.'

'Why would he go out if he was lying low?'

'Well, I checked his movements via his phone data for that day and time and he went to Sunnyhill Road in Streatham.'

'Okay, but he could've been going to see a friend or a girlfriend. Or he had to drop something off.'

'Yeah, there are a hundred possible reasons for the journey — all of them legit. Except ...' He grinned.

'Fucking hell, Brains. Stop playing to the audience. We all know you're a genius. Except what?'

'Except in Sunnyhill Road, there's a garage, Streatham A1 Motor Repairs. It's owned by a Douglas Houseman now, but — and it's a big "but" — its previous owner was one Errol Gallagher.'

'Now that is interesting.'

Brains tapped away at his screen. 'This is young Douglas.' A mug shot appeared on screen of a young, IC1 male, with a crew cut and hard eyes. 'Twenty-two years old. Did time in borstal for possession with intent to supply, GBH and ABH. Then did a two year stretch in Pentonville for possession with intent. Since he got out, he's been squeaky clean and running the garage.'

'Where did an ex-con get the money to buy a garage in Streatham?' Hannah asked.

'Maybe he didn't. Maybe he's just fronting the business for Errol?'

'And, if that's the case, maybe Tyrell was dropping the stolen drugs off there.'

'That's what I was thinking,' Brains said.

'They could still be there.'

'They could indeed.'

Hannah slapped Brains on the shoulder. 'See? I told you you're a genius.'

'I do my best.'

'Give me that address,' Hannah said. 'I'll go down there and have a nosey.'

Brains scrawled the details down on a post-it note.

Taking it, she headed over to where Sarah and Callum were trawling through CCTV footage. 'Hey, do you mind if I borrow Callum? Brains has come up with some intel that I want to check out.'

Sarah looked up from her screen. 'What intel's that?'

Hannah told them both about the garage.

'And you reckon that's where the drugs are?' Sarah asked.

Hannah shrugged. 'It's possible. Definitely worth a look.'

'Shouldn't we call the governor first? Let him know?' Sarah said.

Hannah paused for a moment, remembering Wise's words. *Call me before you do anything.* But he had enough on his plate right then. What if this turned out to be nothing? She didn't want to waste his time. 'We can do that afterwards. When we know if there's something to tell him about.'

Sarah stood up. 'Then I'm coming too. Safety in numbers and all that.'

Hannah smiled. She wasn't sure what use Sarah would be if there was trouble, though. The woman was barely five feet tall, after all. But she couldn't see the harm in it either. 'You got your car here?'

Five minutes later, after leaving Brains moaning about being left alone, Hannah and Callum were in Sarah's Ford Focus heading to Streatham. Compared to nearly every trip she'd made with Wise, the journey to Streatham was a dream for once. London was a ghost town. Not only was there no traffic on the roads, but even the pavements were empty.

They had a straight run down the A3 to Clapham North where they turned on Bedford Road, zipped through Brixton and then they were in Streatham twenty minutes after leaving the station.

'Bloody hell,' Hannah said as they parked up in Sunnyhill Road. 'If only every day in London could be like this.'

'It is Sunday,' Sarah said.

'Most people are probably sleeping off last night's hangovers after the England game,' Callum chipped in from the back.

They all climbed out of the car. 'I'd forgotten the World Cup's on,' Hannah said. 'What happened?'

Callum gave her a look of total disappointment. 'How can you forget the World Cup's on?'

'We have been a bit preoccupied, if you hadn't noticed.'

Callum winced. 'Shit. Yeah. Sorry.'

'We lost anyway,' Sarah said, locking the car. 'Two-one.'

'Does that mean we're out then?' Hannah asked.

Callum looked at her as if she was from a different planet. 'Don't you know anything about football?'

'Sorry,' Hannah said. 'It's not my thing.'

'I thought you were cooler than that,' Callum said as they crossed the road.

'You'll find I'm a source of continual disappointment,' Hannah replied.

The garage itself was easy to find, even if it was a strange location and set-up. The driveway went through where the bottom of a house should be, leading through to the garage at the rear. Blue metal shutters covered the entrance with 'Streatham A1 Motor Repairs' painted across them.

'Doesn't look like anyone's home,' Sarah said. 'We might've had a wasted journey.'

'Don't give up yet,' Hannah said, and hammered on the shutters. She stepped back, watching and waiting for someone to answer.

Nothing happened. She stepped forward again and gave the doors another good pounding. Still nothing.

'Great,' Hannah said. 'Maybe we should go and get a coffee somewhere and try again in a bit?'

'It's Sunday,' Sarah said. 'And it's a garage. No one's working in a garage on a Sunday.'

'I could do with a coffee though,' Callum said. 'And we did come all this way. We might as well wait for a bit.'

'Come all this way?' Sarah repeated. 'We're in Streatham, not Southampton.'

'Why don't you have a fag and cheer yourself up?' Hannah said. 'Then we'll go have that coffee.'

Sarah didn't need telling twice. She had a cigarette out and lit before they'd gone two steps back towards Sunnyhill Road.

Just as they got close to the main road, though, a young lad in an oversized tracksuit and hoodie turned into the driveway, staring at the phone in one hand. Tucked under the other arm was something wrapped up in grease-proof paper.

It was Douglas Houseman. No doubt about it.

'Hello, Douglas,' Hannah said. 'We'd like a word.'

He looked up, all startled, and did a quick double take of the three officers as his lunch tumbled to the floor. Then he was off, like bloody Usain Bolt.

'Stop, you idiot, we're the police,' Hannah shouted after him, but Houseman wasn't listening. He was sprinting as fast as he could. Left with no choice, Hannah set off after him. Luckily for her, Callum followed, and he was a far better runner than she was. He closed the gap on Houseman as if it was nothing, his long strides eating the distance.

Hannah was almost tempted to slow down and let Callum do all the hard work, but she kept on as fast as she could, grateful that she hadn't come to Streatham on her own.

Callum was ten yards ahead of her, his hand reaching for Houseman's collar. Houseman, though, wasn't going to make it easy. He ducked down so Callum's hand flew over his head and, somehow, managed to twist and turn so Callum went running past. Houseman shimmied right, cutting between two parked cars and ran out into the road, heading back the way he came.

Hannah cut right herself, timing it just right more by luck than skill, and collided straight into Houseman, letting his head crack straight into her shoulder. He kicked out as he went down, catching Hannah in her left knee. Pain shot up her leg as she stumbled, almost falling herself.

Then she saw the knife in Houseman's hand as he thrust it straight at her.

42

Hannah threw herself backwards as the knife came at her. She landed on her arse on the cold tarmac, but somehow managed to kick out herself at her attacker. Her big size-nine biker boots knocked Houseman's knife arm out of the way and struck him in the chest at the same time.

He fell to the side, giving Hannah a chance to roll away, and then they were both on their feet at the same time, facing each other. But Houseman still had that big knife in his hand.

Callum came flying out of nowhere, straight into Houseman, tackling him down. Hannah didn't know if Callum knew Houseman had a knife, but she wasn't taking any chances. She grabbed her collapsible baton from her coat pocket and flicked her wrist, opening it up.

She stormed in as Houseman got the better of Callum in their tussle. She brought her baton down as Houseman brought his knife up, cracking it into his arm with all her might.

They all heard the bone break as the knife went flying and then Houseman was howling in pain. But Hannah had no mercy. For all she knew, this was the fucker who was going around cutting off people's balls. She shoved Houseman off Callum and threw him face-front onto the road, then pulled his arms behind his back and cuffed him, ignoring his screams as she moved his broken arm.

'You alright?' she asked Callum, offering him a hand to help him up.

'Where did that fucking knife come from?' he asked as she pulled him to his feet.

'Out of that wanker's jacket,' Hannah replied, resisting the urge to boot Houseman in the face. Still, she did nothing about her smile when she bent down to tell Houseman the good news. 'Douglas Houseman, I am arresting you under section fifty-two of the Offensive Weapons Act 2019, for possession of an offensive weapon with intent to do harm, for threatening behaviour with intent to do harm, plus resisting arrest and assaulting a police officer. You do not have to say anything, but it may harm your defence if you do not mention when questioned something you later relay on in court. Anything you do say may be given in evidence.'

'I need a fucking ambulance,' Houseman spat back.

'All in good time.' Hannah straightened up and saw Sarah walking towards them. 'You alright there?'

Sarah stopped and looked down on Houseman. 'You two looked like you had it well in hand.'

Callum put Houseman's knife into an evidence bag. 'It was a close call though.'

'Nonsense. I never had a doubt you'd sort him out.' Sarah winked at Callum. 'Not a big lad like you.'

'Can you call it in and get a wagon down here to pick him up?' Hannah asked.

'My pleasure,' Sarah said, getting her phone out.

'Tell them to pick him up from the garage,' Hannah said. She looked over at Callum. 'Can you do the honours?'

'With pleasure,' Callum replied. He hooked a hand around Houseman's good arm and hauled him to his feet. It must've bloody hurt still because Houseman screamed his head off again.

'Give it a rest,' Hannah said. 'No one's around to be impressed by your wailing.'

'This is police brutality,' Houseman said, tears in his eyes, as Callum led him out of the road and back onto the pavement.

'You should've thought about that before you tried stabbing the pair of us,' Hannah said.

'I thought you wanted to kill me,' Houseman said.

'Tell it to the judge,' Hannah said as she pulled on some disposable gloves. 'Now, before I search you, is there anything in your pockets you want to tell me about? Any sharp objects? Needles? Anything like that?'

'Fuck off, pig,' Houseman said.

'Delightful.' Hannah tapped the man's pockets first, just in case he did have anything sharp in them, but felt nothing other than his phone, wallet and keys. Sure enough, that was all she found when she searched him properly. She handed the phone and wallet to Callum and dangled the keys in front of Houseman. 'Which one of these opens the garage?'

'I'm not telling you,' Houseman sneered. 'Anyway, you can't go in there without a search warrant.'

'Oh, I can,' Hannah said. 'I could do that the moment you decided to attack me with a knife.'

The kid looked horrified. 'You're joking.'

'Oh, I don't do jokes.' They walked Houseman back to his garage and Hannah tried keys until one slipped into the lock. 'Bingo.'

'You can't go in there,' Houseman said. 'I'm sorry about the misunderstanding outside and all but there's no reason for you to go in there. No reason at all.'

Hannah gave him a wink. 'Apart from the fact you're shitting yourself at the thought of it.' She turned the key and the lock disengaged with a clunk. Pushing it open, she ducked inside, followed by Sarah and, finally, by Callum and Houseman.

A Mini was cranked up on a lift on the right-hand side but otherwise the garage was empty. It was spotless, in fact. For a workshop, it all looked brand new. 'You actually do any work in here, Douglas?'

'Fuck off,' the lad replied.

'It must be hard work being so charming all the time.' Hannah glanced over at Callum. 'Keep an eye on him while we have a look around. Break his other arm if he tries anything.'

'No problem,' Callum replied.

'You won't find anything,' Houseman shouted as Hannah and Sarah set off towards the stairs at the rear of the garage. 'You're wasting your time.'

Hannah glanced back and, for a second, she thought Houseman was smiling. In fact, he really wasn't looking as worried as he had been a minute or two before. Why was that? Hannah would bet her life savings that something was hidden here, whether that was the missing drugs or maybe the firearm that was used to kill Jono. Maybe he thought he'd hidden everything too well — but why shit himself at the thought of them entering the garage?

She followed Sarah up the stairs as the overhead lights popped into life and, sure enough, they found the office. It wasn't anything special. A leather sofa, a fridge with a kettle and some mugs on top of it, a few filing cabinets, and a desk.

'I'll check the desk,' Sarah said.

'Okay.' Hannah walked over to the sofa and pulled the cushions up. Unzipping the covers, she felt inside each one for anything hidden and found nothing. She moved onto the fridge but there was only a solitary can of Diet Coke inside.

That just left the filing cabinets. Hannah started pulling out drawers, but each one was filled with paperwork, receipts and order forms. It actually looked like the garage was a legitimate business.

'Any luck?' Hannah asked Sarah.

'Nope. There's not a thing here,' Sarah replied. 'There's barely even a pen or paperclip in this desk.'

Hannah looked around the office. 'If it wasn't for all the paperwork in the filing cabinets, I'd think they didn't do any work here at all.' She walked over to the windows that overlooked the workshop and looked down. Callum waited by the shutters with Houseman. 'There's not a tool in sight or even a spot of oil on the floor.'

'It's an expensive bit of real estate to not be used,' Sarah said. She came over and joined Hannah by the window. 'They must be doing some work. There's a bloody Mini on a jack down there.'

'Yeah, but something's not right.' Hannah ran her eyes over the office, looking for something she might've missed. 'What about under the sofa? Maybe there's something in the floor or walls?'

'Let's move it and see.' The two officers walked over to the sofa and pushed and pulled it until they managed to manoeuvre it away from the wall. All that revealed though was a mangy carpet with more than a few unsightly stains. Hannah tapped her foot along the carpet but there were no dents or lumps in the flooring that suggested anything hidden beneath the carpet.

Her phone rang. It was Callum. 'Everything okay?'

'Yeah. I just wanted to tell you the wagon's arrived to pick up our friend here,' Callum said. 'They want to take him to the hospital to get his arm seen to before taking him for booking, though.'

'Alright. We'll come down.' She ended the call and told Sarah.

'There's nothing here anyway,' she replied. 'Looks like we had a wasted trip.'

'Not if that knife Houseman had turns out to be the one used to cut Beanz' balls off.' Hannah headed to the stairs.

'You think it is?'

Hannah looked over her shoulder at Sarah. 'I live in hope.'

'Lucky you.'

As they walked into the workshop, Hannah could see Houseman was grinning away, despite his imminent departure to hospital and then onto Brixton to be charged and held in custody.

'I told you there's nothing here,' he called out. 'This is all a waste of time.'

'Wanker,' Sarah muttered as Hannah stopped walking. Something was wrong. The same two questions played through her mind; why was he so scared about them going into the garage but why was he so happy with Hannah and Sarah searching upstairs?

The answers were obvious: he was scared because there was something he didn't want found in the garage and he was happy for them to search upstairs because whatever it was wasn't hidden up there.

So that left the workshop. The workshop they hadn't searched.

'Hold on a minute,' Hannah called out as the uniforms prepared to take Houseman.

'Something wrong?' Sarah asked.

Hannah didn't reply. She was looking around the workshop. Forget the fact that there wasn't any dirt or oil in the garage, there weren't any toolboxes or spare tyres kicking around. In fact, the only equipment that she could see were the two hydraulic lifts, one of which was being used for the Mini. Otherwise, the place looked like it'd been stripped bare.

'What's wrong with the Mini?' she asked Houseman.

'What?' he replied, but that cocky little smile of his wavered.

She pointed to the car that was five feet up in the air. 'What's wrong with the motor?'

'Engine... engine trouble.'

'What sort of engine trouble?'

And, just like that, the smile was gone, and Houseman was back to crapping himself. 'I don't know yet. I just got it in. That's why it's on the lift.'

'Who's the car belong to?'

'Just some bloke.'

Hannah walked over to the lift. 'Considering he's your only customer, I would've thought you'd remember his name.' One of the pillars supporting the car had a control panel. There was a single button in the main box, with a lever underneath and a second lever to the right of that on the adjoining column side. 'How does this work, then?'

'You can't touch that. It's expensive equipment,' Houseman said. 'I'll sue you if you break it.'

One of the uniforms, who'd come to collect Houseman, stepped forward. 'I know. I did a stint as a Motor Vehicle Technician.'

Hannah indicated the control panel. 'Please, do the honours. Let's get this motor down.'

The uniform joined her. 'This one is the safety lever,' he said, pointing to the right-hand one. He pulled it down. 'And this one releases the hydraulics.' He pulled the second lever down, taking his time as the car began to lower. 'You've got to be careful. Too fast and the car could tip over.'

'Leave it alone,' Houseman shouted. 'You've got no right to use that.'

'I think you protest too much,' Hannah said. The Mini clunked onto the ground. 'Let's have a look, shall we?'

Hannah opened the driver's doors first, poked her head in for a quick look, then checked on Houseman's reaction. He was doing his best to appear calm, but it was clear the man was bricking it. She closed the door, taking her time to walk around the car to the boot.

That's when she saw his feet twitching as if he wanted to run for the hills. Keeping her eyes on him, she opened the boot. Houseman was shaking now.

Good.

Hannah looked in the boot. It was empty. She lifted up the cover that hid the spare wheel compartment. The tyre was there, but that was all. She dropped the cover down, then looked at Houseman again. He'd stopped twitching. He almost looked happy again. Like she'd fucked up.

So, whatever he hidden was definitely in the boot and he thought she'd not found it. What a wanker.

She lifted up the cover once more and unscrewed the bolt that kept the tyre in place. She reached in, pulled the tyre out and immediately felt the weight of the tyre wasn't right. Hannah dropped it on the floor but there was no bounce. She looked over at Houseman. 'I think this one needs pumping up a bit.'

He just stared at her, but that little shiver of his was back once more.

'Anyone got a knife?' she asked.

43

It was all spinning out of control. Sarah knew that much, at least. She couldn't believe it earlier when Hannah wanted to rush out the door to go to Streatham. If she could've delayed things, she could've called the bastard and told him to get there first.

But no.

At least, Sarah had managed to tag along to keep an eye on things. Thank God for that. She hadn't known whether she should've been happy or sad when it looked like they were going to come up empty-handed.

Then Hannah had to get all bloody clever and work out that twat had hidden the gear in the car.

'I'm just going out for a smoke,' she said as everyone started backslapping each other and do the bloody happy dance after they'd cut the tyre open and found three bricks of drugs.

Back out in the street, she walked ten yards away from the garage before she got her phone out.

The bastard answered on the first ring. 'What's up?'

'We've got a problem,' Sarah said.

'I don't like problems.'

'We've found the drugs at some garage in Streatham that Gallagher used to own.'

The bastard laughed. 'Excellent. Well done.'

'No, not well done,' Sarah hissed. She felt like she was losing her mind. She looked back to make sure no one was close enough to overhear, but everyone was too busy putting Houseman in the back of the wagon. 'Don't you understand? We have it now. The police. It's going to be logged into evidence and then it'll be locked away until the time comes for it to be destroyed. There's no way you can get your hands on this now.'

'No?'

'No. We're heading back to Kennington right now with it.'

'You driving?'

'Yeah.'

'And there's no way you can take a detour and drop it off for me? You could tell your friends you lost it. Or we could swap it for some washing powder or something.'

'I'm not on my own,' Sarah said. 'And there's no way I can explain to my colleague that I'm just going to stop off at my mate's house to show him the drugs we just found.' She took a deep breath and realised she felt happy things had ended this way. The bastard couldn't blame her for what had happened. 'You just have to face it, it's gone. Write the bloody stuff off as a business loss or something.'

'Oh, I haven't lost anything,' the bastard said. 'I got the money Mad Errol paid that fucking little prick of a wannabe gangster. All three hundred grand of it.'

'So why have you been going around killing everyone then? Why tell me to find your gear?'

'Two reasons, darling. First, no one steals from me. These idiots forgot that, so they had to pay the price for being dickheads. Second, because I can. Now, you're going back to Kennington, right?'

'Yeah, that's right.'

'And, when you get there, the drugs are untouchable?' There was something in the bastard's tone that frightened Sarah.

'That's right.'

'And you're in Streatham right now?'

'We're leaving now.'

'Good to know,' the bastard said. 'Alright. It is what it is. Thanks for the heads up about everything. We'll chat soon.'

The line went dead. Sarah stared at her phone, a sense of relief washing over her. She had done everything the bastard had asked of her and now it was over. She was safe. Her husband was safe.

Maybe there was a way she could fit Houseman up for the murders. Get everyone from looking at Konza as their main suspect. The kid had come at them with a knife, after all. Even Hannah had thought he might be the killer.

With a deep breath, she slipped her phone back in her pocket and turned back to rejoin the others.

'You alright?' Hannah asked. 'You looked like you were having an intense conversation over there.'

'I'm fine. I'm just having an argument with my husband. He's being a pain about me working the weekend. He doesn't want to get off his fat arse and do anything,' Sarah said, hating the taste of the lie in her mouth.

'You ready to go then?'

'Yeah.' She looked over at the garage where some uniforms were locking up. 'We got a good result here.'

Hannah grinned. 'Yeah. The governor will be happy.'

Sarah smiled back as she unlocked her Ford Focus. 'Come on, let's get back.'

44

Wise was in Christina Osakara's kitchen with Roberts, watching the CCTV footage from her Ring camera on her laptop.

Christina hovered nearby, an anxious look on her face. She wore a long grey knitted dress with a roll-neck collar. 'I can't believe there's been another murder.'

If only she knew the truth, thought Wise. There was a murder every two days in London on average, but the past week had been far from average. Still, he looked up, smiled and said, 'Try not to worry about it. These things are very rare.'

'But I heard this man was a witness,' Christina went on. 'Am I in danger by helping you?'

'Not at all. But I can arrange to have some officers to watch over you for the next couple of days if it'll make you feel more comfortable.'

'Won't that make it even more obvious I'm helping you?'

'We really don't think you are in any danger,' Wise said. 'It's really a case of what will give you better peace of mind?'

'I think I'm going to go back down to Deal and get away from it all.'

Roberts looked up then. 'That sounds wonderful.' Her voice dripped with sarcasm. 'Why don't you go and pack while we finish up here?'

Christina stared at Roberts for a moment, clearly shocked that she'd been spoken to like that, then turned and huffed and puffed out of the kitchen.

'Right,' Roberts said. 'Now that Drama Queen's gone, where were we?'

'We just watched Leon come home,' Wise said, pointing to the screen. The time on the screen said 0915hrs. He wound the footage back thirty seconds and hit play. Leon appeared from the right of the screen. He checked out the uniform guarding Cameron's flat, then stuck his finger up towards Christina's camera. That done, he jogged over to the staircase and disappeared from sight.

Wise and Roberts carried on watching but the street was quiet for that time on a Saturday and, not unexpectedly, anyone passing gave the uniform a wide berth. No one went up or came down the staircase though. Wise fast-forwarded the film, hoping to spot something but, again, no one stood out.

'We need some idea of the time of death,' Roberts said. 'Or some way of narrowing down what we're looking for.'

'Maybe the killer knew about this camera,' Wise said.

Roberts looked at him, eyebrow arched. 'Sarah?'

'They seem to know everything else.'

'Christ. We're going to be lucky to have jobs after this.' Roberts let out the biggest sigh in the world. 'Get someone to download all the footage and we'll get one of the new bodies to go through it tomorrow. Do we know when the pathologist is doing the autopsy?'

'Not yet.'

'Wonderful. Well, put a rocket up them as well. We need this all done yesterday.'

Wise's phone rang. He checked the caller ID and answered. 'Hey Hannah. Everything okay?'

'Guv,' Hannah replied, sounding a bit breathless. 'We've had a result.'

'You have? How?'

'Brains found out that Tyrell visited this garage in Streatham that Errol Gallagher used to own on Thursday night. So, me, Callum and Sarah came down to check it out. The current owner's a Douglas Houseman and he wasn't too happy to see us. He did a runner first, then attacked me and Callum with a knife.'

'Shit. Are you both okay?'

'Yeah, yeah. We're good,' Hannah said. 'Anyway, we searched the garage and found three massive bricks of what looks like drugs hidden in a spare tyre.'

'You've found the drugs Konza's after?' Wise glanced over at Roberts, who was watching him intently.

'Yeah. We have. We bloody have.'

'Great. Where are you all now?'

'Well, Houseman got his arm broken while he was trying to stab us, so Callum's gone with him and some uniforms to Lambeth Hospital to get it fixed up before taking him into custody,' Hannah said. 'Me and Sarah are on our way back to Kennington to book the drugs into evidence.'

'Are you with Sarah now?' Wise asked, a nasty thought tickling the back of his mind.

'Yeah, she's driving,' Hannah replied.

'Are you on speaker right now?'

There was a hesitation on Hannah's part. She was probably wondering why he was asking. 'No.'

'Careful how you answer this, but did Sarah make any phone calls while you were at this garage?'

'Yeah. That's right. Is there anything I should know?'

Wise paused for a moment, wondering what he should tell Hannah — if he should tell her anything. In the end, he decided to say nothing. 'I wish you'd called me like I asked before you went over there.'

'Sorry, Guv. I didn't want to waste your time if it turned out to be nothing.'

'Alright. It's done now. Just keep your eyes open on the way back, eh? You can't be too careful.'

'Of course. But it's all good. The roads are empty. Callum reckons everyone has World Cup hangovers. We'll be back in half an hour.'

'Still, take care.'

'I will.' Hannah ended the call.

'What's happened?' Roberts asked.

'We need to move,' Wise said and updated her on what had happened.

'You look worried.'

'I am.' Wise almost didn't want to say anything, as if voicing his fears would make it come true. But people could die that way. 'Sarah made a call at the garage. If she told Konza about the drugs, then this is his last chance to snatch them. Once they get to Kennington, and the bricks are booked into evidence, it's over. Konza has to make a move now.'

'They're not going to ambush a police car, are they?'

Wise didn't need to answer that. Instead, he headed towards the front door and Roberts followed. They left Christina Osakara's house without saying goodbye, and the moment they were back on the street, Wise had his phone out. He called Brains as they headed towards Roberts' Audi.

'Yes, Guv?' Brains answered.

'Hannah and Sarah are heading back to Kennington,' Wise said. 'With three bricks of drugs on them.'

'Yes, I heard they'd got a result.'

'Sarah's car has a tracker in it, right?'

'Of course. All Met vehicles do.'

'Find out exactly where they are and get them an escort all the way back to the nick.' Wise climbed into the passenger seat of the Audi. 'I want ARO support to join them as well. Tell everyone it's fucking urgent.'

'They in trouble?'

'I hope not,' Wise said as the Audi roared to life. 'And send me their location the moment you get it. We'll try and meet up with them on the way.'

'On it now,' Brains said. 'Do the girls know? Should I call them?'

'Not yet. They'll work out what's going on when they see the cavalry turn up.' Wise ended the call. 'I don't want to worry them, though, before then.'

'What route do you think they'd take?' Roberts asked as she started the engine.

'From Streatham? They'll probably take the A3 to Kennington.'

'They won't get hit on the A3,' Roberts said as she pulled the Audi out of its parking spot. 'It's too big and busy. Konza would have to strike before then, on a minor road. Somewhere they can ambush the car easily.'

'Head towards Brixton. Maybe we can intercept them there,' Wise said.

Roberts turned on her blues and twos and accelerated away and Wise prayed they'd reach Hannah in time.

45

'Everything alright?' Sarah asked as Hannah ended her call to Wise.

'Yeah, I think so,' Hannah replied, but that wasn't true. Why had Wise asked her if Sarah had made any calls? And why did he want her to be careful about how she answered his questions? 'He just said, well done — and then told me off for not calling him before going to Streatham.'

She glanced at Sarah out of the corner of her eye. The woman was driving with an intense look of concentration on her face, but Hannah was pretty sure there was something else going on. Was there a nervousness about her?

The more Hannah thought about it, Sarah hadn't been herself since they'd started working on the Cameron Nketiam murder. The woman was normally so calm and measured, but she'd been biting people's heads off all week. Was there something behind it?

Or was Hannah just being paranoid?

She looked out of the car window as they headed up Bedford Road. It was all Victorian terrace houses on one side and new-ish builds on the other. And all so very, very quiet. There was no traffic on the road. No people walking on the pavements.

It was like London had become a ghost town.

They crossed Clapham Road and headed up King's Avenue. The homes switched from terraces to semi-detached and detached, allowing space for more footpaths and trees to fill up space. She could imagine it would look quite beautiful in the summer when it was awash in green but, for now, naked branches reached for the grey sky, begging for sunlight.

They passed a construction site promising more affordable housing, then past a block of flats that looked like it should be demolished. A few St George flags still hung forlorn from windows here and there, waiting to be packed away until the next sporting occasion brought fresh hopes of glory.

Five minutes later, she saw her first person out and about; a woman waiting in a bus shelter, a small shopping bag on wheels beside her. The stranger was no threat, but still Hannah could feel her sense of unease growing.

But if they were in danger, Wise would've said something, surely? He would've told her if there was an issue, especially if it was with Sarah.

Hannah ran street maps through her mind, trying to work out where they were and how far they were from Kennington and safety. By her reckoning, the junction with the A3 was about five more minutes away, up by Clapham North tube station. Once they reached that, it'd be plain sailing back to the nick.

She glanced over at Sarah again. 'Why don't you put your foot down a bit? Get us back quicker?'

Sarah gave her a weird look back. 'Are you sure everything is okay?'

'Yeah,' Hannah said, trying to sound casual about it. 'I just don't like driving around with all those drugs in the boot.'

'Okay. I just don't want to run anyone over. This is a residential area.' Sarah accelerated, but it was nowhere near the speed Hannah would've preferred, even if they were in narrow streets with homes all around them. Anyway, it wasn't as if there was anyone out and about to run over.

The Ford Focus carried on down the narrow road, passing warehouses and a cement works before stopping at the lights on Acre Lane. Hannah leaned forward in her seat, trying to see if there was anything to be worried about, but all she could see was a bus trundling past in front of them. Even so, she felt exposed sitting there in the small hatchback, waiting for the lights to change.

She got her phone out and thought about calling Wise back, but what would she say? That she was nervous? Scared? He'd hardly think more of her if she did that. Might even think less.

Then the lights changed, and Sarah pulled away, crossing Long Acre and heading north up Bedford Road. The road got narrower, if such a thing was possible, and a bus up ahead forced Sarah to slow down once more.

'Fucking hell,' Hannah muttered and shook her head. She wanted to be back at Kennington, not dawdling along behind the Number Seventy-Five bus. If she'd been on her bike, Hannah would've back by now.

Still, at least they were moving, no matter how slowly. If it'd been a weekday, the road would've been chocker and the Ford Focus would've been crawling at a snail's pace, if at all.

Then, Hannah spotted the bridge up ahead. A train shot past along the top of it, coming out of Clapham Junction, no doubt, and heading south. The A3 couldn't be much further on. Relief swept over her. They were nearly there, nearly safe.

A train rumbled past overhead as Sarah drove under the bridge. A white van waited to pull out from the road immediately to their right. Its darkened windows made Hannah look twice as they drove past, before her attention was drawn to the bright yellow pub perched on the street corner, its beer garden ringed by a small grey wall. It was called The Eagle, but she thought The Canary would've been more fitting. God only knew what made someone think painting a building that colour was —

Something hit the Ford Focus hard on Hannah's side of the car. Glass shattered around her as the car slid sideways across the road. Emergency air bags inflated, smacking Hannah in the face, knocking her back against the head rest, as her whole world shrieked with collapsing metal.

Then the car hit something else. Something solid. It was on Sarah's side, and it sent the Focus into a spin. Hannah saw the yellow of the pub looming large and she thought they were going to go through the wall before Sarah's car smashed into something else, the back end tipping up for a moment, before it came crashing down again.

Hannah blinked, trying to clear her head, tasting blood in her mouth. She pushed the air bag down, desperate to free herself of it, then remembered Sarah. She looked to her right, saw Sarah slumped over her own air bag.

Not moving.

There was blood everywhere.

Hannah reached over and shook her colleague. 'Sarah? Are you okay?' The words were hard to speak and muffled in her ears. 'Sarah? Can you hear me? Sarah?'

Sarah didn't move. Didn't respond.

Shit.

Hannah had to get out, get help. This was bad. She reached for her door handle. And saw the van that had hit them square on. Its grill filled her shattered window, locking her in. God only knew where it had come from. The driver was probably drunk from the night before. Well, Hannah would make sure he was nicked if that was the case. He could've killed them. As it was, Sarah looked bad. She needed an ambulance and quick.

Hannah reached for her phone but there was nothing in her pocket. Fuck, she'd been holding it, about to call Wise. It must've gone flying in the crash. Where was it?

It was so hard to think, to focus. She must have concussion or something.

Movement outside caught her eye.

Men.

Dressed in black. Rushing towards the car. Coming to help … no. Not help. They had hoods up, masks on — and guns in their hands.

They aimed the guns at her. And finally her brain kicked back in.

It was no accident.

It was an ambush. Ollie Konza had come for his drugs.

They were going to kill her and Sarah.

Just like Jono.

They were going to shoot her without a second thought. All because she'd not followed orders and not called Wise when she was supposed to. She'd gone haring off without proper backup and now she was going to pay the price.

She thought of Emma, sitting at home, waiting for her to come back.

Not all the men had guns. One had a sledgehammer. He swung it into the driver's side window, shattering it instantly. Hannah got an arm up to protect her eyes as more glass exploded into the interior of the car. She felt a thousand little angry bites as shards struck her skin and tore into her clothes.

The man reached through the broken window and opened Sarah's door. Another man came forward, reached in, and grabbed hold of Sarah to haul her out of the car.

'No!' Hannah screamed. She held onto Sarah as she was lifted out of the vehicle, but she was still messed up from the crash and had no strength left. Sarah's legs started to slip out of her hands. Then, another of the men aimed his assault rifle at Hannah's head and she got the message not to fight.

She held up both hands in surrender.

'Where are the drugs?' the man with the assault rifle shouted. 'Where are the drugs?'

'In ... in the ... in the boot,' she managed to say, spitting blood with every syllable.

'Unlock it. Unlock it NOW!' The barrel of the rifle didn't waver. It stayed locked on Hannah's head. All it would take to splatter her brains across the back of the car was two and a half pounds of pressure on that trigger.

'Okay,' Hannah shouted back. 'I have to reach down to do that. The catch is by my foot.'

'Do it slowly. Any sudden moves and I will kill you.'

Keeping her right hand where the man could see it, Hannah reached down with her left, fumbling for the catch. The by-now half-deflated air bag didn't help, filling up the space around her legs in the footwell. Then her fingers caught on something, and Hannah grunted as she pulled down on the lever. The boot opened with a clunk.

'Get the drugs,' the man with the assault rifle ordered, the barrel of his gun still aimed at Hannah's head. She dared not look but she heard people scrambling and hands digging about in the back. Then there was silence and she saw three men run past the man with the assault rifle.

'Get out,' the man said. 'You're coming with us.'

'I can't,' Hannah replied. 'Your van's blocking me in.'

'Climb out the other door.' As he said it, the rifle twitched towards the door they'd dragged Sarah out of.

Christ, where was she? Hannah was still struggling to think. Her head hurt, her thoughts were slow and there was still that damn ringing in her ears. Most of all, Hannah didn't know what to do. Whether she stayed or moved, she was pretty sure she was dead.

'Move or I'll shoot you where you are,' the man said with another twitch of the barrel.

Shit. Hannah clambered over the gear stick, feeling pain shoot through her body as she did so. It came from every bone, every joint, making her feel sick. She half-fell into the driver's seat and, as she lifted her feet up, hands grabbed her under the armpits and dragged her from the car, before dropping her hard on the tarmac.

As Hannah looked up, squinting against the brightness of the grey sky, another man stood over her with a Glock in his hand. 'Move.'

'Please don't shoot me,' Hannah said as she got to her feet, swaying like a Friday night drunk, hands up in the air. Like that would make any difference.

A hand pushed her in the back, guiding her towards a white van with its side open. Sarah was already inside, lying on the floor, her hands bound with zip ties.

'Move!' The man with the assault rifle shouted. 'Get in.'

Then, from somewhere, they all heard the sirens wailing.

The police were on their way.

Something hard struck Hannah in the back of her head.

The world went black.

46

'Sarah's car's stationary at the junction of Lendal Terrace and Bedford Road,' Brains said over the radio.

'Why?' Wise called back. 'There are no lights there.'

'I don't know, Guv,' Brains replied. 'All I can tell you is that she's not moving.'

'What about backup?'

'We've got some uniforms in a marked car two minutes away with Armed Response just behind them.'

'Shit. Tell them to put their bloody feet down and get there,' Wise said. 'We're still about five minutes out.'

'I'll get there quicker,' Roberts said, her teeth clenched. They were on Landor Road, barrelling down the narrow street at eighty miles an hour, siren wailing, lights flashing. Wise had never driven anywhere with his boss, let alone at high speed, but the woman knew how to handle her Audi S3.

'This is Alpha Charlie Six Two,' a woman's voice said over the radio. 'We have visual. Target vehicle has been involved in an RTC. There are two vans involved. Pulling up now.'

'Approach with caution,' Wise said. 'Repeat, approach with caution.'

'Shit. There are armed men. Repeat, armed men,' the woman said, her voice full of fear. Even over the radio, the sound of sustained automatic fire was loud and clear. 'Shots fired. Shots fired.'

Roberts accelerated as they listened to the frightened police officer.

'This is Alpha Charlie Six Two.' The woman was barely audible over the gunfire. Wise could hear bullets pounding metal. 'We are under attack from multiple armed gunmen. We need urgent armed assistance. Repeat, we need urgent armed assistance.'

'Where are the fucking AROs?' Roberts said as she suddenly swung her car to the left, turning into a single lane road, ignoring the no entry and the red and white one-way signs. The Audi hurtled down the narrow lane, losing a wing mirror to a bollard on the way.

Cars were parked on the right-hand side, all facing towards them, narrowing the road further. Some kids gawped at the Audi as it shot past.

Roberts had to slam on the brakes, as the road turned to the right, to stop herself from crashing into a tower block and Wise could feel the weight of the car pressing down on his side as the car went into a skid. For a second, he thought the car was going to tip over but, with a bounce, it got all four tyres back on the tarmac and Roberts was off again.

Wise could see the gunfight now at the end of the road. Two men in black stood smack dab in the middle of the street. They were in classic firing poses, left feet forward, automatic rifles pressed into their shoulders, taking aim down the barrels of their guns, and firing in controlled bursts at the marked police car ten metres away. There was a parked white van just behind them, its side door open and another gunman inside.

He spotted Sarah's car next, all smashed up on the side of the road, another van wedged into the passenger door, while the driver's door hung open. There was no sign of either Hannah or Sarah.

Roberts put her foot down.

The Audi ate up the remaining distance in an instant.

One of the gunmen had time to turn as the car flew towards him.

Then the Audi hit both of the masked men square on at eighty, maybe ninety, miles an hour. At least one of them smashed into the windscreen before disappearing over the top of the car. Then Roberts jerked the wheel to the left and pumped the brakes as the building on other side of the road raced towards them. The car went into another skid, spinning around. The front wheels hit the pavement on the other side, then the passenger side smashed into a lamppost, sending the car spinning the other way, rattling Wise's teeth and bones. Air bags exploded out of the car, but he pushed his down, desperate to see what was happening, to not be trapped.

How many gunmen were there?

He looked up, past the smoking bonnet of the car, and saw the Armed Response van had arrived. AROs spilled out, dressed in full tactical gear and armed with Heckler and Koch MP5 assault rifles of their own.

Two gunmen remained standing and were in no mood to surrender. They opened fire on the police officers, but it was an act of suicide. The AROs returned fire and cut the gunmen down in a hail of bullets.

And, just like that, it was all over.

Wise got out of the smashed-up Audi, eager to find out if Hannah and Sarah were okay. He held up his warrant card to the AROs as he ran over. 'Police! Don't shoot. Don't shoot.'

Wise reached the van at the same time as the AROs. Leaving them to secure the bodies, he rounded the front of the van, looking for Hannah and Sarah, and saw a figure in black hobbling away down the one-way street Roberts had come storming down.

'We've got a runner!' Wise shouted and set off in pursuit. He couldn't let the bastard reach the housing estate. It'd be too easy for the man to disappear in that rabbit warren. 'Halt! Police!'

The man did as Wise asked — except he stopped, turned and raised a pistol at Wise.

Wise skidded to a halt himself as he saw the barrel of the gun point straight at him.

The gunshot was deafening in the narrow street.

Wise flinched, tensing up in anticipation of the bullet striking him, but it was the gunman who was punched off his feet. It was the gunman who hit the ground and didn't get up again.

'Suspect down. Repeat, suspect down,' an ARO said, moving past Wise, his MP5 locked on the fallen gunman.

'Thanks,' Wise said, but doubted the ARO heard him.

Wise stood for a moment, catching his breath, staring at the fallen figure as the ARO picked up the man's fallen weapon, then checked the gunman was actually dead.

Satisfied the man wasn't getting up again, Wise turned back and headed towards the van. The scene was now swarming with police of every description, with the AROs and the Uniforms from the first response vehicle.

Wise went up to a female officer. She must've been who he'd heard over the radio. She had blood running down the side of her face from a wound up in her scalp. 'You okay?'

She nodded. 'Just got caught by some flying glass.'

'You did good work,' Wise told her before moving on.

Roberts was by the side of the van, on her phone. 'We need urgent medical assistance on the corner of Lendal Terrace and Bedford Road. Multiple casualties with GSWs. Plus two officers unconscious. I want an ambulance down here now. Repeat, I have two officers down who need urgent medical assistance now.'

Wise pushed past her and saw both Hannah and Sarah lying on the floor of the van, their hands bound with zip ties. Blood covered both their faces. He climbed in, checking for pulses and was relieved to find both had strong heartbeats. He quickly checked their bodies for any wounds, but found none. They might be beaten up but that was all as far as he could tell. 'Thank God.'

Looking around, he spotted three wrapped up bricks tucked into the corner by the driver's seat. They had to be the drugs that had caused all these deaths.

He left the van and joined Roberts, only noticing then the bruise above her left eye. 'You okay, boss?'

'Doing better than my Audi,' she said.

'At least we got here in time,' Wise replied. 'It was a bold move going down that one-way street like that.'

'Yeah. We got lucky. How are Hannah and Sarah?'

'Alive for now. I think they're just banged up.'

'I want officers with them in hospital, Simon,' Roberts said. 'If Sarah has been working with these bastards, I don't want her doing a runner while she's being treated for a headache.'

Wise glanced back into the van. 'I'll make sure of it.'

'We got damn lucky here, Simon. Damn lucky, indeed.'

Roberts wasn't wrong about that. There were five dead gunmen on the ground around them. It could quite easily have been dead police officers in their place.

What Wise wanted to know: was Ollie Konza among the corpses scattered around?

47

It was late and the day's pathetic excuse of a sun had disappeared long ago, leaving the world outside cloaked in darkness. Inside MIR-One, a small group of detectives remained, going over the events from earlier, updating their information in real time as new details came to light.

Wise was there, with Roberts too, both slightly banged up from their escapades, but neither willing to go home to rest just yet. Hicksy and Brains were with them as well, making calls and crunching data.

Callum, energy drink in hand, was acting as liaison between the various departments involved in the aftermath of the Bedford Road attack and was updating the whiteboards in Sarah's place. Even Donut was there, going over CCTV footage, an empty chair next to him where Sarah would normally sit.

Hannah and Sarah were both in Wandsworth Hospital, in varying injured states. Hannah had been lucky, escaping with plenty of cuts and bruises to go along with a concussion. Sarah, on the other hand, had a broken arm and leg as a result of the attack. All things considered, they had both got off lightly. Wise had no doubt, though, that if the gunmen had managed to get away with both detectives in their van, then he'd be looking for two more corpses.

'How are we doing with identifying the gunmen?' he asked Brains.

'Good. We've got four of the five names so far,' Brains replied. He got up from his desk, went over to the printer, then returned with mug shots in hand. He stuck three new pictures next to the one of Ollie Konza. 'Konza was shot by an ARO while fleeing the scene.' Brains wrote 'DEAD' in capitals under Konza's picture. 'He had a handgun with him that matches the calibre of bullets used to kill both Tyrell Lewis and Jono. Ballistics are checking to see if it is actually the same gun.'

He moved on to the next picture. 'Gregory Milner. Twenty-two. Shot dead by AROs on the scene.' He wrote the deceased's name under his picture, then 'DEAD' underneath that. 'Next is Ray Fatille, nineteen. Shot dead by AROs on the scene.' Again, he added the man's details under his picture. 'Next, we have the two men run over by DCI Roberts. One is Lloyd Aarons, twenty-four. The other is still unidentified. At the moment, it doesn't look like he's in our database.'

Brains stepped back. 'Apart from Gunman Number Five, the others are all serious criminals.'

'If Konza's gun matches the bullets used to kill Tyrell Lewis and Jono,' Roberts said, 'then that ties everything up. From the initial murder of Cameron Nketiam to the murder of Jordan Hines and Tyrell Lewis to Jono and Errol Gallagher and his wife.'

'That only leaves Leon Tomoral's murder unaccounted for,' Wise said. 'But I think it's safe to say one of these creeps killed him.'

'We've got phone numbers for them all,' Brains said. 'We're looking at where they went over the last forty-eight hours. Hopefully, that will help tie one of them or all of them to Friary Road. Forensics are still working the scenes. So maybe they'll find some physical evidence as well.'

'Good. I'll tell Detective Chief Superintendent Walling that we won't be needing all that extra manpower tomorrow,' Roberts said. 'I know it's been an awful week for you all but, despite everything, we've done well. We got a good result today even though we came close to an absolute disaster.'

No one said anything. If the others felt anything remotely like Wise did, it was hard to feel good about what had happened.

Hicksy shifted in his seat. 'There's something that's been bothering me.'

'What's that?' Wise asked.

'I want to know how these bastards managed to stay ahead of us like they have. I mean, I can kinda work out how they found Beanz and Leon, even Mad Errol to a point, but today? That attack should've been impossible. We only found out about the garage this morning. The girls and Callum went straight over, found the gear and were coming back. There's no way Konza and his gang could've found out about it, let alone known how to intercept Sarah's car.'

'I know,' Wise said. 'It's something we're aware of and we're looking into.'

'Yeah,' Hicksy replied, then looked around at everyone in MIR-One. 'But, as far as I can work out, they had to have someone telling them what we were up to. They had to have one of us helping them.'

Wise glanced over at Roberts, who gave a slight shake of her head.

'We're looking into it, Hicksy,' Wise said again.

'You say that but, if it is one of us, then, by God, I can tell you this — I'm going to kill whoever it is. Jono died because someone here betrayed us all and Sarah and Hannah could be lying in the morgue next to him.'

'I understand you're upset, mate,' Wise said. 'But we are —'

Hicksy jabbed a finger at Wise. 'Don't bullshit me, Guv. Not after what we've been through.'

'I'm not bullshitting you.'

'Then what the fuck is going on?'

Roberts stood up. 'Callum, Donut — why don't you two call it a day?'

Both men looked over at Wise, who nodded. Callum drained his energy drink, dropped it into his bin, stood up and grabbed his coat off the back of his chair. 'Alright. I'll see you all in the morning.'

Donut was a bit more hesitant. 'I don't mind staying.'

'It's alright,' Wise said. 'We'll see you tomorrow.'

Donut shrugged, stood up, picked up his coat and, with Callum, they left MIR-One.

Roberts watched the door shut behind them, then turned to face Hicksy and Brains. 'You're right, Hicksy. We believe someone on this team has been helping Konza.'

'Fuck. I knew it. Who is it?' Hicksy asked.

Roberts glanced over at Wise. 'Tell them.'

'I think it was Sarah,' Wise said.

'No way,' Brains said.

'I don't want to believe it either but it's the only answer I can think of. She even made a call to someone before she and Hannah left the garage with the drugs. That call had to be to Konza.'

'That BITCH.' Hicksy spat the word out. 'How could she? How could she get Jono killed like that?'

'First of all, we need to prove she's the informant,' Wise said. 'Then we need to find out why.'

'Fuck. I'm going to kill her myself when I see her.'

'Hicksy, saying stuff like that doesn't help any of us. We're police officers. Even if it's one of our own, we do things properly. We get the evidence and then we arrest the perpetrator. We don't become criminals ourselves.'

The veteran detective shook his head. 'I can't promise that.'

'Hicksy, don't do anything to make this worse than it is,' Roberts said. 'You don't want to end your career by doing something stupid.'

'Fuck my career.' Hicksy stood up. 'And fuck you too.' He snatched up his coat and stormed out of MIR-One.

Roberts looked over at Wise. 'We do have armed guards at the hospital?'

Wise nodded.

'Well, tell them to keep an eye out for Hicksy and make sure they don't let him in, no matter what bullshit he gives them,' Roberts said. 'I'd rather not have to arrest any more of your team than I have to.'

'I'll make sure he doesn't do anything stupid.'

'I still can't believe it,' Brains said.

'Get on Sarah's phone details,' Wise said. 'I want to know who she's been calling. We have Konza's number and his crew's too. Find that link.'

Brains let out a sigh. 'And what if there isn't one?'

'That would be good news for Sarah but not for the rest of us.' Wise glanced over at Roberts. 'Because if it's not her, then that means we still don't know who the informer is.'

48

All Hannah knew was that everything hurt. Every part of her, from her toes to the hair on her head ached like nothing she'd ever known before. Even trying to open her eyes was a struggle.

'Hannah?' Emma said from somewhere nearby.

'Urgh,' Hannah muttered. 'Where am I?'

'Wandsworth Hospital,' Emma said, squeezing Hannah's hand. 'You got a bit banged up.'

'I feel like I got hit by a truck.'

'By the sounds of it, you did.'

Hannah opened her eyes, then the overhead fluorescent lighting made her immediately shut them again. 'Ow.'

'You were really lucky,' Emma said. 'The doctor says you only have concussion. They want to keep you in for a night or two for observation, but that's all.'

Hannah winced. 'It feels worse than that.'

'Trust me. You'll be okay.'

Hannah managed to open her eyes enough to see Emma sitting next to her bed, a worried expression on her face. 'Why do you look scared, then?'

Emma smiled. 'Because I thought I might lose you and I don't want that.'

'I'm sorry.'

'What are you sorry about? You didn't beat yourself up. Well — no more than you usually do.'

'Yeah. I'm an expert at that.' Hannah tried to laugh, but it hurt too much. 'Ouch.'

'Anyway, I should be the one saying sorry,' Emma said. 'I've been a right bitch to you after you went out and got drunk the other night and ... well, you have a stressful job. It's no wonder you need to let off steam sometimes. I know dinner in front of the TV with me isn't enough.'

This time, Hannah was the one squeezing Emma's hand. 'It is. It's more than enough. I'm the one who's been a selfish cow.'

'Are we good, then?'

'Yeah, we're good.'

Emma leaned in and kissed Hannah on the lips.

'Ow! Ow,' Hannah said. 'You might have to wait a bit.'

'Sorry.'

'What about ... Sarah?'

'Is that the other police officer you were with?'

'Yeah.'

'She's in a room just down the corridor. She didn't do as well as you. She's got a broken leg and arm.'

Hannah tried to sit up, but the movement sent shooting pain through her head and her vision filled with stars.

'You've got to take it easy,' Emma said. 'They really bashed you up.'

Images of the crash flashed through the fog in Hannah's mind, quickly followed by memories of the gunmen — especially that one man who had the assault rifle aimed at her head, the barrel never wavering, her life only a trigger pull away from ending. 'The people who attacked us ...'

'They're all dead. They can't hurt you anymore.'

That was something at least. Still, Hannah had come so close to dying. So close. The man with the assault rifle should've killed her. Hannah should be dead. There was no doubt about it.

From nowhere, her body began to shake. Hannah tried to stop it, but it was impossible. The tears came next, accompanied by big, chest-racking sobs. She couldn't help herself. The shock of it all had to come out. The fear, the panic. The feel of death's whisper on her neck.

Emma leaned in as Hannah cried, slipping her arms around Hannah and pulled her in tight. 'It's okay. Everything's going to be okay. I'm here.'

Hannah heard the words but, somehow, none of them rang true. How could anything ever be okay again?

In her mind, she could see the gunman pull the trigger. She could feel the bullets tear her apart.

Hannah should be dead.

Monday 12th December

49

It was only 7:30 a.m. but Wise was already back at Kennington, feeling no better for the few hours' sleep that he'd managed to snatch the previous night. Armed with a triple espresso from Luigi's, he found Brains at his desk, looking like he'd not been home at all.

'Please tell me you haven't been here all night?' Wise said, feeling guilty that he'd not brought an extra coffee with him.

Brains looked up, the dark shadows under his eyes visible despite his large glasses. 'I might have.'

'Did you find anything useful?'

'I've been mainly working with the phone data so far but yeah, I have.'

'And?'

'I can put Konza at both Western Towers and Friary Road at the times of the murders of Beanz, Tyrell and Leon and the whole crew were in Fife Road at the time Jono was killed as well as Gallagher and his wife.'

'That's amazing. If the ballistics match up as well, then we can close those cases.' More importantly, the man who'd killed Jono had paid the ultimate price. That was some good news he could tell the troops when they got in later — what was left of his troops, that is.

Wise took a sip of his espresso. 'What about Sarah?'

'She hasn't been in contact with any of the phone numbers we've got for Konza or his crew,' Brains said.

'Really?' Wise didn't know what to make of that — if he should be happy or disappointed.

'However, she has been calling one number quite a bit since we've been working on this investigation. I've checked it out and it's a pay-as-you go phone. There are no records to who it belongs to.'

'A burner.'

'Yeah, I'd say so.' Brains rubbed his face. 'The first time she calls it is on Wednesday afternoon, after she visited Cameron Nketiam's widow, Nadine.'

'Hicksy said Nadine had told Sarah about her ex working for Konza. Information she didn't pass onto us.'

'The second call is on Thursday morning — right after our DMM and the third call is on Friday afternoon.'

'After she went to check out Western Towers with Hannah,' Wise said.

'Exactly,' Brains said. 'And it gets worse. The next call between Sarah and the burner is Saturday morning, after we found Gallagher's address, and the last call was yesterday twenty minutes before the ambush.'

'Okay. Now, is there any connection to the burner and Konza?'

'As I said, I can't tell you who has the phone, but I do know that, on two occasions, the burner and Konza's phone were in the same location. That can't be a coincidence.'

'So, either Konza had the phone or someone with him had it.'

'That's what it looks like,' Brains said.

Wise closed his eyes for a moment, feeling anger and disappointment bubble away inside him. 'I can't tell you how much I wanted to be wrong about all this.'

'Me too.'

'Shit.' Wise pulled out the chair from Hicksy's desk and sat down. 'What a fucking mess.'

'What are you going to do?' Brains asked.

'Well, after telling the boss and Walling the good news, I suppose I'm going to have to go down and arrest Sarah.' Just the thought of that made Wise feel sick, though. After Andy, this was the last thing any of them needed. And, yet again, he'd not had a clue one of his officers was bent until it was too late.

He got out his phone and texted Roberts. *Let me know when you're in. Have updates.*

His phone beeped back almost immediately. *I'm in my office.*

'Looks like there's no time like the present,' Wise said. 'I'm going to see the boss.'

'Good luck,' Brains said.

'Keep all this to yourself for now, okay?'

'You can trust me, Guv.'

'I know,' Wise replied but, even as he said it, he knew that he couldn't really trust anyone anymore. Not after Andy and Sarah.

Wise drank the rest of his coffee and headed down to Roberts' office on the second floor. When he got there, Wise found her door open and Roberts herself in jeans and a black roll neck sweater. Instead of battling paperwork like she normally was, Roberts was packing her things into a box.

'Boss,' Wise said, unsure of what he was seeing.

'Ah, Simon. Happy Monday,' she said.

'What's going on?'

'Apparently, running gunmen over in your car isn't quite the done thing, it seems,' Roberts replied. 'I've been put on leave, pending an internal investigation into my conduct.'

'You're joking?'

'Does this look like I'm joking?' She dropped a folder into her box to emphasise the point.

'Shit. Does Walling know?'

'He was the one who told me the good news.'

'I'm sorry. I really am,' Wise said. 'If it means anything, I think you did the right thing. Those uniformed officers would've been killed if not for you. And God knows what would've happened to Hannah and ...' Wise stumbled over saying Sarah's name. Suddenly, it didn't feel right mentioning her in the same breath as everyone else.

But Roberts knew. She understood. 'Are there any updates?'

'Yeah. None of it good.' Wise told her everything Brains had learned.

Roberts slumped down in her chair. 'Christ on a bike, Simon. I was hoping you were wrong about it all. I really was.'

Wise took the seat opposite her. 'Me too.'

'We barely survived Andy,' Roberts said. 'I'm not sure we'll be so lucky this time. Especially as a police officer died.'

'I'll take full responsibility for what happened.'

'I don't think you'll have much choice in the matter.' Roberts pinched the bridge of her nose. 'Part of me is glad I'm not going to be here now.'

'You never know, I might be joining you on leave, pending an investigation.'

'I'm sorry, Simon. I really am. You don't deserve any of this. You're a good officer and a great detective. I hope this doesn't affect your career too badly.'

Wise let out a harsh laugh. 'I think my career's fucked without this.'

'Why's that?' Roberts asked.

Wise hesitated for a second, but he knew the time for secrets was over. It was easy to see a scenario where both Roberts and his careers could be over by Christmas. The woman didn't need any more surprises, especially if SCO10 came after Wise.

'My gaffer thinks we should bang you up,' Heer says. 'He reckons you're a bad one — like your brother.'

'Do you mind if I shut your door?' Wise asked.

Roberts pointed to the door. 'Go ahead.'

Wise got up from his chair and closed Roberts' office door, then returned to his seat. 'What do you know about SCO10's investigation?'

'They're looking into Andy's death.'

'That's only part of it,' Wise said. 'They're actually investigating a gang war that's going on in London. Someone's trying to take over the big gangs and killing anyone who doesn't want to play along.'

'I've heard rumblings about this, but what's it got to do with you?'

'They think my brother is the man behind it all.'

'Your brother? I didn't even know you had one.'

'Not many people do. I've kept him secret as best I could.' Wise told her about Tom and what he'd done all those years ago, his suspected involvement with Andy's death, his meeting with SCO10 at Belmarsh and his offer to go undercover to help catch Tom.

By the time he'd finished, Roberts was white-faced. 'Christ. I had no idea. Does Walling know?'

Wise shook his head. 'I don't know. I don't think so.'

'I don't like this idea of yours to pretend to be your brother. Not if he's as dangerous as everyone thinks he is. It's a good way to get yourself killed.'

'I know, but it's the only thing I can think of where I can help fast-track the investigation. It could take years otherwise and, by then, my marriage and my career could be over.'

'Even so, Simon. It's a dangerous game to play. Undercover work at the best of times takes a very special set of skills, but this?' Roberts sat back in her chair. 'You could get access to the highest levels of his organisation, but the risk levels would be astronomical. I can't see anyone authorising it. I certainly wouldn't.'

'I hope SCO10 see things differently.'

'I'm amazed you've been able to focus at all on your job while all this has been going on.'

'If anything, the job's stopped me from losing it completely. Even then, it's been touch and go.'

'Are you still seeing Doctor Shaw?'

'Yeah. Every week.'

'Is it helping?' Roberts asked.

'Very much so,' Wise replied.

'Okay. I'm glad you've told me,' Roberts said. She puffed out her cheeks. 'I know I'm going on indefinite leave, but if you need someone to talk to, just call.'

Wise stood up. 'I will. I promise.'

'Be careful out there, Simon.'

'I will, boss.' He smiled. 'You too.'

Wise left Roberts' office and returned to MIR-One, glad he'd told her the truth. When he walked into the incident room, he saw the remnants of his team were all in. Even Hicksy was there, his scowl casting the rest of his face in shadow.

He'd update them all on the case, and then head over to Wandsworth Hospital to arrest Sarah.

50

Even dopey from the pain meds, Sarah knew someone was in her room.

She'd heard the door open, heard whoever it was walk in, close the door and then they'd sat in the chair next to her bed. Now, they were watching her pretend to sleep.

It wasn't her husband sitting next to her. He was a small man, and the chair would never have groaned the way it did when the visitor had sat down. Discounting him, Sarah could think of a thousand people her visitor could be, and yet there wasn't a single one she actually wanted to talk to. Especially not if they had awkward questions for her. She didn't have to be the world's greatest detective to know that someone would figure out that there had been an insider on Wise's team, giving all their information away. A traitor who'd got Jono killed.

It was probably better for all concerned if Sarah just carried on lying where she was and let them think she was out for the count on whatever the doctors had given her. Her visitor would get bored quickly enough and leave. In the meantime, Sarah could use the time to work out how she could explain herself if anyone did demand to know what had been going on.

Apart from the phone calls back and forth with the bastard though, she was pretty confident she'd done nothing else to give herself away. And the bastard wasn't dumb enough to speak to her on a mobile that could be connected to him in any way.

So, if it came to it, she could front it all out. Act hurt by the suggestion. Maybe get angry. Threaten to file a complaint. Anything but act guilty. Anything except confess.

'I know you're not asleep,' the visitor said in a voice she knew only too well. 'Let's not muck about.'

For a moment, she thought it was the bastard come to check on her and fear ran through her with such a ferocity, she almost shook with the force of it. Her eyes fluttered open and she saw his bulky shape first, perched on the edge of the visitor's chair, leaning forward, elbows on knees.

It was him. Dear God.

Then, as she focused more, she saw that he was wearing a suit. The bastard didn't wear suits. The governor did. It was Simon Wise sitting there, not his evil brother.

Thank God for that.

'Guv.' Sarah's voice was a croak. Intentionally so. She needed his sympathy. How could she be a snitch if she got banged up and nearly killed for the cause?

'Sarah. How are you feeling?'

'Like I got hit by a truck and nearly killed.'

'You look like you broke a few bones.'

'Just a leg and an arm. Nothing too important.'

'You could have died.'

'I'm glad I didn't.'

'Yeah. It was the other lot that didn't get to walk away. All five of them got killed.'

Sarah tried to smile. 'That's something, at least. After what they did to Jono.'

'It's certainly something.' There was something about his voice that unnerved Sarah. There was no concern in it. No care. There was a coldness that Sarah didn't like.

'Is there something wrong, Guv?' she asked, acting all innocent. A guilty person wouldn't ask after all.

'You tell me, Sarah.'

And there it was. He knew. Or he thought he did. 'About what?'

'Come on. We've been through too much. Don't muck me about now.'

'I don't know what you're talking about.'

'Are you telling me you're not going to confess everything? Even if it might mean you don't get any jail time?'

'Jail?' Sarah didn't have to act much to sound scared. Prison wasn't a place she wanted to go.

'Everybody else is dead, Sarah,' he said. 'You're the only one left to prosecute. Even if you didn't have a broken leg, no one's going to let you walk out of here a free woman. You must know that?'

'I don't know what you're talking about. I haven't done anything.'

'We both know that's not true.' He reached over and took her hand. The hand attached to the broken arm. He squeezed it enough to send shards of pain through her.

'Let go. Please,' she begged. 'I want you to leave now. If you want to ask me anything else, I want my Federation rep with me.' Sarah closed her eyes as tears ran down her cheeks.

'And what good are they going to do you?' he growled as he leaned closer, still gripping her hand. 'How are they going to protect you from me?'

That's when she smelt the cigarette smoke on his breath.

The governor didn't smoke.

Sarah opened her eyes again and looked at her visitor, seeing past the smart suit and clocked the evil in his eyes. 'Tom.'

'That's right, darling. For a minute there, I thought you had me mixed up with someone else.'

Sarah was too petrified to reply.

'Now, what am I going to do with you, Sarah?' Tom Wise asked. 'You are the last one alive, after all, and I can't have you talking, no matter how tempting an offer someone puts to you.'

'You don't have to worry about me. I promise,' she said. 'No one's got anything on me. There's no proof of anything. I was careful.'

Tom smiled. Somehow, his eyes grew darker. 'The trouble with me, darling, is sometimes I worry too much. Maybe even get a bit paranoid about who might be out to get me — who might betray me. And when you start thinking like that, well, it's hard to stop. It's hard to trust anyone, in fact. Especially a tart like you who's already sold out their nearest and dearest for a few quid.'

'I won't say anything. I —' Something sharp cut along Sarah's arm, at the top of her forearm. 'Ow.' She looked down, saw the line of blood, saw the knife in his hand.

'I know you're feeling guilty,' the bastard said. 'So guilty that it's all got too much for you.' He moved quickly then, letting go of her arm and clamping his hand over her mouth so she couldn't scream. With his knife hand, he dragged the bed sheets off her, exposing the top of her legs.

Again, he cut, severing the femoral arteries on both legs. Sarah thrashed about beneath his grip, but she could already feel herself weakening, feel the world shift, grow a little bit darker, colder.

'Stop fighting it,' Tom whispered in her ear. 'Relax. It's better this way.'

Sarah shook her head. She didn't want to die. Not like this.

'Shhhhhh,' he said. The smell of cigarettes so strong now.

Sarah tried to see if there was anyone to help. Someone ... someone ...

It was all so dark now.

So dark.

'Good girl,' the bastard said as he let go of her mouth.

Sarah took a breath, but it wasn't enough. Not now.

She ...

51

Wise was about to get into his Mondeo to head to Wandsworth Hospital when his phone rang. He took it out of his pocket and checked the caller ID. It was DCI Rena Heer.

'Morning,' Wise said on answering.

'Simon,' Heer replied. 'What are you doing right now?'

'I was on my way to arrest someone actually,' he replied.

'That wouldn't be DC Sarah Choi, by any chance?'

A chill ran through Wise. 'How do you know?'

'Can you come over to Hendon now? My gaffer wants to have a chat before you go to see her. Choi's not going anywhere,' Heer said. 'We can tell you more when you get here.'

'The police academy?'

'Yeah, we're working out of some offices at the back. It's nice and private. No one to have a nose around what we're doing.'

'It'll take me about an hour to get there.'

'We'll have the coffee ready for you,' Heer said and hung up.

Wise threw his phone onto the passenger seat and climbed into his car, his mind racing. What did Heer's boss want? Was he going to accept Wise's offer to help? Or did he still want to lock Wise up? And how did they know about Sarah? He thought they'd kept that bit of information tight to the chest. How could that have leaked?

He turned on the engine, all thoughts of arresting Sarah forgotten. He needed answers.

Hendon was on the other side of London and a bastard of a journey for Wise to get there. He had to fight his way through town and up the Euston Road along with everyone heading north via the M1.

By the time he parked up at the Police Academy, nearly ninety minutes had passed since Heer had called.

After checking in at reception, he was told to wait until someone came to collect him. As he waited, he watched a group of cadets run around one of the training pitches. The sight stirred memories of Wise and Andy doing the same, building a friendship despite their very different personalities, full of ambition and eager to do good.

'You took your time getting here,' DS Brendan Murray said, walking over. He wasn't wearing a suit jacket and his shirt sleeves were rolled up past his elbows. The man looked tired, with dark circles under those Richard Gere eyes of his.

Wise stood up. 'Traffic's always bad these days.'

'Well, you're here now.' Murray didn't offer to shake Wise's hand. He nodded towards the lifts. 'We're this way.'

The two men didn't speak as they went up two floors in the lift, then Wise followed Murray down a long corridor. He used a pass to unlock two sets of doors before they reached an open office area.

There were about twenty people in there working away, but Heer was easy to spot in the far corner. She nodded as Wise followed Murray over to her. 'We're in Meeting Room Three,' she said.

'We call it the war room,' Murray added.

Again, Murray used his pass to unlock more doors and the three detectives walked down another long corridor. Windows on one side overlooked the training pitches, squashed under a heavy grey sky.

There was one more set of doors to be buzzed through and then Wise found himself in Meeting Room Three. Immediately, he knew why they called it the war room.

The walls of the windowless room were covered in pictures, maps and headlines. His brother's picture, the one taken by Heer's dead undercover operative, was easiest to spot, perched at the top of what looked like a family tree, except the people under him weren't blood relatives and ninety percent of the headshots were taken from prison records.

A long, jet-black meeting table ran down the centre of the room with enough chairs spread around it to seat the whole team Wise had seen earlier. There were empty mugs on it, next to two French presses full of coffee.

'Help yourself,' Heer said. 'It should still be drinkable.'

'You've been busy,' Wise said, pointing a finger at the information on the walls.

The meeting room door opened before anyone could reply. Two people walked in. Wise recognised both of them. The man in front was Deputy Assistant Commissioner Mathew Steel, one of the most senior officers in the Met. He must be the one overseeing SCO10's investigation. He wasn't a tall man, maybe five feet six, give or take an inch. His hair was cropped short to try and hide how little he had left. He stopped and looked Wise up and down through thin, black glasses. 'By God, you really do look identical.'

The other man with him was Detective Chief Superintendent Walling. 'Simon, good to see you. Do you know Deputy Assistant Commissioner Steel?'

'Only by reputation,' Wise replied. 'It's good to meet you.'

Steel nodded. 'Indeed. Barry tells me you're one of his finest officers.'

For a moment, Wise was confused. 'Barry?'

'That's me,' Walling said.

Wise smiled. 'I'm sorry. I just realised I've never known your first name.'

'Not many people do,' Walling said, clearly keen to keep it that way.

'Was someone pouring coffees?' Steel said, sitting down.

'How do you take yours, sir?' Murray asked, moving quickly to the French presses at the end of the table.

'With a splash of milk, Brendan.' Steel looked at the others. 'Come on. Sit down. We've got lots to get through today. We might as well get started while Brendan sorts the drinks out.'

Wise glanced over at Murray as he sat down. The man didn't look happy to be relegated to coffee duties.

Not that Steel had noticed. 'I hear you've had quite the busy week, Simon.'

'Yes, sir,' Wise replied. That was one way of putting it.

'And you've not yet arrested this ...' Steel hesitated.

'DC Sarah Choi, sir,' Heer said.

'That's right,' Steel continued. 'You've not arrested DC Choi yet?'

'No, sir,' Wise said.

'And who else on your team knows about her activities?'

'Myself, Detective Chief Superintendent Walling, DCI Roberts, DS Roy Hicks and DC Alan Park.'

'That's more than I'd like,' Steel said.

'Roberts is on indefinite leave as of today,' Walling said. 'We can move the others about if we need to, but that might cause suspicion if we do.'

'Why's it an issue who knows?' Wise asked. 'Everyone will know once she's arrested.'

'That's the point,' Steel said. 'We don't want her arrested. We want her to stay in play — but under our observation.'

'But her contact, Ollie Konza, is dead.'

'Choi wasn't calling Konza,' Heer said.

'Then who?' Wise asked, even though he was starting to get a bad feeling that he already knew.

Heer pointed to Tom's picture, confirming that fear. 'Your brother.'

'She was?' Wise didn't know what else to say. He couldn't believe it but, of course, it made sense.

Heer got up from her chair and walked over to the family tree on one of the walls. She pointed to Konza's picture in the line of villains immediately below Tom. 'Konza was one of Tom Wise's most senior lieutenants, running a lot of South London's drug operations. Keeping him out of prison would've been a priority for your brother.'

'Okay, but how does that connect Tom with Sarah?' Wise asked.

'The number she was using,' Heer said, 'is being used by at least two other officers to pass on information of use to your brother's gang.'

'He has quite the collection of officers throughout the Met, it appears,' Steel said. 'Part of what this team wants to achieve is to ferret them out as well as put your brother behind bars. Keeping some of the dodgy ones — like your DC Choi — in play for now is one way of doing that.'

Wise's eyes were drawn to Tom's picture once more. There were eight other headshots under Tom's. If they were all his lieutenants, running operations similar to Konza's, then this really was far bigger and more complex than he'd thought. His suggestion to go undercover, pretending to be Tom, suddenly didn't seem as clever as he had thought it was.

'Can we trust the two other officers in your team who know about Choi to keep quiet?' Steel asked, interrupting his thoughts.

'Well, Hicksy — DS Roy Hicks — was the partner of the officer killed on Saturday, sir,' Wise said. 'When I last spoke to him, he was actually threatening to kill DC Choi when he saw her next. I'm not sure he'd be able to work with her as if nothing was wrong.'

'Maybe DS Hicks needs to go on leave too,' Walling said. 'For compassionate reasons. He —'

Wise's phone rang. 'Sorry,' he said as he fished it out of his pocket. He saw it was Brains but he declined the call and placed the phone on the table. It immediately started ringing again.

'You better answer that,' Steel said, looking unimpressed.

Wise picked his phone up and accepted Brains' call. 'Hey. I'm a bit busy right now.'

'Guv, it's Sarah.' Brains' voice was full of emotion. 'It's bad news.'

Wise switched his phone to speaker and put it back on the desk.

'What about Sarah? What's happened?' he asked, aware that everyone was watching him now.

'She's dead. She killed herself,' Brains said. 'They found her about an hour ago. She cut her veins open.'

Shock ran through the room.

'How is that possible?' Wise asked, feeling his throat tighten.

'No one knows yet,' Brains said. 'The hospital doesn't know how she got hold of the knife or how no one noticed her doing it. Even if they had, though, death was pretty quick. There would've been little chance of saving her.'

'What about the guard we had outside her room?'

'He went to the toilet, apparently. When he got back, Sarah was dead.'

'Shit. Thanks for letting me know,' Wise said. 'I'll be back as quickly as I can.'

'Okay, Guv.' Brains ended the call.

'He's done it again,' Heer said. 'This is your bloody brother's work.'

'We don't know that yet,' Walling said. 'It could be suicide.'

Heer shook her head. 'Don't be naive. He saw a weak spot in his operation and immediately acted to fix it. This is exactly what he does.'

'Rena,' Steel said. 'Let's remain respectful.'

'Sorry, sir,' Heer replied, sounding far from apologetic.

Wise sat back in his chair, taking in what Brains had just told him. Whatever Sarah had done, she was one of his officers, someone he considered a friend. Now, she was dead. Like Andy. Like Jono. 'Whether she did it herself or someone did it to her doesn't matter. Her involvement with my brother has cost Sarah her life.'

Wise looked around the faces in the room. 'What we need to decide right now is how we're going to stop Tom from causing more people to die.'

THANK YOU

Thank you for reading *Talking Of The Dead,* the third Detective Inspector Simon Wise thriller. It means the world to me that you have given your time to read my tales. It's your support that makes it possible for me to do this for a living, after all.

So, please spare a moment if you can to either write a review or simply rate *Talking Of The Dead* on Amazon. Your honest opinion will help future readers decide if they want to take a chance on a new-to-them author. Leaving a review is one of the greatest things you can do for an author and it really helps our books stand out amongst all the rest.

DI Wise will be back in soon.

Thank you once again!

Michael (Keep reading to get a free book)

GET A FREE BOOK TODAY

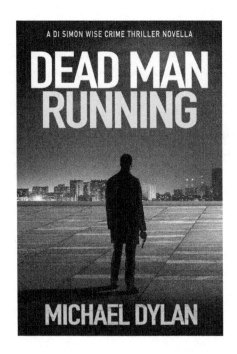

Sign up for my mailing list at www.michaeldylanwrites.com and get a free copy of Dead Man Running, and discover exactly how DS Andy Davidson ended up on that rooftop in Peckham with a gun in his hand.

Plus by signing up, you'll be the first to hear about the next books in the series and special deals.

THE DI SIMON WISE SERIES

Out Now:

Dead Man Running

Rich Men, Dead Men

The Killing Game

Talking of The Dead

Printed in Great Britain
by Amazon